THE SEAL OF JOHN SOLOMON:

THE COMPLETE ADVENTURES

OF JOHN SOLOMON, VOLUME 4

H. BEDFORD-JONES

THE SEAL OF
JOHN SOLOMON
THE ADVENTURES OF
JOHN SOLOMON, VOLUME 4

H. BEDFORD-JONES

COVER BY
MODEST STEIN

STEEGER BOOKS • 2020

A NOTE FROM
MR. H. BEDFORD-JONES

IT WERE untruthful for me to set forth this tale as wholly my own work. At the request of my friends, John Solomon, and Frederick Sargent, F.R.G.S., F.Z.S., I have merely gone over the manuscript of the latter with a view to its present use. I do this since Mr. Sargent realizes that he is apt to intrude too much dry science upon his readers. Those who desire his report *in toto* may find it in the proceedings of the Royal Society.

Since certain portions of this account have reached the press in garbled form, both these gentlemen think it only due to them that their story be given out as it actually occurred, their notes and data being placed at my disposal throughout. I need not apologize for the seeming incredibility of this account. It has too well been attested before the scientific world by Mr. Sargent, who, as everyone knows, has refused a knighthood and the Grand Cross of the Bath as incompatible with his American citizenship.

I have stuck closely to his original manuscript, changing certain more modest portions at the instigation of John Solomon. Against the urgent protests of us both, Mr. Solomon shortly returns to the Orient, and will not see this story in print. His terrible experiences in Themoud have told heavily upon him, and we fear—

However, what will be, will be. Here I give you Mr. Sargent's narrative, and since no man knows the Oriental countries better than he—unless it be John Solomon—surely no captious critic will have the hardihood to call his statements in question.

CHAPTER I

JOHN SOLOMON PREPARES TO DIE

A MAN WITH one hand bandaged and in a sling walked out of the Egyptian Government Hospital at Port Saïd. He passed over to the Church of the Epiphany without a glance and went slowly up the Rue el Tegara toward the Arab quarter. From head to foot he was cloaked in a *burnoose* of dazzling white Oman weave, the hood up.

He paused in front of the church to watch an Arab who was beating an ugly Somali camel. A single word broke from his lips; the Arab looked up at him, ceased his labor, jerked at his camel and trudged off with a low mutter. The crowd flowed on again, and with it the man in white.

Behind, the camel-driver turned over his camel to a negro who seemed to be in wait a few feet away, and hastily waved his hand at nothing in particular; after which he drew up the hood of his dingy *burnoose* and departed after the white figure, now half a block up the street.

As if that wave of the hand had startled them into action, a number of loafers and beggars loitering near the church and hospital scattered suddenly. A Syrian who had been showing laces to the tourists on the church steps flung his goods beneath his arm and darted down into the throng, leaving the tourists open-mouthed. A passing Osmanli jabbed his fez over his ears and veered sharply down the side street past the church toward the Rue Quai du Nord and the tramway.

Three blocks farther on, at the Rue des Cimetiéres, this

Osmanli dropped from his tram and waited. Presently, the tall figure of the man in white swung along, his bandaged left hand fended carefully with his right. Several beggars shifted into sight on the corner, and the camel-driver's *burnoose* appeared somewhere in the crowd. The Osmanli stood nonchalantly on the corner, smoking a cigarette in a foot-long amber mouthpiece.

The figure in white, looking neither to right and left, came up and passed with never a stop, then flickered away into the Arab quarter, heedless of the din behind him. For there was a crowd around the corner, where a howling, cursing, footless beggar clung to the Osmanli. A knife dropped to the street and two Sudanese policemen led them both off.

The man in white paused at a dingy little shop with unwashed windows which bore the sign

JOHN SOLOMON
Ship's Stores.

with an Arbi scrawl below.

The camel-driver met him; a look of inquiry and a nod passed; and the man in white stepped inside.

Here, amid steel cable, coiled rope, anchors, old guns, canvas, and other accessories of a ship-chandler's shop, he found three men waiting. One was an Arab, one a water-seller with his skin, and the third was a negroid Somali with a dirty cloth.

The newcomer nodded to the Arab boy behind the counter and passed to a little door behind. This gave on a narrow passage, through which he entered a larger room; and a most surprising room it was, considering the shop in front.

Divans, wall-niches, *hookahs,* and small tables stood around in confusion. In one corner was a heap of *jezoils*, pistols, *tulwars,* and muskets; in another stood a pile of rugs; two electric fans whirred, while above all was one rich stained-glass window.

In the center of the room were three men. One was an Arab silversmith, who was hard at work. Another was a negro, who stood waiting with fez removed. The third, who sat cross-legged

on a rug, waved a hand at the man in white but said nothing.
The newcomer settled down on a pile of rugs.

The central figure was an anomaly. He was a small, plump
man, wearing shirt and trousers, carpet-slippers, and a *tarboosh*
jauntily cocked over one ear, while he sucked at an empty clay
pipe. From beneath the *tarboosh* a wisp of grayish hair stuck out
on one temple, but his face seemed absolutely featureless. It was
round and plump and nothing else—until he looked up. Then
it was seen that his eyes were very wide, very blue, and might be
rendered very intelligent if he so wished.

In front of John Solomon—for this was the ship-chandler
himself—was a small brass-bound chest full of little red note-
books, while other note-books lay open on the floor around
him. The silversmith finished his pounding, and at a sign from
Solomon gathered up his tools and vanished.

Solomon made a mark in the book before him. The man in
white saw that beside the ship-chandler was a heap of small
silver rings, while another heap lay where the smith had sat.

"Is it the tally?" asked the negro in Arbi, or, as it is wrongly
called, Arabic.

"It is the tally," responded Solomon, picking up six rings from
the pile at his side. "One of these to you, the others to you know
whom, with the message."

"Ha'am, sidi!"

The negro vanished and the water-seller entered, holding out
a hand on which glittered a small silver ring. Solomon took it,
tossed it into the far pile, made an entry in a notebook, gave him
another from the heap, and he, too, vanished.

The Somali entered and showed a dozen of the silver rings in
his dirty cloth. He spoke at length in Somali.

Solomon made laborious search through his note-books,
checking ring after ring, it seemed. Finally he counted them over
and delivered an equal number from the pile beside him. The
procedure was repeated with the Arab; then Solomon went to

the door of the passage, shouted something, and returned with a sigh of relief.

"Werry 'ot day, Mr. Sargent, sir!"

He mopped his face nervously.

"Did—did you get me message at Alexandria?"

I smiled—for I, Frederick Sargent, was the man in the white *burnoose*, which disguise I had assumed for purposes which shall appear presently.

The Seal of John Solomon

"That's why I'm here, John. And I came by way of the hospital."

"You're 'urt, sir?"

Solomon leaned forward, his eyes agitated.

"Didn't Selim—"

"Now, John!" I reproved him relentlessly with a speech he was fond of quoting. " 'Them as asks questions gets lessen they asks, I says.'

"Oh, well, here's the yarn. I got your message at Alexandria, slipped into this pilgrim garb, and came over at once. I went straight to the hospital and found Adan ibn Hamid. He was dying, but he gave over the papers and warned me that the place was watched. Just after leaving I met Selim, and I imagine that his men had a row with a Turk on the way over. Now give us a knife."

Solomon betrayed signs of perturbation which puzzled me, for as a rule the pudgy ship-chandler was about as emotional as his own stained-glass window. Evidently there was something strangely amiss. However, he opened a big clasp-knife and passed it over. I ripped the bandage and splints from my left arm, and with a grin at John drew out a little roll of papers.

He seized on them with a grunt. Beads of perspiration stood out on his forehead, though I thought the room cool enough. When he had cast his eye over them he leaned back and shifted his attention to me. I was beginning to wonder what it meant.

"Lud! It give me a mortal bad turn, Mr. Sargent, when I 'eard yesterday morning as 'ow Adan ibn Hamid was in 'ospital, and them Osmanlis all about! Forchnit it was as I remembered you. Dang it, I forgot! Give me that 'ere ring, sir, please!"

I obeyed. It always struck me as odd that Solomon dropped his h's when he spoke English, but in Arbi or Somali or Osmanli he got out the strong aspirates with hardly an effort. He selected a ring from his pile which he handed me. I could not repress a whistle of surprise.

My other ring, which I had worn for several years, had borne Solomon's name in Arbi; this new one bore a diagram—a square with diagonal cross-lines from corner to corner.

"What's gone wrong, John, in Heaven's name? Your men have worn those rings for the past five years, to my own knowledge— and your place is all mussed up—"

"I've been 'ere for twenty-year now, Mr. Sargent," said he moodily, filling his pipe with whittlings from a black plug. "It ain't a nice 'ouse, so to speak, but it's mine—or it was. It's seen some mortal queer things this 'ouse 'as, but—but—dang it, the old sign comes down and the shutters goes up—"

He paused, blinking down at his pipe. I stared at him astounded, for the poor fellow had all but gone to pieces in a minute.

"Why, John!" I said awkwardly. "What's happened? If you're hard hit, man, let me lend you a bit—"

"It ain't money, sir, thank you werry much," he broke in, and I saw his plump fingers shake as he raised and lit his pipe. "No, it ain't a matter o' money, sir. I've been and called in all them rings, Mr. Sargent, and issued others, and there's still a tidy lot to come in. I've sold these 'ere rugs and things, and next week I 'ands over of me account-books and such to the Crédit Lyonnais for safe-keeping, and—and goes. But it ain't a matter o' money, sir, just like that.

"No, it's a matter o' principle, Mr. Sargent. It's all werry well to run risks, I says, and a werry fine thing it is to be a brave and upstanding man like you, sir; but I'd sooner 'ave me *Times* and me pint o' 'alf-and-'alf than the biggest tombstone in the world—just like that. 'Owsoever, that's neither 'ere nor there, as the old gent said when 'e kissed the 'ousemaid on the nose."

Solomon sighed heavily and bent a gloomy eye on his rugs. I, who had never once known him to be other than his genial, optimistic self, was frankly amazed and said so.

"Look here, John, what's the answer? You wired me over here from Alexandria to get some papers from a native in hospital—a bare dozen blocks away from here. I do it, then find myself guarded like a pearl of the harem, and find you preparing to clear out. Why didn't you send Selim over there? Let me in on it, John! Good Lord! the natives haven't turned against you?"

"That's what I was 'oping you'd say, sir, and I thanks you werry much. No, the natives ain't turned—not yet, sir. It's me that's been and turned, so to speak."

Here a bell sounded and Solomon clapped his hands. The camel-driver entered.

"Well done, Selim," said John in Arbi. "I know the tale. Who was the Osmanli?"

"It is not known, *sidi*. He was taken to jail with Yusuf, my mother's son, who begs for alms on—"

"Very well. Let Yusuf's fine be paid. Go you to the coffee-

house of the Pilgrimage. There you will find one wearing the
ring—a *hajj* named Omar ibn Kasim the Hazrami. Between
you let that Osmanli go to paradise before he talks with another
Osmanli. That is all."

Selim withdrew. I shot a startled look at John, for it was a
new thing for him to turn his hand to deliberate assassination.
He shook his head slowly.

"It'ad to be done, sir. You see, that Osmanli'e was watching of
you.'E knowed'e was jugged for watching of you, and if'e passes
on the word, why, you're a dead man, Mr. Sargent, and sorry I
am to say it. So'e won't pass on the word—like."

I nodded. Plainly John had drawn me into something pretty
extensive. However, I said nothing, for I saw that the story was
coming. After puffing a while he began:

"You see, sir, ever since they killed Nazim Pasha there's been
a quiet revival o' the customs all over Islam—like the Wahabites
started. When you was'ere last I told you about that there Senussiyeh affair down on the Red Sea. That was one thing. I give that
King Solomon treasure over, as you know, which stood me in
fair solid wi' the sultan, if I do say it as shouldn't.

"'Owsoever, too many people knew this'ere ring o' mine, sir,
and what good is a secret if so be as it ain't a secret, says I? This
Adan ibn Hamid,'e come a matter o' several'undred mile to see
me and give me them papers. Five minutes after'e reached Port
Saïd a Turk shows 'im me ring and tries for the papers. Five
minutes later Adan goes to 'ospital, stabbed clear through, but
'e keeps the papers.

"I saw as'ow I was suspected, Mr. Sargent, so I sends for you,
sir. I'd been looking for Adan some time, in a far-sighted way,
so to speak, for I guessed what was going to 'appen."

"But what the deuce does it all mean, John? Confound it!" I
exclaimed irritably. "You're worse than an Arab story-teller! It's
a new thing for any one to be threatening *you*, and I can't make
head nor tail of it. The fact that the Osmanlis are mixed in it

would indicate that you've run your head up against Constantinople—"

"Wuss than that, Mr. Sargent!"

Solomon actually groaned out the words.

"I've been and run me 'ead up against the 'ole bloomin',
blushin', damned Moslem religion—or I'm going to do it, which
is werry much the same. I'm a going to die inside of a week, sir!"

I received this announcement in blank amazement. John
Solomon was shattering precedents with a vengeance, it seemed,
for he had sworn for the first time in the five years I had known
him! It crossed my mind that he had a touch of the sun, but I
dismissed the thought.

"Going to die! What do you mean?"

"Just like that, sir—I'm a going to die, only I ain't. In other
words, sir, I've *got* to die—and only you and the Crédit Lyonnais
and them as wears this 'ere new ring will know as I ain't dead!"

He rubbed his hand over a stubby chin.

"What's more, sir, I be growing of a beard, which I'd advise
you to do the same. 'Cursed is the 'airy woman and the 'airless
man,' as the Arabs say, sir, and if so be as you says the word—
why, you and me goes on a little trip."

I knew John Solomon, and my plans for making an expedition through the Libyan *hinterland* vanished like smoke. Not
only because of our old friendship, but because an expedition
with this man would be certain to bear fruit in adventure, and
possibly in scientific discoveries, I did not hesitate.

"I'm on, John. What's the yarn?"

"I ain't got the time for it right now, sir."

His eyes shifted, so that I knew he lied. Then they came back
to my own with a light of desperation gleaming in their placid
blue depths.

"To be frank, Mr. Sargent, I 'ave me back against the wall, and
it's mortal risky! There ain't nothing to be gained in a material
way, so to speak, but—but—I'm danged if I can watch them
there Turks carry on like this!"

He stopped his vehement outburst abruptly and puffed for a moment.

"You know that there coffee 'ouse of the Pilgrimage, up near the Mosque, where I sent Selim? Well, sir, you go to the Eastern Exchange Hotel and stop there till you 'ears word as 'ow I'm dead and buried all shipshape and proper. Then, sir, go to the coffee 'ouse disguised, for you won't be going back to the 'otel.

"There you'll find this 'ere Hazramaut man—Omar ibn Kasim. 'E'll know what to do, sir, 'cause why, I don't know yet myself, though I will to-night. In the mean time you might go to the American Consulate, down on the Quai François Joseph, and ask for the report on the case o' the Rev. Uriel Gairner. Also, take this 'ere letter"—he handed me one from the sheaf I had fetched him—"and burn it when so be as you've been and read it. That and Omar will give you the yarn."

It occurred to me that I could hardly go to the Eastern Exchange in my present rig. This matter Solomon remedied by fishing out of somewhere an outfit of European clothes I had left with him a year or two previously and forgotten all about.

"Uriel Gairner, eh?"

I repeated the name as I got into the things.

"And Omar ibn Kasim, *el Hazrami?* All right, John. Is it worth while to wire Alexandria for my effects? If I've got to let a beard grow again I'll have to have money to do it on, as I didn't even bring a letter of credit along."

"Werry good, sir."

Solomon produced a check-book from his brass-bound box, put on a pair of spectacles, and wrote his name.

" 'Ere's a blank check, Bank of Egypt, sir. It ain't a matter o' money, as I told you, Mr. Sargent; so don't be afraid to spend it. And—and I'm mortal glad that you're a going to stand by me, sir—mortal glad!"

Solomon put out a hand, and I promptly struck mine into it without seeing any special reason for his gladness. As it was, John came near spoiling the Egyptian Nour-ed-Din ibn Saleh—

which, ungrammatically but forcefully, was *me*—through his reticence that afternoon.

However, I was soon transformed from my pilgrim guise into the garb of a respectable tourist, and, with the rather valuable white *burnoose* and the *ihram,* or pilgrim costume, in a small satchel, I said, "Good-by!" to Solomon's "Temple," as it was known among the elect. I dropped from my tram at the corner of the Boulevard Eugénie, and with a sigh of satisfaction entered the Eastern Exchange Hotel, myself once more for a brief space—until my confounded beard should grow. And I did not quite foresee what trouble that beard was to give me.

CHAPTER II

TANGLED THREADS

MY FRIENDS tell me that at this point I must describe myself—in fact, that I should have done it long since. Well, the sooner a bad job's over with the better, so here goes!

First, I am not a titanic hero of romance, being barely six feet. Second, I am not blessed with strength at all. I am a great deal stronger than most men, but that is not a blessing; it comes from scientific cultivation of muscles, hard work on the desert, and a cast-iron stomach.

I have rather bushy eyebrows, black hair and eyes, high cheekbones, and a truculent air, I am sorry to say, for it is wholly an assumption on my part. As a boy I always had the ambition to travel in Arbi-speaking countries, and, having specialized in Oriental tongues at college, at twenty-one I had cut loose and gone.

At twenty-eight, finding myself a member of many societies—royal and otherwise—I had made a highly unsatisfactory trip "home" to the States. Now I was back again, just in time to get John Solomon's message and come to his assistance.

I have kissed the *Kaaba,* have prayed before the tomb of the Prophet at Medina, have journeyed from the Caucasus to the Afghan valleys, and am well known at Damascus as a Persian gentleman of undoubted piety, even though a *Shiah.* My monographs on the geology of the Pushti Kuh and Zagres ranges, as well as others on that weird peculiarity of the Arabian deserts which the Arabs call *nefud,* and which I shall touch upon later, have won some little attention—but I think this is sufficient.

To return: Fear, I have observed, is seldom caused by any concrete, definite thing; but it does come from an indefinite danger. A man may look into a rifle unafraid—though I never could—but when he looks at a jungle which may spit forth bullets at any moment he feels cold chills in his back. In other words, fear is largely a matter of imagination.

During my five years of gradually increasing intimacy with John Solomon I never remember having seen that plump little man much disturbed. That afternoon, however, he had not only been disturbed, but he had been in actual distress—in a state of pure funk.

I knew that he had a large force of men scattered through the Orient—a secret-service system all his own; that more than once he had faced very definite peril without a tremor; and that from the dingy little shop in Port Saïd extended threads that led into coffee-houses and throne-rooms alike.

Set down where he was, dealing with Moslems more often than with Christians, much more at home in Arbi than in English, it is not strange that others have asserted that John was a convert to Islam. It must be confessed that he held secrets rigorously guarded from all Christians; that he possessed gifts of regal splendor and letters of friendship from Sultan and emir and *sheik;* that he had small regard for the law of Christian nations, and that on at least two occasions the head of Islam had decorated and honored him.

None the less, Solomon has put himself on record as never having swerved in the faith of his fathers. Sitting like a benevolent spider in his den, pulling at his threads of treasure and masquerade and empiry, cloaked in mystery and garbed in silence, his was a nature peculiarly adapted to gaining the respect and confidence and fear of Arab and negro, Somali and Wahabite. Of what then was he in such fear?

The abstract thing, Islam, I concluded as I thought the thing over at dinner. Solomon had so long worked hand in glove with the Moslem world that when the parting of the ways came he would know best what perils surrounded him. With the horns of the Crescent closing around him, with his decision to give battle, whatever the cost, he might well fear the terrible, vague power of Islam. Yet he had determined to give battle. Why?

"Any one who didn't know him would think him posing," I reflected. "It does seem absurd to imagine him setting himself up against the organization of Islam—but he smashed the Senussiyeh in Arabia, which was some job.

"What on earth can be up? He was so worked up over it that he couldn't bring himself to tell me this afternoon, that's sure."

I recalled that in the cipher cable which had brought me from Alexandria he had warned me against the Osmanlis, and again during the interview. This was the most puzzling thing of all.

The Osmanlis, those pure-blooded Turks who rule the empire, are the latest born of the children of the Crescent, and few in numbers compared to their subjects. The religion of the Prophet, the *furquan* or "Illumination," was not given to them, but to the Arab people; they, conquering it, were conquered by it. Compared with the Arabs, they respect the precepts of the Koran little—but the government is theirs.

Then why should this be an affair of Osmanlis only? If John Solomon had in some manner offended Islam, or if there were some Moslem plot afoot, as was most likely, there was no reason for its being restricted to Turks, especially since against the unbeliever all races of Islam are knit together solidly. Why was John afraid of Osmanlis, not of Arabs or Egyptians?

Remembering the letter he had given me, I drew it forth, rereading it before I burned it. It was written in English, penciled. For the life of me I could see nothing especial about it except that it was written by a woman. It read:

> MY DEAR MR. SOLOMON:
> I am sending copies of father's sketch-maps back to you by the man you lent us. He seems afraid to stay with us longer, and

I am sorry. However, Esmer Bey is traveling a little way with us.

He is a very fine Turk, quite a gentleman, is exploring for the Ottoman government, and is quite English in every way. Father is delighted with him and he has helped us a great deal with the Arabs we have met.

Our Afghans are with us, and will stay, I think. Father does not know about the maps, so you see I am risking a great deal in sending them. Please do not worry about us, as everything is going well.

Yours sincerely,
Edith Gairner.

The letter was small, much crumpled, and on thin paper that burned quickly as I held it to my cigarette. Edith Gairner—well, the writing was clear cut at least, with none of those flapdoodle things spreading all over the paper that girls learn to make nowadays. By "father" she evidently referred to the Rev. Uriel Gairner whom Solomon had mentioned, and I determined to visit the consulate in the morning and find out about the mystery.

Now, let me say here that I knew John Solomon quite well enough to obey his orders to the letter in full certainty that all would be as he said. And so I fully intended to do had not Providence, as John would have said, intervened. That intervention was destined to give me no little agony, but it was also destined to prove that my years of study and slow absorption of learning had not been wasted on an aimless existence.

It was the next morning that I called upon the consul. I found that official an elderly Missourian, full of years and sadness, who wore a fez about the consulate in blissful ignorance of its import, to the no small delight of the Moslem servants. He was a new appointee, was already heartily disgusted with the place and the people. He received me with open arms and a proffered corn-cob pipe, which I declined with thanks.

"Well, sir, that was downright queer," he ejaculated after I had set forth my errand.

He pulled at his whiskers reminiscently.

"I came from Gibraltar on the same steamer with the reverend gent, and a strange man he was—dummed strange! He's a mish'nary from Westerville, Ohio; can't talk politics worth a whoop, but jabbers Arabic like a house afire. Dummed fine daughter, though, Sargent!"

"Well what about him?" I asked a trifle impatiently. "Where is he now?"

"In the bughouse, I guess, if they got one out in this dummed country. Say, if you ever see a crazy man he was it! One day he started to tell me a long rigmarole about how he was going to prove the Koran false, and how he knew where there was a bunch of Crusaders landed right in the heart of Muhammad's country, *et cetry, et cetry*. I says to him: 'You'd do a dummed sight more good if you introduced baseball and chewing-tobacco out here, also a little healthy politics, Mr. Gairner!' Say, I thought his daughter'd bust her sides laughing! He seemed real sore about it, though."

"Any report on him?" I asked again.

"No, sir; that's all I know about him, and there ain't any report here to my knowledge. Where he is I don't know, either, except that he hired out a bunch o' men and started for some forsaken place. He wanted to bother me with it again, but I says to him: 'Give me official business and I'll eat it, but don't come around me with no fairy tales. Anyway, it's downright wicked of you to drag that girl into such foolishness.'

"So he went off mad. Dummed if I know what his scheme was, Sargent! My vice—he's over at the club now—he was real thick with the girl, but I guess she kept her mouth shut.

"Say! Hold on a minute! Dummed if that kid ain't got some camery pictures of the pair of 'em stuck around his desk—wait till I go see. You see, I couldn't sanction any such religious fandango, not officially, and—"

His voice died away somewhere in the interior.

I was not greatly interested in the reverend gentleman. As I readily conceived, Gairner was of the type I had often met with—one gone forth to destroy Islam—probably led astray by some of the fantastic legends which abound amid the Arabs.

Gairner's knowledge of Arbi, and the fact that he had started on this trip from back home, would argue that he had previously been out here; but I could not recall any such name as that of a missionary I ever knew—and I prided myself on knowing most white men who could speak Arbi and live among the Arabs.

After five minutes the consul returned with the pictures. I looked them over. Except that the father had a patriarchal beard and big feet, I could make out nothing at all, for all of them were either sun-smeared or else the faces were in the black shadow of sun-helmets. So, returning them with perfunctory thanks, I got the latest Reuter's from the consul and returned to my hotel, dismissing altogether the affair of the Rev. Uriel Gairner.

During the next three days I kept close to the hotel, and closer to my room. On the chance of its coming in handy, I brushed up my Osmanli, for—as every scholar knows—though the Arbi characters are used by the Turks, as by the Persians, Hindus, Malays, and others, the Osmanli tongue is essentially Turanian and not Aryan, I had not used the language for a year or two; but, though it is hard to learn, it is harder to forget, so I soon found that I had it by the throat very satisfactorily.

But unrest was growing on me during those four days since leaving Solomon. Still fresh from the States, I was eager for the environment of the Orient once again. The very street smells, the chatter of passing natives, the sight of *burnoose* and fez and camel, all reacted powerfully upon me. I had dipped into native life on coming to Port Saïd, and had left it when I left Solomon's Temple, and brief taste is as fire to the blood. I defy any man to spend eight years in Islam without either hating it or hungering after it, each intensely. I hungered.

Besides this, I was obeying Solomon's instructions to grow a beard. Now, my own unadorned features marked me out at once among the tourists, for they were burned deep, even after my

trip home, and I was painfully conscious of the glances contin-
ually flung at me.

When to this was added the effect of my black stubble of
beard, I looked and felt more like a wild man than a civilized
human being from America. Theoretically Port Saïd is an excellent place in which to grow a beard; practically the Eastern
Exchange Hotel and its patronage have other views on the
subject. I was not accustomed to being the focal point of numerous glances every time I entered the dining-room, and nervous-
ness grew upon me at each meal, while between times I kept
to my room and spoke Osmanli to the chandeliers. Then Fate
happened along and took pity on me—at first.

It was the fifth morning after my interview with the consul.
In utter desperation at my confinement, I sneaked down the
servants' stairs to the street, felt better on exchanging a few
hearty Arbi curses with an insolent dragoman, and strolled
down the three blocks to the Continental. Here I ordered a pot
of tea and settled down over this to peruse a fortnight-old copy
of the weekly *Times*.

At first I paid no attention to the people around me, though
the room was comfortably filled with tourists and others. Once
or twice a strident American voice rang out and made me wince.
I was rather vaguely aware that the vacant seats at my table had
been occupied, and that an order had been given in English; then
a low-pitched tone reached me in excellent Osmanli:

"*Tchabouq oliniz, shimdi!* Make haste now!"

Being interested in a review of Albert Inness's latest book—I
had known Inness when he was on the Geological Survey down
in Somaliland—I merely glanced up without noting other than
that two fezzed Osmanlis sat opposite, and went on reading.

"The dog of a Nazarene wonders what we say!" chuckled one.
"Safe enough, *agha!* The last news from Esmer Bey was that he
expected to join the Nazarenes at Maan, where they would of
necessity leave the railway. What of the *padishah, agha?*"

For a bare instant the meaning of the words escaped me; then

I jerked up my paper lest something in my face betray my knowledge of Osmanli. Esmer Bey—why, it was that same Esmer Bey of whom the letter from Edith Gairner had spoken! Was it possible that here I had run across some loose thread broken from Solomon's net?

"The same!" rumbled a second voice without the quick animation which had distinguished the first speaker. "A *firman* was given this Nazarene *papaz*, for his influence was strong and we were fools. It cannot now be revoked. Esmer Bey wired us of papers at Jerusalem; what of them?"

"The man was killed, *agha;* but the papers were not obtained. Osman Sened had full charge of the business, but he got into a feud with an Arab beggar, was arrested, and was stabbed in the back as he left the court before we could communicate with him. The messenger sent by the Nazarenes died in the hospital and was buried. We searched the grave, but found no papers."

The second voice ground out a sullen oath. By this time I was aware of the fact that the gods had indeed favored me, and I was listening without shame. The two Osmanlis would not suspect that any one in this room would know their tongue, much less this rough-chinned individual reading the *Times*.

"Who is in this party of Nazarenes besides the *papaz* and his daughter?"

Fingers drummed on the table. I took it that he of the rumbling voice was newly arrived. Since he was addressed as *agha,* or lord, he must be possessed of authority.

"None, lord, of the unbelievers. There are two Afghans who will no doubt fight for their salt; these were given the Nazarene by Suleiman. The others, both camel-men and camp-men, are Arabs hired by virtue of the *firman*—may Allah curse the thing!"

"And Esmer?"

"Has ten of our men, besides Arabs. He also bears a *firman* of exploration and another authorizing him to do as he wishes. Perhaps by this time he has killed the infidels."

"Fool, why kill them until they have served us. When the work is done will be time enough."

"Then think you that there is such a place, lord?"

"Is it not named in the *sura* of Al Araf, in the *sura* of Al Furquan, and elsewhere? Think you that the *Kitab*, the book of books, revealed to our Prophet by Allah himself, is a lie?"

There was a note of heavy irony in the voice which did not escape me. I know my Koran well, as of necessity I have had to, but it was hard to guess to what place they referred. Yet—why that ironic note? What was it the consul had said about Gairner trying to disprove the Koran?

"And Suleiman—is he aware of anything?"

"It is thought not, lord, but he deals with many men, and is watched."

"Aye, and he has served us well in other days. Still, these Nazarenes—Well, we shall see! Now I must join Esmer at once. You had orders; what have you done?"

Much of the conversation had gone over my head, but this was more like it, I thought exultantly. I wanted another look at these gentry, so I unfolded a sheet of the paper and lowered it until I could look over without turning my eyes directly on the two.

The *agha* was a heavy-jowled man with graying beard; the other was much less dangerous-looking—a man with furtive, spying eyes. He flung a quick look at me; I carelessly met his eye for an instant, then returned to my paper.

"You can leave here by the noon train. It reaches Port Ibrahim in time for the caravan to start and reach Ain Musa by nightfall. Ten of the fleetest Sheharat camels are in waiting. With them are two of our men. The others are pilgrims who will be glad of the chance to hit straight across to the railroad. You will need one more man, but we can get him easily enough; there are pilgrims in plenty."

"Good!"

The heavy-jowled man betrayed satisfaction.

"Then we will strike for Akaba and so across to Maan, where I will take some means of getting into touch with Esmer, who no doubt will have left word. The caravan is at Port Ibrahim? Good. Let us go."

Lighting fresh cigarettes, the two rose, paid their score, and departed.

I looked at my wrist-watch. There was a fever in my blood. It was ten-thirty. An hour and a half and the train would leave for Suez and Port Ibrahim, bearing this mysterious *agha* who was going to join Esmer Bey. The temptation was terribly strong!

I remembered that letter written by Edith Gairner, and how she had spoken of this Esmer Bey. Things began to clear up a little for me.

"Quite a gentleman—has helped us a great deal—father is delighted with him." And again, "Our Afghans are not afraid."

Recalling how the two Osmanlis had spoken of these Afghans, and that they had been furnished by Solomon, I concluded that they were men to bank on.

But—of what could men be afraid? It seemed certain that Gairner and his daughter had reached Maan, on the Mecca Railway, and had started for some place of which I was still ignorant—some place whose very existence seemed doubtful, though named in the Koran.

I knew well enough what a mad thing it had been to attempt. Arbist though this missionary might be, protected by a *firman* from the Sultan though he was, a journey into the heart of Arabia might well frighten the bravest coast Arab. I had done it in disguise—had crossed Arabia twice; yet I would never have dared it with a woman.

Unfortunately for myself, I possessed the natural chivalry of the Anglo-Saxon, and the thought of the woman almost decided me. Gairner himself would have troubled me little, and but for those mysterious Osmanlis he might have made the trip safely, for the *firman* of the Sultan will effect much. But with Esmer and this *agha*, whose cruel eyes and heavy face held all the cunning of his race, plotting against him, there would be little chance.

And in the mean time Solomon was—waiting for his beard to grow! I think that this thought, ludicrously enough, settled my decision. Right or wrong, I would have a try at being that extra man with the *agha's* expedition. If I failed, well and good; John and I would then work together. The chance had been offered me, and I determined to take it.

"Confound it! I'm sick of being stared at like a lunatic by these spick and span tourists!" I thought as I entered the hotel hastily. "Let's see—I'd better drop John a line in case I make good with it. Then I'll visit the Arab quarter and get what I need, and just about make the train. I'd better not visit John's place if he's watched."

Once I mark out a course for myself I seldom vacillate—though I wished later on that I had vacillated there and then. I sat down and wrote Solomon what I had heard and what I proposed to do, addressed it in care of the Crédit Lyonnais, and posted it. Let me confess here that it never recurred to me that, in his own words, John had his back to the wall and was dependent on me for aid. I doubt whether I would have hesitated even had I recalled it, for this opportunity was too good to miss.

So at ten-fifty-five a white-*burnoosed* Arab left the Eastern Exchange. At eleven-ten he dropped from a tram in the midst of the Arab quarter and made certain purchases. At eleven-forty he left another tram on the Rue l'Arsenal and walked over to the Gare, where he bought an entire first-class compartment in the noon train, having certain changes of costume to attend to.

And at twelve-five I was on my way to Port Ibrahim. Ever since I have considered that the most unlucky moment of all my life—and yet in a sense the luckiest, considering what came of it all at the end.

CHAPTER III

THE ROAD TO MAAN

IN THE shelter of a line of palms, not far from some native buildings, knelt a group of camels, their loads beside them, ready to go on at an instant's notice. More than one passing Arab paused to glance appreciatively at the beasts. To the eye of the desert-bred they were superb—long-limbed, heavy-muscled racers from the easternmost Sherarat tribes such as no Arab needs to recognize by brand or mark.

Near them lounged a group of men, pilgrims by their two-pieced garb, though *burnooses* were piled on the sand near by. Below glittered the waters, hot in the afternoon sun, while close at hand passed the great liners to east and west, and out beyond the pile-built Port Ibrahim stretched its tenuous railway line across the floodtide shoals to Suez.

Nor were there liners alone on the water, for native *dhows* and small craft, rarely passing through the canal because of the tolls, spread their sails in all directions. The group of men under the palms paid no heed to all this, however, for the attention of all was centered on the pilgrim who sat on the rug among them and made little marks in the sand.

He also was a pilgrim, though over his cotton garb he wore a white *burnoose* of Oman weave, which left head, heels, and instep bare—as is commanded. His powerful, scrubby-bearded face was intent on his works.

Seizing the rosary which the opposite pilgrim held up, he ran his fingers along the beads to the one-third mark of red

coral, then set down a dot in the sand. It was the Ceremony of
El Raml—the fortune-telling of the beads. When finally the
labor was done all leaned forward in complete absorption. (This
was not the first time that I had won my way into good Moslem
society by my arts!)

"O you, called Sa'ad ben Ali!" I chanted in a sing-song
voice. "Behold! Allah reveals that you come from the land of
Tunis"—this was no guess, for he carried the cross tattooed on
his temple—the mark of a Tunisian over all the world—"that
in your waist-cloth is much money, and that you are a merchant
in the land of your fathers."

I made one good hit, for the bearded Sa'ad scowled and
clutched at the filthy pilgrim-cloth about his loins, the scowl
being for the other holy ones around.

"By my father's bazaar," he growled, "it is a lie that I have
money. The other is true—but what of this pilgrimage of mine?"

"Allah reveals to me, O you who make the *hajjat el farz* from
the land of Tunis, that of some money shall you be robbed, and
some shall you keep; yet—there is a bad omen in this thing,
Sa'ad ben Ali!"

"It will be a bitter pomegranate for pilgrims who steal from
me," muttered Sa'ad with an evil glance at his comrades.

They grinned.

"Allah reveals to me that at a place called Maan, which is
where I know not, you shall leave this caravan, O pilgrim, and
finish the pilgrimage otherwise—or it may be before you reach
Maan. Say! Is this truth or untruth?"

"By the ninety-nine beautiful names of Allah!" swore Sa'ad
in astonishment, while a mutter of surprise broke from the rest.
"How knew you this thing, *Hajj* to-be?"

"Am I to reveal the secrets of my art?"

I shrugged my shoulders.

"God is gracious and merciful! Who—"

A *burnoose*-clad man broke into our midst with a hasty ejaculation. He was no pilgrim, I noted. Probably he was one of the two Osmanlis waiting with the caravan.

"Who are you?" he shot at me, then turned. "On with the loads! Our lord comes."

The others scattered hastily.

"There is no God but God," I returned composedly, throwing the beads to Sa'ad. "I am a pilgrim, so give me alms in Allah's name, for I have no money, O stranger!"

The Osmanli chuckled.

"Saith not the *Sura* of the Cow that a pilgrim's best provision is the fear of God? Then fear Him and get hence."

At this I whined with the true beggar-whine, for I saw other Osmanlis coming.

"O protector! In the name of Allah, let me be even as one of these dogs of yours! Give me a camel to drive, for I know the trade-routes, and God will bless thee forever and pluck thee out of Eblis for thy holiness—"

"Silence!"

The Osmanli turned as the others came up. I saw the mysterious *agha* approaching with the second Osmanli. I had gained on them by means of a good boatman and certain coins. A few words passed, and to my surprise I heard my heavy-jowled friend, who wore a *burnoose* like the others, addressed as Yelniz Pasha. He looked me over.

"A strong dog of his shoulders," he commented in Osmanli; then, in Arbi: "Your name, pilgrim?"

"Nour-ed-Din ibn Saleh of the house behind the mosque Abou Dahab in Al Kahirah in Egypt, Protector," I rattled forth glibly. "I have made the lesser pilgrimage, and now that my brother's child has fallen upon days of sickness—"

"Allah curse thy brother's child! Where are your papers? Think not to steal off in my shelter. Light of the Faith, lest there be a reckoning with the English—"

As I had procured the proper pilgrim's papers at Alexandria immediately upon the receipt of Solomon's wire, I shoved them forward, hardly daring to hope that I would succeed in my purpose. Yelniz glanced at them cursorily, returned them, and whirled on his heel with an anxious glance at the westering sun.

"Take the unattended camel and add a *ratib* to thy prayers if thou hast lied!"

"Allah bless thee!" I shouted. "I have not lied!"

And that was the manner of my setting forth again into Arabia, to my own great future sorrow. Later, indeed, standing before that terrible fiery Seal of which I shall have further to say, I vowed that nevermore would I put *burnoose* upon me, and that vow I have kept.

FOR SOME months now I had not been into the desert. The hot gleam of the sands, the pitch of the camel, the very reek of the beasts themselves, was sweet in my nostrils. In some measure my wanderlust had slipped behind me, except that I had naught to keep me at home. And from the day I left Gibraltar westbound, the East had called me.

Nor is it any vague, easily controlled thing, this call of the Eastern world. It is like an itch in the blood, an alien impulse that grips on men and draws them into the dim distances despite their will-power. I knew well that inside of a week I would be cursing the sands and the brazen sky and the stink of camels, yet stay away from it I could not. I cast all thought of John Solomon from my mind, and as I followed the camel of Sa'ad ben Ali I determined to play my own hand in the game regardless of consequences.

I was well armed—openly with dagger and pistols, secretly with an automatic slung beneath my arm-pit, under the pilgrim's shoulder-cloth. The spice of danger allured me, as did the mystery of the journey itself, and danger there was, for my trip home had rid my body of much of its acquired tan, and save for my head and arms, I had had to stain my body with walnut-juice. A week, however, and there would be no more need of that.

So I started out confidently enough, but at the sunset halt for prayers my confidence received a peculiar setback. Yelniz had ordered that the party recite only the *farz* or obligatory prayers, and omit the rest. The pilgrims protested, for to them the *ratib* or self-imposed prayer-penance meant much; but Yelniz turned on us with a look that silenced all opposition.

As I rose, after the *salaam* over each shoulder to all brethren of the true faith, I felt an unaccountable oppression. The sun was dropping with Orient swiftness over the rim of the world; in all directions the untracked desert stretched yellow and crimson and dun, and now for the first time, I think, I realized my loneliness.

What was more, for the first time I realized that I had done an insane thing in thus obeying the impulse to accompany Yelniz Pasha, and in cutting myself off from John Solomon. The latter had spoken of a journey, and without doubt he had meant that I should accompany him over this same route, to the same end.

If John intended to pose as a Moslem—probably as an Afghan or Kurd, which would explain his blue eyes—he could have done so with some success under my wing, for I knew every twist and turn of Islam and could be *Shiah* or *Sunni* at a moment's notice. And John had surely been in deadly fear.

I felt a swift, keen regret at my own thoughtlessness; and as the rapid journey was taken up again across the darkened sands my regret turned to remorse. Nor was it unmingled with fear— that same fear of the indefinite which had so laid hold on John Solomon. It was not fear of Yelniz Pasha, but it was fear of all that Yelniz Pasha stood for, as if the night had clamped down on the desert and my spirit alike.

What would John Solomon think of me—of that letter of mine? Beyond a doubt it would disarrange all the careful plans of my plump little friend, and despondency came over me at the idea. It was partly the despondency of weariness, for camel-riding is no light task after some months of idleness; but I also saw my whole action in the clear light of reason, and my regret was very bitter. Also, it was destined to be very lasting.

So it was in no very cheerful frame of mind that I rode into

Ain Musa with the rest, unloaded and fed my camel, and turned in beside Sa'ad ben Ali under a black two-man tent of camel-hair pitched beside the beasts. So tired were we all that eating was put off until the morning by common consent.

With the false dawn we breakfasted, then began the march, or rather flight across the desert of the Sinai Peninsula. While we pilgrims were at our prayers, Yelniz Pasha conferred with his aides and vanished into the town, returning with a sullen Arab *sheik*, who seemed anything but pleased at coming. One of the pilgrims was unceremoniously left upon the sands to reach Mecca as best he might, and with his howls of protest dimming behind us, we followed the *sheik* out to the north.

What with the rest and food I found my spirits rising percep-tibly, and when Ain Musa had fled behind into the thin horizon I had cast off the lingering remnants of my depression and was again myself, alert lest I betray the least sign of my infidel heart. The other pilgrims would hardly suspect me, for they were all from northern Africa, and were like sheep, except for Sa'ad ben Ali; my danger lay not in them, but in the Osmanlis and in the Arab *sheik*. And my trial came at the midday prayer.

"Nour-ed-Din! Ho, Light of the Faith, come here!" cried Yelniz when I rose from my short prayer.

He and the *sheik* were standing a little apart. I saw that the Arab was short and ugly. I did not care for his looks overmuch.

"This man is from Al Kahireh—*Sheik* Yusuf," said the Osmanli. "He claims to know the trade-routes. See if he has lied or no."

I met the glittering eyes of the Arab boldly enough, though my hand was ready to slip out that automatic any instant. It was true that I had been over this route to Akaba several times before, but the *sheik* could easily prove me a liar if so minded.

"What wells do we reach this night, son of Saleh?" queried Yusuf searchingly. "With whom have you traveled these routes before? Has any man deigned to give you title of protector of the caravan?"

Now, it is a curious thing how swiftly the mind works at times. Between this question of the *sheik's* and my answer I do not think that five seconds elapsed, yet I considered many things. I might lie, but I must lie circumstantially, giving the life-history of every man I mentioned and my own into the bargain. And somewhere this hawk-eyed son of the desert would catch me tripping.

Even as he spoke, however, Yusuf put up a hand to stroke his beard. Whether it was done intentionally or not I have never known to this day, but the glitter of a ring caught my eye; I was so close that I could see the diagram on the ring—the seal of John Solomon—and my heart leaped in hope.

"O Beloved of Allah," I answered humbly enough, straightening the folds of my *burnoose* so that my own ring sent a little shimmer of sun-glare back into the Arab's face, "I was in your caravan last year, in the train of the merchant Ajman ibn Kail—"

"Enough!" broke in Yusuf with a nod of recognition. "I know the man now, Protector, for at first his beard deceived me. He is safe."

"Good!" rumbled Yelniz.

He seemed to be fond of that guttural *"eyi."*

"Know, Light of the Faith, that we go not to Akaba but to Maan direct? To-night we reach the wells of Kalaten-nakal, and after that these other pilgrims must not suspect."

"It is well, Protector," I made answer. "I will lie to them if they suspect."

And there was an end of that.

Only the night before I had half-formed a purpose of blocking Yelniz Pasha's advance in some manner, getting away, and rejoining Solomon. Now, however, that plan must be abandoned. Upon reaching the wells of Kalat that night Yelniz would abandon the caravan-route to Akaba and strike direct across the desert to the Mecca Railroad.

It bespoke his desperate haste with a vengeance. The distance was a good hundred and fifty miles, and twelve waterless hours

in the desert sun will kill any man alive, so that the pilgrims
might well rebel. There was little danger that they would know
their position, however, and with Yusuf's guidance and our
unexcelled racers the distance could be covered in two days.

As we rode onward that afternoon I was devoutly thankful
that the *sheik* had so unexpectedly proven to be one of Solomon's
men. My barefaced lie had been picked up and carried forward
without an instant's pause, but it was unlikely that I would get
any chance of talking with the *sheik*. However, once we reached
Maan I could bid Yelniz farewell and wait for Solomon.

That much of the trip would be fairly easy. Once on the
other side of the railway, however, Solomon and I might have
to fight. There the Bedouins had no fear of *askaris* or other
Turkish soldiery, and lay in wait for caravans on every hand.
The sultan's *firman* had doubtless protected the Gairner party,
for now that the great Ibn Rashid emirs of Arabia have been
subdued to fealty the sultan is feared in the land; but none the
less, after the disastrous Balkan War all Islam was more or less
disorganized, and the Osmanlis were forced to fight for their
very existence as a race.

"Well, *inshallah bukra!* Let tomorrow take care of its own
evils, by Allah's grace!" I concluded helplessly. "I don't suppose
John can get through without me, so I'll have to wait at Maan.
But what in thunder does it all mean? I'll bet old Uriel didn't
have a notion he was going to buck up against the Osmanlis
like this!"

An hour after sunset we reached the Kalat wells, much to
the delight of Yusuf, for there was a full moon, and like many
desert-bred Arabs, he detested travel by moonlight. In so small
a company we had no opportunity of speaking in private. As we
had camped near the wells, I ate a frugal supper of dates, dough,
baked hard in the ashes, and excellent coffee. Sa'ad ben Ali was
proud of his skill at coffee, but it was his last brew in this world,
though we had no presentiment of that fact as we turned in
together beneath our two-man tent.

We were up and off before the dawn. Yelniz informed us cynically enough that there would be no halt for prayers until midday, and if we did not like it we could pray while riding. As he delayed making this announcement until the wells and town were ten miles behind, the pilgrims were forced to make the best of it with a bad grace.

I alone knew that the trade-route had been abandoned, none of the rest being used to Syrian desert travel. The *sheik* led us at a terrific pace, pushing the racers to the utmost. The camels stood the pace fairly well. At noon there was a two-hour halt, then the journey was continued, no further stop being made until after dark. Plainly Yelniz was in desperate haste to reach Maan! This was brought out savagely enough the next day. Except for Sa'ad the Tunisian, who wore his pistols as if he knew how to handle them, the pilgrims were faint-hearts, intent only on getting to Mecca, always willing to steal, but afraid to face a weapon. Two hours after the midday halt, no water having yet been reached, the terrible pace began to tell on the camels, and one of the Osmanlis' steeds began to stagger heavily.

Yelniz at once ordered us to pull up, and commanded Sa'ad ben Ali to change camels with the Osmanli. This the Tunisian stoutly refused to do, for he knew the consequences of falling behind the party in that trackless waste, and he flatly charged Yelniz with favoritism.

The pilgrims at once took sides with Sa'ad, protesting loudly against the injustice of the order. I wisely drew to one side with the *sheik,* for I saw the evil light in Yelniz Pasha's eyes as he listened. He repeated his order with ominous calm, and the furious Tunisian snatched at a pistol.

Before he could pull it out a weapon cracked. Sa'ad pitched forward from his camel to the sand and lay in a heap. The shouting ceased. Yelniz quietly ordered his man to take Sa'ad camel, and in a horrified silence the march was taken up again, the foundered camel being left to follow as best it might.

I knew that did necessity arise I would meet with the same

fate—perhaps. But in spite of all my desert training the last drop of my water was gone an hour later, and the skin flapped idly against the camel. Still, if the beast could stand the pace—

"Ah!"

A hoarse cry from Yusuf, and I saw a black dot on the horizon ahead. Our pace remained unslackened, but to my vast disappointment the dot grew, not to a group of trees, but to a file of a dozen camels coming toward us.

As we drew closer it was seen that the others also were in mad haste, and as I pitched along beside Yusuf I noted that they also were mounted on racers. The *sheik* would have veered from the course to avoid danger, but Yelniz commanded him to keep on.

Closer and closer we came, until there were perhaps five hundred yards of sand between us, when suddenly the other string of racers swerved and came plunging down on us with a burst of shouts from their riders that drew an order to halt from Yelniz. The *pasha* sat his camel for a moment; then excitement leaped to his face and he turned to his aides with a yell in Osmanli.

"By Allah! It is he!"

Who? I could see only that the others were muffled in *burnooses* against sun and flying sand, and bore modem rifles. Fifty yards distant they halted in semimilitary fashion and one of them rode out to meet Yelniz. I quietly moved my beast nearer to the aides, who were watching the meeting of leaders with absorbed interest.

"The *agha* has good eyes," muttered one of them dry-throatedly. "What in the name of Eblis is Esmer Bey doing here?"

Esmer Bey! Small wonder that I started.

CHAPTER IV

ON TO THEMOUD

S HADING MY eyes from the sun-glare, I saw that
Esmer Bey—if this was indeed he—must be an extremely
powerful man, though his flowing *burnoose* hid the lines of his
figure and I could make out only his general size.

Neither he nor Yelniz left their camels, but sat side by side
for an instant. Then Esmer called something to his men, and
his voice startled me again. It was vibrant, powerful, with a ring
as of brazen metal crashing somewhere within its depths—the
imperious voice of a son of the true Osmanli breed with under-
tones of Mongol cruelty lingering beneath it.

At his word his men came forward. Yelniz turned, and as they
drew up to join us I caught the rumbling voice of Yelniz raised
in protest and decision.

"… But give us water instead, and all return together to your
wells. I tell you I am too weary to talk now."

"By the Prophet, why did you not come from Jerusalem to
Maan, as ordered? Say!"

It occurred to me that this was strange talk from *bey* to *pasha;*
but as the two parties closed up I caught a fleeting, vague impression of Esmer's face under its hood, and wondered no more.
Every move, every word of the man showed that he was a living
volcano of energy, while the more sluggish Yelniz was plainly
afraid of him. And with good reason, as events proved to me.

"You sent word of a messenger with papers," replied Yelniz

sullenly. "They wired me from Port Saïd that he had slipped through. I came—"

"Where are his papers?"

"Gone. He is dead. No man saw the letters."

"The letters gone—thou fool!"

Esmer's voice was positively vitriolic. Even Yelniz straightened up beneath its sting. But the other paid no attention. Directing his own men to supply us with their fresher supply of water, he assumed command of the whole party by tacit consent.

I was too eager for a taste of the precious water to pay much further heed to the Osmanlis. Esmer's men had canteens instead of skins, and at close quarters I made out that they were regular desert troops, and Osmanlis to a man.

The aspect of our new comrades utterly cowed the pilgrims, already terrified by the death of Sa'ad. Now they were only too anxious to finish the trip and be rid of their unwelcome protector. No sooner was the water divided than Esmer, who appeared to have no need of the *sheik's* services, led the troop off at a swift pace. I conjectured that we were not far from our destination, and once I settled down to the swing of my camel I began to realize more than ever that something very astonishing was going on.

I knew that the men who wore John Solomon's ring had long been picked; that the little ship-chandler had a well-nigh perfect system of these aids scattered down the Red Sea coasts and elsewhere; that he was granted a huge yearly subsidy from Medina and Mycea for running guns and pilgrims and that to be one of Solomon's men was tantamount to being above the law.

Adan ibn Hamid, whom I had known in other years as one of the best of this secret-service corps, had been sent with Uriel Gairner—and he had been afraid to go forward, according to the letter he bore back from Edith Gairner. He had quitted the caravan, had reached Port Saïd, and had there been attacked and sent to die in a hospital.

Of what had he been afraid? Not of Esmer Bey, certainly; yet here was Esmer also, away from the caravan on which he was presumably spying, and evidently in hot haste to connect with Yelniz Pasha, his nominal superior. I concluded to get into touch with Yusuf in some manner and find out what I could.

This did not prove so hard as I anticipated. With the sunset a low group of palms came into sight ahead, and with them something that stretched in a glittering, tenuous line across the desert—the railroad to Mecca. We pilgrims greeted it with yells of joy, firing what pistols we had into the air, while the Osmanlis rode on with ironical faces.

By dark we were in camp. Under the trees to one side were stationed the camels, one of the soldiers on guard; and as the wells were all but dried up we watered the beasts by twos and threes. Esmer superintended all in person, driving the men with his furious energy, while Yelniz retired almost at once into the larger camel's-hair tent which was put up for the two leaders. No other tents were erected, as we were too worn out to be fearful of sleeping beneath the stars.

To my delight, Yusuf quietly assumed the place of the slain Sa'ad and attached himself to me, the Osmanli soldiers keeping to themselves. Esmer did not seek the large tent until the evening meal was over. While this was preparing he directed me to attend to watering the camels with Yusuf. The *sheik*, instead of resenting the curt order, accepted meekly; and once out of ear-shot I turned to him eagerly.

"Are you here by Solomon's orders, *sheik?*"

"Allah forbid! Know, O Nour-ed-Din, that I had orders to gather a caravan of the chosen who wear his seal," and he held up his ring. "They were to report to me at Ain Musa. So was it done, and I was awaiting his coming when this dog of an Osmanli came and commanded that I guide him to this oasis."

"And where are we?"

"On the railroad, some ten miles from Maan. I could not refuse him, for he had orders from the government—may Allah blast it!—and could have forced me."

"Do you speak Osmanli?"

"I? Am I a village dog to soil my tongue with refuse, Egyptian?"

I nodded, thinking swiftly. The *sheik* had not penetrated my own disguise, so much was certain. If John Solomon had intended leaving Ain Musa with a caravan of his own men under Yusuf's guidance, the best thing Yusuf and I could do would be to go back and rejoin him.

Still, the thought of those two Osmanlis in their tent stuck persistently in my head. I outlined to the *sheik* what I knew of the business. Yusuf added one bit of knowledge, though to me it seemed utterly unconnected with the trip at the time.

"Yesterday I heard Yelniz Pasha talking, Egyptian, and more than once he made mention of the place called Themoud, accursed of the Prophet."

I recalled the words of the Osmanlis in the Continental Hotel at Port Saïd: "Is it not so named in the *Sura* of Al Araf?" Themoud! Why, that was the place of legend and fairy tale, the great city north of Medina and Mecca, supposed to have been destroyed for its sins by God and blotted out in fire and earthquake.

Yet I saw no connection. Besides, casting back over the *Suras,* I remembered the words of the prophet to the men of Themoud: "So that on the plains ye build castles and hew out dwellings in the hills." Gairner was going into the stony desert, not into the hills. What was more, the very name of Themoud existed only in legend and was synonymous with utter destruction. So I cast aside the *sheik's* half-hopeful suggestion and asked as to his plans.

"I have fulfilled my orders, son of Saleh, and this night I return to meet our Lord Suleiman—if it be not too late. Since I shall get no pay for this service, I will take one of the fresh camels belonging to the soldiers."

My heart leaped—this was the very thing! If I could only overhear that coming conversation in the tent I could go back to Ain Musa with Yusuf. And I was more than anxious to get some inkling of this Osmanli plot if I could.

Yusuf heard me out, and as we returned to camp suggested quietly that since I understood Osmanli I might creep up to the tent and listen. The whole band, both pilgrims and Osmanlis, were too worn out to stand watch, save for the man on guard at the camels.

"Him will I take care of," concluded the *sheik,* and pointed to Esmer Bey squatted over the little fire of camels' dung. "There is a moon to-night, but that cannot be helped. When the hour calls go and listen. I will prepare the camels for flight."

I nodded. Save for the guards fifty yards away, the Osmanlis were already lying about the fire. In the tent gleamed a dim light.

No sooner were the camels under guard again than Esmer Bey went down to the wells to drink and wash. When he returned, I knew, the long-deferred consultation would ensue. Giving my white *burnoose* to Yusuf to take to the camels, after our meager supper I lay down and waited until all things sank into silence, when the figure of Esmer loomed up in the shadowy gloom beneath the palms and passed into the tent.

I dared not risk missing any part of that talk. Knowing that my browned body and filthy pilgrim clothes would mingle perfectly with the sand hue, I slipped off and cautiously approached the tent. The ease of it surprised me; stepping over the group of sleeping Osmanlis, I came quietly to the back of the tent and squatted down in the sand. The tent was between me and the camels, so that I was well out of sight of any one.

From inside came the sleepy tones of Yelniz, who was being rudely awakened by Esmer Bey. The latter had gained nothing in temper from having been forced to bottle up his thoughts during the afternoon. At his curt command Yelniz told what he knew of Adan ibn Hamid's death, saying that since there was nothing to be done at Port Saïd he had made all haste to get trace of Esmer at Maan, thinking to follow with men.

"Follow—me!" came the ironic rejoinder. "You would do well

if you could, Yelniz Pasha. Now pay heed. The Nazarene and his daughter have more evidence than we hold, though I could not find out what it was. I joined the day after they left Maan, and two days later they sent this Adan ibn Hamid back with letters. I, too, sent off a man to Maan to wire word of his coming to Jerusalem and Akaba, but he escaped the net, it seems.

"For a week we traveled fast to the northeast, and another to the north, using both our *firmans* to get passage. There are two devils of Afghans with the Nazarene, and they suspected me, though he did not.

"Finally we came to such desert as even I, who have passed half my life in Yemen, never saw before. There were no Arabs and less sand; the camels wore out their feet on rocky, sand-dusted soil blasted by Allah, and there was no wind of any kind, save the hot breath of Eblis. On the seventh day of this I left them."

"Coward!" Yelniz jeered mockingly. "Did the infidel girl repulse you?"

"Nay; she is as good as my wife, or will be," returned Esmer coolly.

This I by instinct knew for a lie, and instantly I began to hate Esmer Bey.

The Turk continued: "I stole certain maps which the Nazarene had made, and came back to get you and troops—"

"Why?" queried Yelniz impatiently. "You should have waited. We do not yet know if it be not like chasing the lion in the jackal's lair."

"Be quiet!"

The metallic, vibrant voice fully betrayed Esmer's swift anger.

"On that seventh day of the second week I saw in the distance a hill, long and shaped against the sky like a man's nose. From the apex ascended smoke. Does *that* smell of jackal, O prince of sheep's brains?"

For a moment there was silence. Then Yelniz, showing no anger at the taunt, rumbled forth his amazement:

"By the ninety-nine names of Allah! Can you find your way back?"

"Can I read the Koran when it is spread before me?"

The insolent scorn in the voice of Esmer rang hard.

"I have maps, and the direction was north east for a week, then north, into the stone desert. What more could man desire? The Man's Nose That Smokes—it might have been fifty miles away, or a mirage, for the air was clear; none the less, I have seen it, and now remains but to plan. Where there is smoke there are men, and where there is a mountain of that shape—and men also—there lies—"

"What we must get," broke in Yelniz's heavier voice, with a trace of the other's energy creeping through it. "If we get it not, Esmer, we and ours lose what we have—"

"Less talk and more work! You sent men from Jerusalem?"

"No; I thought you had men—"

Esmer broke into a furious storm of cursing. The virile power of the man impressed itself on me anew; but I waited eagerly until Yelniz also grew angry, at which Esmer regained his temper and smoothed things over.

A week to the northeast, and then north! Small wonder that my pulses throbbed, for now I knew—yet I did not know all. This information would be invaluable to John Solomon if I ever saw that gentleman again, which at present seemed doubtful. And yet—and yet—what the deuce were the Osmanlis on the scent of?

So I lingered, and all unwitting flung away the golden opportunity Fate had proffered me. The next words of Esmer Bey bound me to my place as by a chain; the incredible was true!

"Listen, Yelniz! There must be men there, and we have none save our dozen Osmanlis here in camp. We can either wait at Maan for your men or push on to Themoud. Remember, these Nazarenes must be disposed of beyond consular reach, while at the same time—"

"I know—I know!" grunted Yelniz irritably. "Also, this

messenger with letters came to some one at Port Saïd. Was it
to Suleiman?"

"Let that wait. What of us?"

"Wait also. There may be men at Themoud—may the
All-merciful blast the place!—but not many. A nation could
not remain hidden for ages; a few might. We can get Arabs—"

"Good, O Prince of Cunning!"

Esmer's reply was good-humored.

"We must also collect camels, for the journey will take two
weeks or mayhap, more.

"I have it! At Maan the *sheik* of the Ma'az tribe lies netted in
jail; let us promise him immunity for his murders and robberies
on condition that he leads his men with us. We can proclaim a
jehad against Themoud by means of my *firman*, which no one
can read; the Ma'az men are the finest devils out of Eblis for
fighting, and there are a hundred of them."

"*Tchoq eyi!*" grunted Yelniz. "Very well, Esmer. And what of
these Nazarenes, who also have a *firman?*"

"What is that to us? At Themoud there is no need of *firmans*.
The *papaz* can be sent to partake of his own paradise. The girl
will enter my harem."

I was trembling in a fever of excitement. There are legends in
Arabia; I, who had studied long to make myself a teller of tales,
had heard often of the Man's Nose That Smokes, and more often
of the place called Themoud. The latter, indeed, dates back to
Diodorus Siculus and Ptolemy, but so interwoven with fantastic tales of genii and beasts that never were by land or sea had
all these tales become that I was hard put to it to credit even
Esmer's words.

Yet—did Themoud actually exist? It was said to, of course; but
only as a city of the dead set in a choice portion of Eblis, placed
on earth by King Solomon or Mohammed, according as the
story-teller chose, as a warning to other unbelievers. The smoking mountain shaped like a man's nose had still more fantas-

tic explanations, nor did any one really think that such a place existed.

Small wonder that every pulse of me was throbbing! In that instant I believe that I would have sold my very soul to know that it was to be my fate to reach this place, to know that I was to bring it before the world in all its marvel. Yet had I foreseen how dearly I was to buy this reward I think I would have crept silently out into the sand and perished.

Yelniz returned an evil chuckle to Esmer's last statement, and started to speak. The words were lost on me, however, for from the trees fifty yards away on the far side of the tent, where the camels were guarded, a single shrill cry trembled on the starlight. An instant later there was a shot, and another, with a shout in the voice of Yusuf, the *sheik:*

"Hasten, Egyptian; hasten!"

CHAPTER V

THE CIGARETTES OF ESMER BEY

T**HE EGYPTIAN** was not overly noted for his slowness at other times; yet before I had gained my feet the two men inside the tent had taken the alarm, while the wakened Osmanlis were starting up beyond.

Yusuf had been discovered, of course. It crossed my mind that I must reach the camels and get away, for the *sheik's* shout would betray me as an accomplice. I darted around the side of the low tent, drawing my automatic as I did so; wild yells were rising from the pilgrims, mingled with shouts from the Osmanlis; but no more sound came from *Sheik* Yusuf.

There was no time for hesitation. I could not go around without drawing a bullet from the Osmanlis; I must go through them, scatter them, and so gain the shelter of the camels. For the rest—flight.

So I started to rush, but got no farther than the start, for I had overlooked the important fact that tents have ropes, and Arab tents very long ropes. At my third step I tripped and plowed forward into the sand with a muttered curse.

The very impetus of my fall lent me swiftness. In an instant I had rolled over, and sprung to my feet again. Turning to take up my course, I found myself gripped by the shoulder, and the heavy figure of Yelniz Pasha swung into me and flung me back. His great jowled face peered into mine; I felt myself pressed back against the tent side, while the Osmanli gave a shout that bellowed over the tumult.

Desperate, unable to free my arms, seeing my fate close upon me, I managed to twist up my right hand, got the revolver against the brown *burnoose*, and pulled the trigger. Yelniz screamed— staggered—and I pulled free.

Without glancing back I dashed at the bewildered Osmanlis. The strident tones of Esmer Bey came from somewhere close at hand, but, dropping my automatic, I struck out with both hands as I leaped into the group of men. In my heart was desperate fear that Yusuf would desert me.

"A genie!" went up the yell, and the Osmanlis scattered before me, two or three reeling down under my blows.

I broke through the others and ran for it, hoping against hope that the *sheik* would wait for me.

I had but fifty yards to cover, though it was hard running in the loose sand. At each step I fully expected to hear a bullet whine over my shoulder, but none came; and I had covered half the distance and was straining my eyes to make out the figure of Yusuf among the cluster of bubbling, snorting camels before I was aware of the danger that menaced me in the shape of something that touched my bare back once very lightly and then slipped down and away.

Twisting my head as I ran I was startled to see a figure right at my heels, running step for step with me, its hand outstretched and at my shoulder. Though I had not seen Esmer Bey without his muffling *burnoose* and head-handkerchief, I knew instantly who my pursuer was. And I knew that he would have me in another moment.

Without warning I whirled and shot out my fist. So close was the Osmanli upon me that my arm drove over his shoulder, and we came crashing together. In a flash I realized the folly of my course. Had I but gone a few steps farther Yusuf would have been at hand to relieve me of Esmer; but it is upon just such trifling things that the fate of men turns. Now Esmer had me in a grip of iron and was shouting to his scattered men.

I tried in vain to send my fists home. Esmer had locked his

arms around me, and a second later he deftly tripped and sent me to the ground beneath him. Here, however, I made shift to get a grip on his throat. I think I have said that I was stronger than some men, and I caught a gasp of surprise from Esmer as I broke his hold and sank my fingers among his neck muscles.

For a moment I fancied that I would get away from him. I threw myself up, managed to bear him back, and drove up my knee into his stomach. Then, just as I had wrenched free of him, a mass of men flung themselves upon me.

Thus far I had uttered no word, and now I could not if I would. I struggled in vain; the bodies above suffocated me, ground me down into the sand by their weight and held me there helpless, and when I was all but strangled they piled off, and I found myself bound firmly hand and foot. I had failed.

What was more, I knew that Esmer Bey must be a man of steel. This Osmanli, who was a reversion to the old racial type which had swept the world into chaos until it became effeminated, had put at naught all my strength and science, and had flung me like a child. To say the least, it was irritating.

Sobbing the cool air into my lungs, I lay staring up at the stars and listened. I heard shouted orders from Esmer, followed by shots, and then one defiant, exulting *"Allahu!"* which drifted faintly to me and told me that *Sheik* Yusuf had made good his escape.

"Serves me right!" I thought bitterly. "If I'd obeyed orders John Solomon and I would have been leaving Ain Musa by this time with a good crowd of his men. No! I did all right, confound it!"

And perhaps I had done right, after all. At least I had learned that this Osmanli plot was directed primarily against the place called Themoud—unless Esmer Bey had made a mistake about seeing the Man's Nose That Smokes—and secondarily against Gairner. Also I now knew approximately where this place was; but the core of the whole matter still lay beyond my ken.

Why? Osmanlis are not interested in mere exploration as a rule.

I proceeded no farther with my meditations, for just then two soldiers picked me up and carried me inside the tent of Esmer, where an evil-smelling candle was burning. I caught sight of the body of Yelniz in the side shadows, but cannot remember that I felt any great regret over his death. Esmer's voice, not exactly pleasant to hear, came from without, and a moment later he entered and I obtained my first view of him, divested of his *burnoose.*

Esmer Bey, at this time some thirty-five years of age, was at the height of his renown—for I learned all about him later on and insert that knowledge here. Osmanli to the core, he had an almost Caucasian cast of feature which served him well. Following that open break between the Porte and the Grand Senussi, of which I have spoken before and in which Solomon was somewhat concerned, Esmer Bey had visited the *hinterland* of Libya, had succeeded in reconciling the two present-day heads of the Moslem faith, and had aided the Senussi in his protracted struggle with the Italians.

This had brought Esmer into prominence at Constantinople, and his rare ability, combined with his fanatical doctrine that the Osmanlis should no longer ape the Christians, had speedily placed power in his hands. At the time I was ignorant of all this, but I did know that Esmer was undeniably handsome, with his square chin, high brow, and deep eyes; only his high cheek-bones betrayed the Turanian in him, together with the latent cruelty that ran through the power of his whole manner and look.

Powerful he certainly seemed, proud without being arrogant, secure enough in himself and in my bonds to order the guards outside. Then and only then did I remember that I had a part to play. I expected an examination after the usual oriental manner; but in this I was disappointed.

Now, I do not apologize for what followed. I ask you only to remember that I was Nour-ed-Din the pilgrim, and that I was playing my part as best I could. In Anglo-Saxon eyes I did wrong, perhaps, and yet—for the moment I was an Egyptian.

"Your name?" asked Esmer, sitting on the prayer-rug in the center of the tent and looking calmly at me. I was sitting, arms bound behind me, against the tent-wall.

"H-m!"

He continued to gaze reflectively at me when I had given my name. His calmness made me uneasy.

"Well, this *sheik* has escaped after slaying two men, O Light of the Faith, and you have not escaped after slaying Yelniz Pasha. It would interest me to know the reason of this slaying."

"The reason?" I repeated blankly. "By the Prophet and the Book, master, I know not! I had but wakened with the first shot, and as I stood up Yelniz Pasha caught hold on me, and not seeing who it was I fired—"

"Do not blaspheme, Egyptian," broke in his quiet, thrilling voice. "I am not unused to dealing with your kind, so no more lies. Where did you get this automatic pistol? Such things are not worn by pilgrims."

He nodded at the weapon which I had so unthinkingly dropped in my panic after shooting Yelniz, and which had been flung inside the tent. I knew the futility of lying, and yet I dared do nothing else than lie, lest my disguise be pierced by those hard, smoldering black eyes. I flung myself desperately into the part, and I think I played it well.

"By the holy tomb, I swear that I lie not! See, *sidi,* at Port Saïd I stole it from an infidel dog whom I was guiding through the streets—"

"Peace!"

Esmer leaned forward suddenly. There was such bitter, intense malignity in his face that I shrank back involuntarily.

"I said—*lie not!* You had no business near my tent, dog. Say! Who sent you to murder Yelniz Pasha?"

I think he saw that I was genuinely startled at this. I saw the plausibility of such a charge, and could not keep the alarmed amazement from my face.

"I am an Egyptian, *sidi*. I had not been in the land three days when Yelniz Pasha took me under his protection. Are poor pilgrims, unknown and untried, hired to slay such men as Yelniz Pasha, lord? It is not so in my country. I have friends and money, *sidi*, and I will pay *diyat* for this fault of mine—"

"*Diyat!*" scoffed Esmer, laughing a little. "This is no matter of bloodfine, Egyptian. Not twice a thousand camels would pay for the life of an Osmanli. Ah—"

As if seized by a sudden thought, he drew some matches from his waistcloth and left the tent with a single bound. A moment later he reentered, coolly resumed his seat, brought the candle to his cigarette, and looked at me again.

"By the genii of Suleiman! Those straight-gazing eyes of yours all but deceived me. So!"

And of a sudden his voice literally bit into me.

"You were spying, eh? And to judge by the hole you left in the sand you were there for some time. Now, O son of Saleh, how much of that conversation did you hear?"

"I know not, lord, for I knew not the tongue," I made humble answer.

I saw that Esmer, having found the traces of my resting-place beside the tent-wall, was not to be trifled with any further. Still I might yet save my identity from those searching black eyes with a flame of Eblis in them.

He sat in silence a little, puffing at his cigarette until it had burned to the last half-inch. Then with the utmost deliberation he leaned forward and pressed the glowing end full against my bare foot.

Taken by surprise, I cried out once, then sat motionless while that searing pain pulsed through my blood. My hands clenched hard and dug down into the sand behind me, but I ground my teeth together after that first involuntary cry and gazed steadily into the mocking eyes of the Osmanli.

It was by no means in keeping with my part to maintain such stubborn silence, and when I realized this I writhed in my bonds and groaned. The cigarette was extinguished against my flesh.

"Whence come you, Egyptian?" asked the Osmanli softly. "There are more matches and more cigarettes. Answer?"

I groaned again. I had never thought that a cigarette-ember could bring such awful suffering; Esmer had burned into the tender instep and I was almost nauseated with the anguish of it.

Yet what to say? Give up the secret of John Solomon, I would not at any cost, for already my desertion of Solomon had caused me too bitter self-reproach. Esmer drew out another cigarette, and at that I broke silence—an idea in my brain.

"No more, *sidi,* in the name of Allah! Oh, would that I had never met the accursed Nazarene! May Allah do battle with him; may his hands perish; may he be burned in the flame; may Eblis—"

"Peace!"

Esmer, a satisfied light in his eyes where that little dancing flame still leaped, put away his cigarette without lighting it.

"I thought we would have the truth out of you! What of your relations with this unbeliever?"

"O Protector of the Faithful," I whined, the lie taking shape, "I swore upon the Koran and upon the holy cities and upon the Prophet that I would say nothing of this matter to any one!"

"It is written that oaths made to unbelievers are of no account," Esmer said coldly. "Let my cigarette absolve your oaths. Speak!"

I had a manifold purpose in this lie of mine. By this time, perhaps, John Solomon would have carried out his purpose of dying, and the less he was suspected by Esmer the better. Moreover, if Esmer could but get the idea that the Rev. Uriel Gairner was not quite so helpless as he had seemed the Osmanli might advance with more caution and less speed.

Nor was my own outlook pleasant. So long as I could keep a

cool head and parry with lies the questions of that acrid voice, Esmer might not suspect my disguise; but let it be discovered—

"O *sidi*, I was hired by the Nazarene *mullah* in Suez, and served him as guide while he was there. When he left he sent me with letters to the consul of his Frankish nation at Port Saïd. This consul questioned me and then conferred with many men from a Frankish war-ship in the harbor.

"Then one day the consul gave me much money and this pistol, and told me that I was to follow Yelniz Pasha, if I could. He said that Yelniz Pasha was feared by the Nazarene *mullah*, and ordered me to find out if harm was intended. He promised me great reward.

"By the blessing of Allah I joined this caravan at Port Ibrahim. That is all I know, protector; by my father's head I swear it! I know no word of Turkish, and what you and Yelniz Pasha said this night was hidden from me by Allah's will.

"*Sidi*, I have told the truth. Now cut my bonds, in the name of the Compassionate, for they are eating into my flesh!"

Esmer Bey had received this amazing invention of mine unmoved, but none the less he believed it, as his words showed.

"That has a ring of truth to it, pilgrim. So the consul confers with Americans from a war-ship? Bad!"

He lowered his head on his breast, his fingers tugging reflectively at the pointed beard which accentuated the strong line of his jaw. Once more I raised my voice in querulous complaint, playing my part out to its finish. Now it was win or lose all; if I had read my Osmanli friend aright I would win, and in any case I had not much to lose.

"Loosen my bonds, O Light of the World! Loosen my bonds and I will serve thee, O Mighty One, O Blessed of Allah, O Beloved of the Houris of Paradise, O Most Bountiful and Gracious, O—"

"*Bismillah!* Peace!"

Esmer straightened up impatiently and cut short my wails.

"You shall go back to Port Saïd and tell this consul that no

harm is intended, that Yelniz Pasha was slain by accident, and
that you saw nothing of me or mine."

I caught my breath, for—I had won!

"So shall suspicion be removed," went on Esmer. "This shall
be your *diyat* for the death of Yelniz Pasha—that you remove
suspicion. Remember! It is written that all true believers shall
help one another against the infidel, and think not to escape me
if this fine be not paid. My arm is long—"

While he was speaking the Osmanli drew a knife and leaned
over to cut the bonds about my ankles. I could hardly realize
my own good fortune; not only did Esmer believe my astound-
ing lie, but he was actually going to send me back to Port Saïd
in order, as he thought, to double-cross the imaginary consul.
Oddly enough, remembering the man of whiskers and baseball
and politics, I laughed inwardly.

But as his knife began to bite into my ropes Esmer Bey
suddenly straightened up and replaced it in his girdle. Without a flicker of emotion on his face he leaned back once more.
Slowly he drew a cigarette from the case beside him, looking
down at the little tube as he knocked it against his closed left
fist and freed it of loose tobacco. When he looked up at me his
eyes were smoldering strangely.

"Who are you?"

"What do you mean, *sidi?*" I could not keep the alarm out
of my voice, try as I might, for his whole aspect had changed
in a second.

"Who are you?" he repeated slowly, leaning forward.

A very devil of cruelty gleamed out of those black eyes of his.

"A Frank—an infidel; but of what country?"

He switched suddenly to English.

"Answer me, you fool! To play thus with Esmer Bey!"

Suddenly stricken, I glanced down at my ankles. Then in a
flash I realized all that had happened—the ropes, tightly drawn
as they were, had rubbed away the stain. The sun had not yet
burned my body Arab-brown, and a ringlet of white skin around

the ropes had betrayed me utterly. With an effort I gathered myself together.

"I am an American," I replied, throwing away all pretense as I met his eyes squarely. "My name is Sargent, Esmer Bey, and I also am on my way to Themoud."

I think it speaks volumes for the man that he showed neither astonishment nor anger in that moment.

"Yes?"

His tense voice lifted slightly.

"You are a fine actor, Mr. Sargent; a very fine actor. But for those ropes you would have gone free in another minute or so. Now, however, I want to know only one thing. Who put you on my trail?"

I had played the game and lost, and I think I flung back my shoulders a little as I realized that I was no longer an Egyptian but an American.

"That I will not tell you, Esmer."

He slowly leaned over and held his cigarette above the vile-smelling candle until the heat sent a little red glow crawling up the tube. Then he began to puff slowly.

CHAPTER VI

PAYMENT

A WHITEWASHED HOUSE of mud-brick stands
on the outskirts of Maan, with its own wells and date-
palms, all surrounded by a low wall, also of mud-brick. It is far
from the bustle and squalor of the railroad—yet, because the
caravans pass by it as they come into the city from Jof and Hail,
there are bazaars opposite the low mud wall, throngs of pilgrims
about the bazaars, and swarms of beggars who find the mud wall
an attractive spot for displaying their sores and so gaining the
alms of the pilgrims.

On a certain day in the pilgrimage month of Shawal there
was unusual bustle and crowding in the narrow street between
the bazaars and the mud wall. Thin-bearded Moors, sturdy,
red-whiskered Afghans, gaunt Somalis, fat, crafty Persians—
all jostled together in blissful forgetfulness of the seventy-odd
jarring sects of Islam.

So had the crowd stood and jostled for six days past. Each
day the tide ebbed and flowed as caravan or train carried off old
faces and left new behind, yet every day the crowd had stood
there. The wonderful part of it to each newcomer was the silence
that at times swelled into a buzz of talk, then died away again.
True, the bazaar-keepers cursed, but below their breath and to
each other only.

At one side of the entranceway through the low mud wall two
ancient lepers, whose leprosy was so hideous that they had long
since grown rich on alms, had been sent off to beg elsewhere. In

their place stood two erect Osmanlis, with fixed, glittering bayonets, and a little behind them and between was a dark object, from which ran chains to a ring in the wall above.

Over the three figures was a painted scrawl in Arbi. It was this that caused the occasional buzz of talk in the unwashed, holy crowd, as those unable to read sought its import from others:

> *In the name of Allah, the Compassionate, the Merciful! Let all ye true believers gaze upon this Frank who sought to defile the holy places with the feet of an infidel—the false pilgrim of an accursed race! Harm him not upon pain of death, but let his punishment be observed and told afar. "Knowest thou not that God hath power over all things?"*

The subtle irony of the final quotation from the *Sura* of the Cow always drew smiles of appreciation from the newcomers, startled as they invariably were. Then invariably they would wait to see the punishment of the Frank, and in silence, for it had been commanded that there should be no shouting and no tumult since Esmer Bey was occupying the house behind the low mud wall. And this was that for which they waited.

At the *moghrab*, after sunset, the *eshe*, or darkness, the *soobh*, or daybreak, the *doohr* or noontide, and the *asr* or afternoon, just as the muezzin a few blocks away was mounting the stairs of his minaret to call the faithful to prayer, two figures would appear in the gateway.

The first of these was Esmer Bey, who would gravely acknowledge the salute of his two guards. Behind him was an Osmanli bearing a large whip. Esmer Bey would ask a single question in some strange tongue, and then a little sigh would go up from all the crowd around.

For at the question the huddled figure against the wall would lift itself slowly and wearily until all the crowd could see the clean-shaven Frank, now burned to a dark brown from head to foot, look up at Esmer Bey and snap out a single word. As the first note of the muezzin's call would float down softly, Esmer

Bey would sign to the man with the whip, who would silently take up his position.

Then, as every one from Esmer Bey to the lowliest beggar bowed toward Mecca, the whip would fall once for every *sura* repeated by the crowd around, until Esmer Bey would rise and vanish. The four or five thudding blows would draw no cry from the Frank, and when he settled back against the wall the flies would cloud down over him once more, covering all save a little glint of silver on his hand.

This was undoubtedly the most popular place of prayer in all the city, though none knew the meaning of that question. Indeed, more than one bet had been placed as to how long the unbeliever would last, and many a pilgrimage had been delayed until such bets had been settled. It was a glorious sight for all of the true faith.

But—how shall I speak of those ten days that had passed like ten ages of torment since that night in Esmer Bey's tent? Even now I can scarce bear to recall the things that passed, for the very memory of if is horrible. Esmer was infinitely cunning, infinitely diabolic; after promises he settled down to the most terrible torture that was ever dreamed of, for it was torture of mind and body alike.

It is enough to say that by now I had settled down to counting the hours and minutes between the times of prayer, for each of those whip-strokes cut around my body, and that monotonous question was slowly but surely torturing me into weakness and breaking down my will. It was so easy to answer it!

A thousand times had I prayed for death, but Esmer was too deep, too cunning. He wanted, not to wear down my body, but to wear down my mind. It was now the seventh day that I had been chained to the wall. With dulled senses and torpid brain I saw the sun gleam down and die, and heard the anticipatory rustle of breaths amid the crowd. Twice to-day I had fainted beneath the whip-strokes. Now as Esmer stalked out I knew that it could not last much longer.

Strange that we of the Western world are so apt to regard the means as the end! On that afternoon I felt that surely the finish of all was at hand. I was too weak to move, and the torture of the flies was beyond words. Yet I now know that all this was but the means to a greater end—it is easy to be philosophical in an armchair.

"Your answer, Mr. Sargent?" asked Esmer, standing over me while the crowd held its breath and wondered. "Who sent you on this mission?"

I lifted a haggard, skin-drawn face and glared at him with hatred in my eyes. Across my cheeks there was a red weal where the whip had fallen three days before—and sometimes the redness of it stands out to this day.

"No!" I mumbled, my will not yet broken.

The other shrugged his shoulders and turned.

"He will die, *agha*," muttered the Osmanli with the whip.

Disregarding the muezzin's call, Esmer turned again and looked down at me, a cold calculation in his eye.

"He will not die," he returned. "But to-night remove him to the room next mine. When his strength comes back we will try a better way. The dog is strong."

The drone of prayer, that cursed first *sura* of the Koran, welled upward from town and walls and street, the deeper and more hollow reverberations of the pilgrim-filled mosque sounding up through it all like the note of an angry hornet surrounded by wasps. But at the second of the *farz* prayers, as the whip came down for the second time, I fell forward, mercifully.

I wakened soon—almost too soon, for Esmer had barely gone and half the crowd were still on their knees, reciting penance *suras*. At all events the torture was over for the present, I thought; what was to come mattered little, so that I could but be away from this place of terror. The thought put new life into me, and I waited for the night almost happily, so miserable was my heart.

Suddenly I looked up to find a stately, elderly man come out of the crowd and stand before me. He was a person of some account, for he wore a rare-woven *abba* from Jof a handkerchief on his head girt with a thick band of camel-hair interwoven with gold thread, and a silver-hilted sword. He spoke to my guards in Arbi.

"So! A Frank! Of what nation is he, brethren?"

"How should we know?" responded one of the surly brutes with more respect than either had been wont to show the crowd. "It is not allowed to harm him, O *sheik!*"

"Nay, nay; I would not harm him," came the grave answer. "Let Allah punish him! But once when I was a young man I visited many lands, even as far as Constantinople, and learned the tongues of the unbelievers. Can he talk or is his tongue torn out?"

"He can speak your own tongue well enough," laughed the soldier half-suspiciously. "It were best not—"

The *sheik,* for such he undoubtedly was, quietly opened his *abba* and showed the jeweled Order of the Mejidieh; instantly the two soldiers saluted, and at the same time I almost cried out, for there was a little silver ring upon his hand.

"I think there will be no harm in an old man's gratifying his vanity," said the grave Arab, smiling and stroking his beard again. "You, brethren, no doubt speak the tongue of the Franks also, and can follow what is said—"

"Not we," grunted the Osmanli disdainfully.

A little glimmer as of satisfaction lit the somber eyes of the *sheik* and was gone.

Sudden wild hope leaped into my dulled heart as I looked up. I still wore John Solomon's seal-ring, for it had not been worth tearing from my hand; had this Arab seen it and come to help me? I fell to trembling, and waited.

"Be careful," came slow and difficult words in English. "I can do nothing now; but if you make yourself the escape and reach the date-bazaar opposite of the gateway you will find friends."

Now, it sounds like a little thing, no doubt, but only by a tremendous effort did I restrain myself from shouting aloud at those English words, garbled though they were. I mumbled something, I know not what, and as the terrible spasm of my joy laid hold on me, darkness came with it and I fainted again.

WHEN I awakened it was with a blissful sense of ease and comfort. My body, at least, was at ease, for I lay on an old rug in a bare room, my wrists still wearing handcuffs, but brought together in front of my body. The sun was streaming in from a small, high window in the tumble-down wall.

I knew that I lay in the room of which Esmer Bey had spoken—next to his own. Then I remembered the old Arab *sheik* and lay back with my eyes closed.

"If you make yourself the escape and reach the date-bazaar—"

I knew that date-bazaar well; I had stared across at it day in and day out until I knew every line of it; I knew the cross-eyed Syrian who kept it, bargaining in his shrill falsetto with caravan men and pilgrims. But how to reach it I knew not. I was ironed and a captive; sleep had brought some portion of my strength back, but I was terribly sore and stiff from whip-weals and burns. If I was to get away it would be by my own unaided efforts.

Had I but a knife I felt that I might do something with it, for all pity had been burned out of my soul in the past ten days. From that first moment of my awakening all energies were bent on reaching the date-bazaar. I think it gave me new life to dream of it, even as a remote possibility.

I had doubtless slept the night away, for by the warmth of the sun I concluded that it was nearly noon. I was unwashed, naturally, but clean-shaven; this last was intended as a torment, yet it was a grateful boon to me. A little after the murmur of voices came to me; then a door in the wall opened and Esmer Bey appeared, with a soldier who bore dates, camel-milk, and barley-bread cake. Esmer stood looking down at me, a slightly sardonic smile on his powerful face.

"Are you feeling better, Mr. Sargent? You had better recover strength before a week is out, since you go with us to Themoud—unless you tell me what I want to know before then."

With that it came to me—for he plainly thought me weaker than I was.

"Where am I?"

I whispered the words faintly, staring up wide-eyed.

"In my house—at least it is mine for the present."

He smiled down at me and motioned the soldier to set down the food and drink.

"Think you that sense will come to you, O Nour-ed-Din?"

I made no answer, but closed my eyes and turned away my head weakly, at which he laughed again and went out. I heard him caution the soldier to remain on guard outside my door, and as the steps died away I turned and fell upon the provisions.

A week to escape in! A week to get to that date-bazaar a hundred yards away or less! What might come when that place was reached did not worry me greatly; I would be with friends, and that was enough. It was an untold comfort to think of what that little silver ring meant, up here on the fringe of the desert.

And what did it mean, after all? It occurred to me that the diagram was something Solomon had been too much agitated to explain that day, and I had forgotten it since then. Looking at the ring, I could see nothing strange about it—merely a square with lines running diagonally from corner to corner.

Yet, it must have some meaning, or Solomon would not have adopted it. He was a strange man, full of odd whims and fancies, but underneath every one of these there was a basis of solid common sense. He did nothing without an object.

It slowly grew upon me that somewhere, at some time, I had seen that diagram before. I could not place it, however.

Perhaps an hour later I had a second visit from Esmer. This time his brittle mood had passed into suave affability.

"Perhaps I have been a little hasty, Mr. Sargent," he said quietly. "It has just occurred to me to ask you a few other questions."

For, odd as it seems to me now, he had tortured me solely to gain an answer to that one reiterated query of who had sent me to trail him. I answered nothing to this.

"Tell me, now; do you know more of Themoud than passed between Yelniz and myself that night?"

"No," I answered faintly, seeing no harm in telling the truth.

"Then you do not know my object, or Mr. Gairner's object?"

I shook my head, and saw a light spring into his eyes.

"Why, then, let us abandon this foolish business!" he laughed lightly. "Mr. Sargent, I cannot tell you what this object is; but I swear to you by all I hold sacred that it must be accomplished."

Earnestness came into his voice; in another man it would have been fanaticism, but Esmer was no ordinary man.

"It is greater than you or me, Mr. Sargent, this object of mine. I am but an agent, as Yelniz Pasha was an agent. Come! If you are a friend of Mr. Gairner's then say so openly and fear not."

I wanted to laugh in his face.

"Fine talk, Esmer Bey," I said feebly. "Fine talk; but too late now. You'll get no more out of me with all your wheedling; only some day I'll pay you back for your work."

He stood looking down. There was that little dancing devil in his eyes, but I did not fear it now. His voice remained quite passionless, though.

"You will change your mind, Mr. Sargent. I just received a wire today which had been delayed for a week coming *via* Damascus, concerning a friend of mine in Port Saïd. A Mr. Solomon, poor fellow—he died the same night as Yelniz Pasha. A fire burned his place, and he was identified afterward—"

He had studied me as he spoke, and instantly I decided that before this complication my best course was to disarm his suspicion by admitting my knowledge.

"Solomon!"

I stared up and put wild bewilderment in my eyes.

"Solomon—dead?"

"Yes; Mr. Solomon is dead and buried by this time."

Esmer continued to study me.

"Come! Don't you think we have played the farce long enough?"

I shook my head wearily and closed my eyes.

"I don't know him—never heard of him," I muttered, and an instant later the door slammed.

I smiled for the first time in many days. I had allowed Esmer to read the fact that the news of Solomon's death had hit me hard, as he thought; this would let him know that I had come from Solomon, and my pretense of continued obstinacy would not fool him. He would consider the road open behind him now, and would pay small heed to me or to those who had sent me; I alone knew that John Solomon had not died.

Trust John to be identified! So he had burned down that old shop of his! No doubt some one's body had been placed in the building to be later identified, and there was little doubt in my mind that it had been an Osmanli body. Since the "death" had taken place ten days ago, John must be well into the desert by now.

And now—how was I to reach the date-bazaar?

I was ironed; there was a guard at my door; and doubtless there were sentries at the gates. Also I had a house to get exit from, and that worried me most of all. Fortunately my ankles were free; I rose and walked about the room, trying my strength.

Getting out of the window was impossible; it was too high and too small to let me through did I reach it. No; I must go by means of the door, and that meant silencing the guard.

But how was I to silence him?

I tried my strength by lifting the old rug I had lain on—and stopped abruptly, staring down at it.

It was a common enough *kuz kilim*, or bride's rug, and very heavy, but bore in varying colors the same pattern as that on Solomon's ring! Then I remembered—I had seen that diagram on rugs before, and on the robes of a so-called wizard who lived in a little town across the Persian line near Basra. The thing itself was called the seal of Suleiman, meaning the ancient King Solomon, and was supposed to have magical properties, though no one knew what those properties were.

"Well," I thought, dropping the rug, "I'd better attend to the business in hand. Now, can I get my hands around that guard's throat; and, if so, can I strangle him?"

It was not a nice thought, I assure you, though at the time it seemed perfectly natural to me. After various exercises I determined that I could not be sure of myself by any means. After a day or two of returning strength I could try it with better success, and in any case it would be best to wait.

I *must* succeed! If I failed, if I were to be discovered, Esmer Bey would put me out of his way like a fly. I felt that he would do so anyway, now that he guessed my secret, and would not bother to take me with him into the desert. Therefore I must checkmate him.

And gradually, as I lay in the darkness that night and listened to the *eshe* prayer droning up from all the Moslem world, the plan came to me.

CHAPTER VII

OUT OF THE FRYING-PAN—

IT WAS the third evening after I had been transferred to the house. I had by no means regained my strength in full, but as I guessed that Esmer was meditating some devilish scheme to get rid of me in an effective way I dared put off the attempt no longer.

He had not visited me again, but that fear was strong in my mind. Covert grins from my guard when he brought my food only increased my apprehension. He refused to speak, however, even when I addressed him in Osmanli.

He was a wiry fellow, this guard who kept my door from sunset to sunrise, but I had little doubt that if I once got my hands about his throat I could take care of him. Strange as it may appear, in the seven continuous years which I had spent in Arbi-speaking lands, most of them in disguise, I had never found occasion to fight.

Once or twice caravans with which I was had been attacked, and once when a valuable Nejd stallion had been stolen from me in Hail I had caught the thief and delivered him to the emir's justice; but as a rule, traveling as a simple teller of tales or a fortune teller, I met with no accidents. Arabia is well ruled, save for the untrodden desert portions, and in its way holds far less crime than America.

My assumed air of truculence, my green turban—for I had made the holy pilgrimage before—and my evident poverty had always carried me safe. On this occasion it was very different, however. Exposed to that crowd, I had been in deadly fear that some one would recognize me as the Damascene or the *hajj* or the story-teller; if those fanatics knew that I had already made the pilgrimage not all the power of Esmer Bey could have kept them from tearing me to pieces.

So I am not ashamed to confess that I was beginning to get my fill of Islam. The dangers of discovery had been terribly brought home to me, and my torments had sickened me to the soul. I had been mad—mad to try this thing—mad to leave John Solomon there at Port Saïd. But there was a magic in the name of Themoud that tugged at my brain.

I did not know what the crux of the whole affair was, but I did know that if I found this mysterious Themoud to be really existant, I would have done a great thing. Still, that a place could exist in legend from the days of Mohammed down to our own times without being discovered, that a tribe or a nation could remain unbelievers in the heart of Arabia without feeling the sword of Islam, was incredible. Only Esmer's talk of terrible and unheard of deserts could explain it.

The hours passed slowly, very slowly. After the *eshe* prayer I waited until the hum of voices had died down through the house and all was quiet. If I had only had some tobacco! I think I had fooled Esmer very neatly as regarded my real condition, but I hated him so bitterly by this time that I could not bring myself to ask him for so much as a cigarette. And to-night, if all went well, I intended to pay out my debt.

So when at length I could stand the unbearable waiting no longer I groaned—softly, then louder. At the same instant I left my bed and moved to the door. I had a better plan than throttling the sentry, and I wanted to save my strength for Esmer Bey.

A movement outside and the door opened. My eyes, used to the darkness, made out the form of the sentry who had left his rifle outside. He was barely three feet away from me. I waited.

"What is the matter?" he asked in Osmanli, knowing that I spoke the tongue.

I did not answer, but at his step forward I brought up my handcuffs, then swept them down. They were double, of old make, and very heavy. Consequently as the iron struck him fair on the temple the Osmanli simply crumpled up and went down.

Pulling him away from the door, I removed his *burnoose* and head-cloth, thinking to don them. Here I was blocked, however, for my irons prevented. Searching the man I found cigarettes and matches, but no key. That was probably in Esmer's possession.

Making shift to bind the man, I lit a cigarette, and after one deep inhalation I started for Esmer's room. My door proved to open on a court full of starlight—deserted. As it was at the corner, with a wide entrance on the right which doubtless led to the gates outside, I turned to the left where a smaller door showed.

This was closed, and as I opened it I heard heavy breathing. Now, with the memory of those days of torture behind me, I had had a purpose in lighting that cigarette. It was not a nice purpose nor a creditable one, but I defy the most forgiving man to go through such an ordeal as mine and still preserve his lofty ideals.

I had my hands around Esmer's throat before he wakened, and strength seemed to flood back to me at his first struggle. But he was muffled in a rug, and I had such a grip on his bare throat that he could make no outcry—man of steel though he was. He gurgled, strangling, and groaned to himself as I pressed my face close to his so that the glowing tip of my cigarette branded his cheek until it died out. He could neither kick nor hit, though he wrenched one arm free. After a moment he relaxed.

God forgive me, I had meant to strangle him into death, but I could not. Very cautiously I let the air into his lungs until I made sure he was not shamming, then rose and struck a match.

A search disclosed no keys on his body, but presently a bunch of them came to light, hanging on the wall. Handling them over one by one, I got the bunch into my teeth and tried three on the handcuffs thus; the fourth and last slipped into the lock, turned, and set me free.

"Thank Heaven!" I breathed fervently.

I was glad I had spared Esmer's life; later I regretted it. I felt weak and sat down to rest.

Ten minutes later Esmer was fast bound and gagged. I had a splendid new *burnoose* with head-cloth, two revolvers—automatics both—spare clips of ammunition, a hip-belt of cartridges, and—it was lucky that I fetched this supply—clean linen and sandals. I felt like a new man.

How easy the whole thing had been—seemingly! Yet every instant of that time had passed like an age to me, and when at last I strode boldly to the gates, where a single sentry stood on guard, and looked over at the bazaars across the way, my heart-beats nearly stifled me.

The sentry challenged me, but with an automatic in my hand I walked straight up to him, then shoved the cold steel at his throat. As he started back I saw that he was the man who had whipped me—and the only one who had spoken a kind word for me.

"Be quiet!" I said softly. "A word and I shoot. Drop your rifle."

He dropped it.

"Listen, Osmanli! When I lay by the gate and you came to torture me, you would have spared my life. Take yours in exchange. Give me your belt."

Astonished and utterly cowed by the menace of that automatic at his throat, he unslung his belt like a man in a dream. I tied his hands—for I had no fear of him—then his feet, and gagged him. Drawing him inside the gates that he might not see where I went, I left the accursed place—free!

The date-bazaar was dark and silent, for it must have been near midnight. A knock at the locked doors, however, fetched a guttural voice from somewhere inside:

"Who is it?"

"A friend of Suleiman who seeks friends here."

As if by magic the doors swung open. A hand pulled me inside and on through the darkness into another room, also dark. Five minutes passed with rustling of garments and voices; then a light sprang up.

The room was small and bare, with only a mat of rugs in one corner, with brass grinder, urns, and coffee-cups ready for use. In a farther doorway stood the *sheik* who had spoken to me that day by the mud wall, and the Syrian bazaar-keeper stood by him with a light. The Syrian turned and vanished and the *sheik* came forward.

"Welcome, Frank," he said gravely, motioning me to the pile of rugs, and himself sitting beside me.

An Arab entered and, without a word, began to grind up some coffee. Then the old *sheik* began to unburden his mind, sedately and frankly.

"I know not who you are, Frank,"—and he spoke no more in English—"nor does that concern me. You are in trouble and you wear the ring of Suleiman, therefore have I done what I could."

He lifted a hand to his beard, watching the coffee-maker, and again I saw that he also wore the ring with the diagram.

"But know this, Frank. You have offended my religion in thus trying to gain the holy places in disguise, and I hold no friendship with you. What I can I will do for the sake of the ring. So ask me not to further your journey to Mecca."

Now, I saw that it would be useless to proclaim the writing on the mud wall as a lie, nor indeed was it a lie altogether. So I accepted the old man's dictum gravely, nodding and lighting a cigarette.

"Know you where Suleiman now is?" I asked.

"It is not known, Frank. I have heard that he crossed the railroad with a caravan, but not by any trade-route. It is long since I have seen him, and only by accident did I chance to see the ring upon your finger—my own came to me a few days since by messenger."

This information caused some rapid thinking on my part.

First, Esmer Bey would take it for granted that after escaping I would double back to Port Saïd and to safety, and if there was any search made it would be in that direction. But Solomon had crossed the railroad and gone out into the desert.

I knew the general direction of Themoud, so it seemed to me that the best plan would be to head through the deserts for that place, where I was certain to find John and the American party. Also, they must be warned of Esmer's approach. Questioning the *sheik*, I found that Esmer had done as he and Yelniz had planned that night in the tent.

The Ma'az Arabs, Bedouins famed for their pillaging and outlawry, though but a small band, had been broken up and their *sheik* captured a month since. Esmer had released the *sheik* and sent him out to gather his men—as I knew from his own lips he would set forth on the march in a few days.

Outlining the situation of John Solomon, though careful to say nothing of Themoud or the Man's Nose, I asked the old *sheik* if he could send me forward with a caravan. He shook his head gravely as the coffee-maker brought us the first tiny cup of brew.

"That no man could promise, Frank. All men shun those northern deserts as the pestilence. A week northeast, and after that north? No one would attempt it unless it were some reckless Hazrami—for those men of Hazramaut fear neither man nor genie. Best give over this plan."

"I will not give it over," I returned stubbornly. "Suleiman is in danger somewhere out there, and for his sake you must either grant me a protector and give me camels, or else let me go my way alone, in which case the blame of Suleiman's death will be yours."

That touched him and angered him as well.

"Know, Frank, that for three days camels have stood ready— and no common load-bearers but racers every one—of my own stock and breeding. Of these there are four, and with them is my own sister's son for your protector."

He paused as a second cup of coffee was brought to us. I ate a wheat-cake and sipped at my coffee, after the old man had tasted it in all propriety.

"And will your sister's son go with me on this journey?" I asked.

"He will not, if he is not a fool!" came the biting answer. "What he shall do is to go with you until others of the desert-born are met with, when he shall turn you over to them, saying that you are a trader, and ordering that they further you on your trip."

"Very fine!"

I laughed slightly.

"And when he is out of sight or before I shall be slain and my beasts taken—"

"Am I a dog?"

The old man lost his sedate manner and flashed into anger.

"Is the blood of Ibn Rashid unknown in this land? By the Prophet's beard, Frank, think you there is no honor in Nejd? It is not for your infidel hide that I do this but for my honor to him you serve; thus it shall be done, so say no more."

He was undeniably angry, and to appease him would be a hard task. What was more, I remembered the jeweled order he had worn, and in conjunction with his words it seemed plain that he was of the house of Ibn Rashid, the great emir, in which case his orders might well be obeyed by every Bedouin and outlaw in the desert. To this day I have never learned his name, nor found out whether my guess was true, for Solomon will not talk about some things; but I fancy that he was a far greater man in the interior of Arabia than he was in Maan, which belongs to Turkey direct and not to the emir.

It was unfortunate that I had angered him, for no sooner had I thanked him for his aid and tried to smooth things over a bit than he offered me a third cup of coffee. Now according to the coffee etiquette of Arabia this is equivalent to asking a guest to be gone. Noticing my astonishment and even dismay, he vouchsafed to explain.

"It were unwise to remain in the city, Frank, for your face is well-known and wide search will be made. Allah forbid that I should be inhospitable even to a *Kafir* (unbeliever), but the camels wait and the night is not yet gray-haired."

"I am ready," I replied, drawing myself up with what dignity I could muster.

This seemed to fetch him out of his imperiously wrathful mood somewhat. He came to his feet and stood looking at me a moment, stroking his beard and smiling as if at some hidden thought.

"Well, well!" he said slowly. "God is great, and is assuredly with those who do righteous deeds. You are an infidel, Frank, but you are a man and faithful to your salt; may Allah watch over you! Tell Suleiman that there is something afoot among these Osmanlis—"

"He knows it already, to his sorrow," I broke in dryly.

"Like enough. But tell him this: That the Beni Rashid have no love for Osmanlis, and that while there are men and horses in Nejd he shall ever find protectors there, if need be. And so—*bessalama!*"

"*Bessalama,*" I repeated, and followed the Syrian, who had reappeared through the back doorway; nor did I ever see the grave *sheik* again.

Passing through several rooms, unlit and ghostly, we emerged into a filthy alley and wound through a maze of back streets for ten minutes. I thought I knew Maan fairly well, but the Syrian totally confused me. However, I followed him in blind trust. At length we wound out of the city and came upon a roadside well, near which stood a large group of palms, feathery-dark against the sky.

Here the Syrian left me and plunged into the darkness beneath the trees. I heard voices: then my guide reappeared and motioned me to follow, and I was aware of other shapes in the gloom behind him.

For a moment I half-thought that I had been led here to

be made away with through some devilish plan of Esmer Bey,
but I thrust aside the suspicion and went on. Presently I found
myself at a camp of half a dozen men who were hastily loading
and saddling four disgruntled camels at one side.

The Syrian turned about and vanished as a tall shape came
forward. In the half-light I knew that this must be the guide of
whom the old *sheik* had spoken. Truly, he must have been of the
Rashid breed—tall, spare, perhaps forty years of age, with the
starlight glinting on silver-mounted weapons, his eyes looked
squarely into mine for a moment and he smiled.

"You are the Frank expected?"

"I am he," was my answer. "But let me be no Frank—merely
the merchant Nour-ed-Din ibn Saleh, of Egypt, I pray."

He nodded.

"And I, Ishaq ibn Taril. All is ready."

"Ibn Taril" was an assumed name, but it was a name of the
emir's family, which confirmed my conjectures. However, I
wasted no time then or afterward in wondering who my guide
was.

I found that the camels were laden with a little merchan-
dise—pipe-bowls and other light articles—and with many
water-skins, only two of which were filled. This Ishaq explained
by saying that there would be no lack of water for the present,
but I would have need of the skins after parting from him. How
he knew my plans I cannot say, unless the Syrian had imparted
them in a few words; but know them he did.

The camels were all magnificent beasts, from a camel view-
point of quality. Ishaq saw me eying them and laughed quietly.

"No caravan-pace of three miles a day for us, Light of the
Faith! These two we shall ride, and the other two you shall take
when we part; in this way you may have the fresh beasts to go
forward into the stony desert with."

I saw that he had everything planned out for me, so I climbed
into my seat without more ado. He watched me covertly, for it
is easier to ride a bucking bronco than it is to keep one's seat

during the first minute aboard a desert-bred racer; the brute heaves upward at the first touch of the rider on his back, and is eager to be off without delay. No one was holding my beast, but as soon as my seat was assured Ishaq sprang to its head and called one of his men.

The tether of an extra camel was fastened to my saddle, and the Aral mounted his own racer. I grinned covertly, for he all but went over the side as the camel plunged up, nor did he gain his saddle for a moment later, a man leaping at the brute's bridle.

I had swiftly determined that if possible I would persuade Ishaq to travel at night only, for this would have a threefold use: We could have cooler travel, would not be likely to meet Bedouins, and I at least would be surer of my direction, having no compass and being forced to go by the stars, and never having done desert travel except with a caravan.

A word from Ibn Taril and his whip fell. The keen night air cut my whip-sore face; I drew up my *burnoose*-hood as we plunged through the trees at the lonely stars of the desert. Esmer Bey was behind me, and ahead lay Themoud, the mysterious, which no man had as yet unveiled.

CHAPTER VIII

—INTO THE FIRE

I HAVE OFTEN remarked that a system of artesian wells, with irrigation such as we have in our own Western States, would do wonders for this western portion of Arabia. That first night, and after sunrise the next morning, we passed charming stretches of oasis-dotted country where date-palm, tamarisk, and acacia flourished above stretches of wheat and barley and *temmin,* to say nothing of fruit and vegetable-patches.

In places we came upon long, dry *wadies,* or gulches, strewn with parasitic thorns and the bell-nests of the loxia, all of which would be washed away with the wet season—if one should ever come here—while the *wady* beds themselves glittered with sands of quartz and mica and porphyry and many colored granite, with streamers of colocynth clustering along the deeper portions.

By noon, however, all this had vanished behind us, and we halted at the edge of the real desert. Ishaq had a small tent, which we pitched in the shade of a *ghada* bush. After eating a few dates I fell asleep at once.

Despite his family, Ibn Taril was as much delighted as a child that evening when I told his fortune before we started out. In no long time he had forgotten that I was an infidel Frank, and we got on famously. He consented to my night-travel idea, and provided me, fortunately, with a pair of *za'al* or black woolen twists for the ankles, such as all southern Arabs wear for use as superior ligatures in case of snake or scorpion bite. I thought little of these at the time, but their value was to be proven later on.

We had four days, or rather nights, of monotonous desert travel. At times we stirred up ostriches or camels, the presence of the latter apprising us that Bedouins were not far distant, and one morning we drifted into a small oasis, a mere hole in the desert stretches, where there was an encampment of Arabs. These were up and about us instantly; but a few words from Ishaq quieted them, and we rode on after watering.

Seeing that my guide did not wear Solomon's ring, I did not mention it to him; but on the fourth morning of our journey I was destined to find that he was not only aware of its import, but knew also that there was something forward. Since then I have often wondered at the manner in which both he and the elderly *sheik* knew of the Osmanli movement in a general way, and I have since found that Solomon was regarded by the whole Wahabite people as a buffer betwixt themselves and the Turkish power. No one can say definitely as to that, however, except Solomon himself—and such things he does not talk of even to me.

On that fourth morning, after a swift, unrelenting flight to the northeast, we reached a small oasis with a bare dozen palm-trees clustered about its single well. As we rode up in the sunrise we saw several low, widespread black tents under the trees, with a good-sized group of camels near by. A number of armed Arabs came forth to meet us.

Their show of force died away as my guide flung back the wide hood of his *abba,* and a little murmur of surprise sounded, while their chief came forward to hold Ishaq's camel. My companion had already informed me that his company would extend no farther, so I was not surprised at his first speech as we rested beneath the *sheik's* black tent.

"I bring you a guest, Ibn Harun," he said abruptly and peremptorily, as one who expected his orders to be obeyed.

The *sheik,* on removing his *burnoose,* disclosed a bandaged arm.

"What is this—has there been dispute?" Ishaq continued.

"Somewhat, *sidi*," and I thought the Arab looked embarrassed. "A company of men insisted on passing without paying our tolls, and—"

"So the men of Ma'az take the law into their own hands?"

Ishaq rose to his feet and pushed away the tray of food that had been brought to us.

"Explain!"

Torn between two fears, as it seemed, the other obeyed. The name of Ma'az brought Esmer Bey back to my mind; but as the Arab told a rambling tale of desert battle and captives I paid little heed, being hungry. This was some dispute which should have been referred to the emir at Hail, I concluded, and this guide of mine resented its settlement in outlaw fashion.

Not until some of the other Ma'az men led with an ill grace two bound captives into the tent did I look up from my *temmin* cakes and dates. The first of these prisoners was a coast Arab, wounded with a sword-cut over the head; the second was almost as black as a negro, but from the very aspect of him I knew him for a Hazrami—one of those wild adventurers out of Hazramaut who may be found all over the Moslem world, decorating a gallows or leading an army indifferently.

Then I sat up very straight. The Hazrami had turned proudly to resent a shove, and I caught a silver ring glinting on his hand.

In a flash the whole thing came to me. Solomon's caravan had been stopped by the Ma'az Arabs, doubtless under Esmer's orders. Just then Ishaq stepped forward, twisted the bound Arab around, and looked down at the ring on his hand also.

"It seems you have plucked at big game, Ibn Harun!" exclaimed my guide dryly. "Hazrami, what of this? Where is your master's caravan?"

The Hazrami grinned, while the Ma'az *sheik* glowered sullenly, daring to say nothing.

"Dispersed, *sidi*, and most of us slain. We twain fell to the lot of these dogs, and whether our lord lives or dies I know not. But—we slew!"

"Aye, by the Prophet's beard!" broke in Ibn Harun sourly.

Ishaq took one step forward and seized him furiously by the beard.

"You dog!" he cried, his voice tense. "And you dared to offer me food, having thus disgraced your authority? Loose those two men!"

The Arabs standing by obeyed, for they seemed to know this guide of mine.

"Harken, Egyptian!"

Ishaq turned to me as he flung the *sheik* back.

"Go with these two men; take three of our camels and leave me the fourth, and depart whither you will. We are at the edge of the stony desert, and I can help you no farther."

"And you?" I asked, rising in some dismay, for I sorely lacked rest.

"Fear not for me. If these jackals dared bite at me they would feel the lion's claws. Allah go with you! First fill your water-skins."

And so the three of us went forth from the low tent, nor did I ever see Ishaq ibn Taril again.

No word passed among us as we led the three racers to the well, watered them, and filled the skins; only the Hazrami laughed a little whenever he looked at the score of Arabs who crowded about the tents, watching us with evil eyes. All were men, and armed. Half an hour later we were alone on the desert.

With my first bewilderment gone, I managed to get his story out of the Hazrami. The other man rode as if dazed, his head sunk.

Omar ibn Kasim—for this was no other than the Hazrami I should have met at the Port Saïd coffee-house—had left Port Ibrahim with John Solomon, being his second in command. They had a party of thirty men and speedy camels, the caravan being under the direction of that same *Sheik* Yusuf who had led

Yelniz Pasha to Maan, and who had met Solomon on his return barely in time to take command of the march.

From him John had learned my story. As Yusuf knew nothing of the plans of Yelniz and Esmer Bey, however, Solomon had decided to push straight ahead and trust to luck to find me. Five days before this, or on the same day of my escape, they had encountered the whole Ma'az fighting force, consisting of over a hundred men, hastening in to Maan to meet Esmer.

Solomon had refused to pay tolls, and whether Esmer had sent out word to stop caravans or not I never learned; but in any case a dispute arose, and the Ma'az outlaws made a furious attack. Half of John's men were knocked over in the scrimmage. The rest were scattered with the Arabs in pursuit of them; Omar ibn Kasim had stuck to John until a bullet killed his camel, when he had wisely surrendered, being left alone.

It may be imagined what my feelings were on hearing this tale of desert outlawry. Toward noon we pulled up and camped, and, in spite of all my weariness from the night's journey, I consulted with this Hazrami, who was a man of some ability.

"Go on," he advised calmly. "Whither we went I know not, save that it was to find a place no other man had found, in the midst of deserts worse than the plains of Eblis. If Suleiman escaped he went on; let us do likewise, and to the north, not to the northeast."

So the three of us went forward; and since the wounded Arab refused to move by night, preferring to stay and die on the sands, we, perforce, traveled by day. Without warning we plunged into one of those inlets from the sandy southern desert which the Arabs call *nefud* or sand-passes. And that was the beginning of our misery.

Ridges, slopes, wave-ruffled hills of red sand where the wind had twisted and furrowed beautifully and terribly; a sea of red flame to the eye, its upflung heat striking like a wave—this, in brief, is the *nefud*. I had never met one so far north, though they stretch in four northerly courses from the red desert northwest;

but there was no doubt of the thing. Dried-up lizards rustled about our camps, and occasional ostriches dusted away into the horizon from before us; but other than this there was no life.

We had three days of this blinding, heat-struck travel, and by good chance on the third evening we came upon what is called a "navel"—a cuplike depression extending down to a basaltic rock where a spring issued forth to die in the sands ten feet away. There was not a tree, not a shrub, not a sign of life; but there was death, for here our wounded Arab died at midnight, babbling of green fields and smiling at the stars. He was a coast man, and the desert sun had stricken into his wound.

The water in that spring was very thick with sulfur; I remember it discolored the silver rings Omar and I wore. We made shift to bury the Arab and started off at dawn, leading his camel, our water-skins newly filled; but we spent three hours getting out of that hole in the sands. It was about two hundred feet deep, with steep sides, and our beasts were almost exhausted by the continual slipping back when at length we gained the desert level and started to the north.

We left the red sands of the *nefud* during the afternoon, to the intense relief of ourselves and our poor beasts. Both of us were keenly alive to our danger. We were hitting into the unknown; neither of us had any knowledge of water-holes or oases, and if we found another spring it would be by pure good luck. Our supply of water was sufficient for a week, however, and by pushing our camels we could cover an immense distance in that time—if nothing happened.

And cover distance we did, but to small purpose. I am not sure of the number of days, but I think it was two after leaving the red sands that we came to the rock desert and a little spring surrounded by a plant with blood-red leaves, whose name I did not know. Before we suspected anything wrong the lead camel broke forward to the water and gulped at it; then he rolled over, grunted once, and died.

We rode from that place as if the pestilence were upon us.

Omar ibn Kasim, to whom I had told all I knew of Themoud and Esmer's tale, stated that we must now be among the same rocks which Esmer had so dreaded. So it appeared, for with the next day we were wandering through a desert wholly unlike any I had ever seen in my life or heard of.

All was rock—blistering to the touch, strewn with thin sand and setting at fault all the teachings of geology. Now we would pass through an airless valley of white calcareous marl, ringed with sand-hills; an hour later we would be among great splintered sections of gneiss and colorless quartz, from which would upleap fragments of pink feldspar or green hornblende, shimmering and radiating with the terrible sun blaze. Again would come a stretch of black slate, or perhaps a twisted, calcined mass of basaltic rock, carven and fantastically shaped by the blown sand.

By the mercy of Heaven in the midst of this desolation we came upon a spring that was neither poisoned nor salt. It was small and nearly exhausted, yet it gave us all an abundance of water, and enough besides for two skinfuls, before it went dry. This, according to my reckoning, was the sixth day after leaving the *nefud,* though Omar held that it was the eighth. I cannot say for certain.

Now, in the midst of the rock we came upon things which then I took for mirages of a sun-smitten mind, but afterward found true enough. For there were salt plains—salt amid the basalt and the marl and the granite; pillars of salt, great rocks of salt, blown sand of salt-dust. Even the Hazrami could hardly stand this, and I remember his groans and prayers floating after me as I rode ahead. But fortunately he could not turn back, as I had all the water.

Amid the rocks and the salt had been bones often enough. And, more than bones, we came sometimes upon a body half unearthed by the winds, mummified and still recognizable. In that intensely dry, hot, windless region decay was unknown; weapons lay amid the bones or dried remains, bright and untarnished.

At one halting-place, in the shade of an immense black rock of basalt, we found a man clad in chain-mail, with helm and shield and bones all about him. A broken sword-hilt was still clutched in his right hand, and the skulls and bones around were split and hacked, while a great lance-head was half buried in the mummified muscles of his throat. I suppose the vultures or scorpions or lizards could not eat through the chain-mail—and he was spared for perhaps a thousand years. What old struggle and combat to the death had this been? One thing—the man in armor wore golden spurs, and there was a cross on his helm.

We wandered ever toward the north through this horrible place; how long I know not. Once we found a camel standing erect with his head flung up as he had died—a ghastly thing enough, for the salt had covered him, then had whirled away and left him preserved against all flesh-seekers through eternity.

Then—our water gave out.

We had halted about midnight, after pushing on desperately, on a small eminence that seemed of lava in the starlight. In that maelstrom of rock and salt I was not surprised to find lava, for the place was plainly a huge volcanic upheaval.

We found the water-skins holding perhaps a gill each. This we drank, then cut open the skins and sucked the moisture from the inside, and slept till dawn.

"Best stay here and die by noon," mumbled the Hazrami as we woke with the first glimmer of the true dawn. "*Ya Rahman! Ya Rahman!* God of mercy—look!"

Even as he had spoken, the sun had shot up, bathing all that blasted horror in light. Such a sunrise I have never seen before or since. Perhaps my brain was fevered, for all the colors of the spectrum seemed to glint and glimmer from the salt-crystals and the gaunt, burned rocks.

At Omar's frenzied cry I turned and looked. He was pointing at the red disk of the sun, which now hung, poised above the horizon-rim. Outlined against it, clear cut and sharp, was a mountain shaped like a man's nose—it was exactly as if some giant lay prone behind that desert line, with only his nose show-ing. And from the apex of the peak a thin line of black trembled and waved upward across the sunrise and was gone.

"The Man's Nose That Smokes!" I shouted hoarsely. "Come!"

In feverish haste we unhobbled the poor camels, who were now nearer dead than we, for we had given them little water, and were off. But deep down in my mind I knew that we would never make that distant peak; we had not a drop of water, there was no shelter from the sun, and the saltdust was strangling us and the camels alike.

"Truly this is a land of Afrits and genii!" I heard Omar groan an hour later as we wound down into a valley whose lava-bed was flowered with salt.

Close upon the words my camel stumbled on a fragment of rock scarcely larger than his own hoof; he went to his knees, and I rolled gently over his neck to the rock. There was a darting pain through my ankle, a cry from Omar above me, and horror seized me as a scorpion flickered away. It was the yellow scor-pion—I gave up.

Then it was that Omar came to the rescue. Whipping out his knife even before he reached me, he made a merciless inci-sion around the wound that drew a scream of pain from me and awoke me to life again. Then, seizing those *za'al* or black woolen fillets which Ishaq had given me, he wound both about my leg above the wound, drew them tight, and laid me in shelter of my camel, who was too weak to rise again.

"Stay here, *sidi*," he cried hastily. "I go—and by the blessing of the Compassionate I will return with Suleiman!"

Already the poison was throbbing in my leg. I shrieked at him not to desert me: but the Hazrami climbed into his saddle again, urged his poor beast up, and was gone.

Some hours after my camel died as he lay. I cannot bear to look back on that terrible day. The shadow of the poor dead brute was all that preserved my life. The pain of the scorpion's sting shot up to the groin, and I lay in a horrible nausea for hours.

Over and over the temptation swept upon me to take out one of my automatics which were in the camel-bags and end the thing mercifully. Toward noon I could resist no longer, and I tried to reach up to the bags, but could not. I was literally too weak to move, and once this realization came over me, my fevered brain leaped beyond control.

Visions—only such visions as could come from that smitten country—visited me. Curiously from a psychological standpoint there were no such mirage nor dreams of water at all as would naturally be expected.

Instead, the impressions my brain had gained during the journey took on life. There was that mail-clad warrior, with golden spurs and cross-adorned helm, who came and smiled at me, snakes in each of his eyeless sockets. There were others behind him—men dressed like Arabs of old, with scimitar and mail; skeletons that walked and gibed, and other things more horrible still of which I cannot speak.

Behind them all came other men clad like the first, in chain-mail. These, however, rode horses—beautiful, sleek Arabs; and over their mail they wore white coats, broidered with the diagram on Solomon's ring. There was a woman among them, or perhaps an angel; she had wonderful gold-brown hair. She came and held my hand for a moment. Then one of the men gave me water—and while I drank it turned to liquid fire that scorched and seared me, so that I screamed and fell senseless. And as I did so I heard Solomon's voice.

CHAPTER IX

THE PEOPLE THAT WAS LOST

"**I**'M BETWEEN the devil and the deep sea with a vengeance," I said, and laughed.

I lay on a bed with a precipice on one side of me and John Solomon on the other. More exactly, I was lying at a great window in a room built of massive masonry, and there was a five-hundred-foot drop overside.

At first glance I hardly recognized John. His plumpness was gone from him; there was a jagged, half-healed scar across his forehead; his expressionless face had suddenly leaped into lines and wrinkles of age. In fact, had it not been for the clay pipe and the odor of vile tobacco he might have passed for another man.

I had been here two days, sleeping most of the time. My scorpion-wound was all but healed.

At the present moment John was engaged in reciting what had happened to him.

"Well, Mr. Sargent, I got out o' that brush wi' the Ma'az men with three men left out o' thirty, and four camels out o' fifty. Forchnit it was that I 'ad water. We got within sight o' the Man's Nose, sir, same as you. Then one o' the men went mad, just like that. It was 'im give me this 'ere swipe over the eye, and I 'ad to shoot 'im, and sorry I am to 'ave to say it. Then, while we was a fighting, the camels up and went. Lud, it give me a mortal bad turn, sir, to see them beasts vanishing in the distance, and me with two men afoot! No, sir; not a drop. All the water was on the camels, and there we was. We started to walk that night,

and toward sun-up we come to a salt pool. One o' the men was
bound 'e'd drink, which same 'e did, and went stark mad likewise.

"'E just wandered off in the rocks, sir, and the last we seen of
'im 'e was dancing with a corpse 'e'd been and pulled out o' the salt
sand. Dang it, Mr. Sargent, it was downright 'orrid; it was that!
The other man, 'im and me laid down in the shade of a rock all
day and started out again at dark. About midnight it was when
'e borrowed me gun and shot 'imself dead."

John paused and wiped at his brow. As his story unfolded
to me I began to see why he had changed so terribly. My own
sufferings had seemed bad, but Solomon's had been far worse.
Indeed, I have never understood how the little man survived
that tramp through the awful salt horror.

"Well, Mr. Sargent, I don't just know 'ow I come 'ere, as the
'ousemaid said when the old gent found 'er in the butler's pantry;
but 'ere I be, and 'ere you be, and a werry good job for us it is.
But—but—dang it, there's a many as didn't get 'ere."

He gazed out the window, blinking.

I gave him the message of the old *sheik* who had helped me
away from Maan. As he made no answer I followed his gaze,
raising myself on an elbow.

As I found later, I lay in a room of the castle, built on one of
the crags of that granite mass which from a distance assumed
the outline of a man's nose. My window looked out on that
terrible rock and salt desert. A cool breeze entered the room.
Close beneath the lowest crags of the mountain I could see a
great mass of ruins—columns and plinths, fragments of walls
and buildings—that stretched to right and left. Beyond it was
that same desert through which I had passed.

Omar, I learned from John, had come within sight of the
castle, and Solomon had led out a party of rescuers, who had
pushed on to find me after hearing the Hazrami's tale. Just then
a stunted, weak-faced man with fair hair entered the room,
bearing cups of thin gold, which held water. The man wore skin
leggings and a wool coat of white, broidered in gold with that

same design of Solomon's ring. When he went I remembered my last dream, and eagerly asked where I was. John laughed shortly.

"In Themoud, Mr. Sargent, and this 'ere place is built on the Man's Nose."

"And this is where the Gairners were bound for—did they reach it?"

"It is, sir, and they did. What's more, that brown-'aired angel o' yours is right 'ere in the next room."

With which he sighed, rose, and went to a door with a low word or two. There was a rustle of garments, and John stood back.

"Miss, this is Mr. Sargent. Miss Edith Gairner, sir. Mr. Sargent is all right now, miss. Werry sorry I am as 'e didn't come with me, but that weren't me own fault."

And that was the only reproach I ever had from him for my desertion. He slipped out of the door, and a moment later Edith Gairner was sitting beside me.

In the light of all that took place before and after that moment, I suppose I should make her out as a very goddess of beauty. I wish I could, but it would not be the truth, and unfortunately this is not fiction. Nor was she slender and willowy. In short, Miss Gairner was a rather tall, determined-eyed girl, dressed in a soft, clinging garment of white wool, with the diagram of the ring, or Solomon's Seal, worked in small size on each breast.

She was not beautiful, as most men reckon beauty; but there was something about the firm lines of her suntanned face that I liked at first glance. Intuitively I felt that she would be a good comrade—better than many a man I knew. Her figure, brought out by the clinging woolen garment, was like her face—firm, well-modeled, yet with just a hint of girlishness about it all when she was in repose.

"Well," I smiled at her, as neither of us spoke for a moment, "did you people have as much trouble getting here as John and I did?"

It was an inane thing to say, for her face clouded.

"Yes, Mr. Sargent, I'm afraid we did. You see, our men decamped and left us a short time after Esmer Bey went back, and if it had not been for our two Afghans we might have been murdered. As it was, father—"

She paused and looked away. But I was not thinking greatly about her father, for her words reminded me that I had not yet told Solomon my story, and he knew nothing of Esmer's preparations, unless Omar ibn Kasim had told him. Eventually I found that he had.

"Father found that the men had stolen some of his instruments, and he rode back after them, with Yar Hussein, one of the Afghans. Neither of them returned, though we waited a week beside the last well, and as father had mapped out a course to be followed, Akhbar Khan and I left most of the supplies for him and pushed on alone."

"Do you mean that you and one Afghan crossed that Tophet of rock and salt?"

I stared at her incredulously. She nodded, cool-eyed.

"And you heard no more from your father?"

"Nothing. But he had the Sultan's *firman*, so he can hardly have come to any harm."

Here Solomon reentered—he said afterward that he thought we could get acquainted better by ourselves—and I told them what I knew of Esmer. Under the girl's brown eyes I remembered that I had not shaven since leaving Maan.

As I finished the tale John dropped a powder in one of the gold cups of water and held it out.

"Drink this, Mr. Sargent, if you please. We'll 'ave a new man of you in the morning, sir. Then we'll show you over this 'ere place, and werry interesting it is, and 'ave a bit o' talk as won't wait much longer."

"Just a minute!"

I paused with the cup ready.

"I want to know what this whole business is about. What are you after here, Miss Gairner?"

Her eyes laughed, though not her mouth, but John checked her.

"In the morning, sir, if so be as the poison 'as worked out."

Knowing John, I drank and lay back, choking over the nauseous draft, until a swift drowsiness crept upon me and I was asleep.

I awakened to a day destined to be the most intensely absorbing of all my life, I think. It is hard for any one not a scientist to imagine my feelings, placed here among an unknown race of people, whose every production bore evidence of a high rate of civilization.

To begin with, two men entered with a tub and bathed me, then supplied me with a white woolen garment like their own, Solomon's Seal on the breast. Every trace of soreness had gone from my leg, and though the hair on my temples had become grayed within the past three weeks, I felt like a new man. When I was dressed Solomon entered with Miss Gairner. John added a sword-belt to my costume, but refused any explanation.

"Do you know what day this is, Mr. Sargent?" asked the girl, smiling. "Sunday! And as soon as we have breakfast we'll go to church."

I laughed, thinking that of course she was joking. The two attendants brought in cakes and honey, with a peculiar, bitter hot liquid somewhat like tea. While we were eating I was startled at hearing the deep tones of a bell reverberating through the castle. A knock came at the door, and one of the attendants beckoned to us silently.

What followed was awe-inspiring, to say the least. Leaving the room, we entered a high corridor, pierced with long loopholes at intervals. This led into a great hall through which a few white-cloaked figures were hurrying. Our guide led us from this to a second corridor, and so through a high gateway with portcullis and drawbridge. As we emerged into the open I glanced back in amazement.

The castle of Themoud was almost a perfect model of Norman

architecture—massive, square-towered, with a forty-foot wall. It seemed new-built; but as this country knew no rain, a building might last forever without crumbling.

We walked along a hewn road in the rock, the castle and desert behind us, the huge peaks of the Man's Nose all around. Suddenly, after entering a shadow-darkened valley, the path twisted and opened out into a marvelous prospect.

Ahead of us was a vale five miles across, with peaks on the farther side. It was slightly below us, yet far above the desert level; I subsequently found that it was nothing more than the crater of a long-extinct volcano.

In the center lay a small lake, with a line of trees marking its outlet on the far side. All around waved fields of wheat and oats, rippling like silk in the morning breeze and sun. The plain was dotted with stone houses, low and comfortable looking. Beneath spreading trees I caught sight of herds of animals, small but sleek horses, and a few sheep, while to right and left on the higher ground were flocks of sheep and goats. I did not note all this at the time, however, for we turned aside abruptly.

Before us, at the end of the hewn road, was another massive building in the form of a cross, pointing toward the risen sun. Into this we followed our guide, amid a number of others. All these people seemed fair-haired. One or two whom I saw were of exceptionally strong build, but the majority seemed weaklings, with degenerate faces.

The men all wore swords, which they left at the door of the church—for such it was. The women were dressed in the same flowing white mantle; most of them were beautiful in an insipid fashion. Frankly, I disliked both men and women at first sight.

The interior of the church was astonishing in the extreme. It was lit by great clusters of candles in a dozen places, and seemed to have been built originally for a vast number of people. At present there were a scant three hundred grouped in the front ranks of the great stone pews; of these only eighty were men.

As I sank down beside Miss Gairner I looked up. Overhead

towered the high roof without a ray of light from the outside, for windows the church had none. But—something after the fashion of Westminster—there were banners hung from the walls, and great carvings of armorial bearings beneath the banners. I know nothing of heraldry, but it required no student to tell that these were coats-of-arms of the days of chivalry.

Contrary to our present-day custom the chancel was very dim. Suddenly a sonorous voice rang out, and with one accord every soul in the church knelt. I was surprised to find myself following a prayer in what seemed a softened dialect of Arbi, with many old words and colloquialisms such as may be found in antique copies of the Koran, but entirely recognizable to me.

Ordinarily not a religious man in the accepted sense, I am not ashamed to say that on this Sunday morning I entered into that service with a devout heart; while John Solomon, who to my certain knowledge had not entered a church for years, simply plumped down on his knees and stayed there. We all had a good deal to be thankful for.

Toward the end of the service I became interested in a scroll-like carving running along the back of the high stone pew before me, and I was so absorbed in making out the devices engraved on the shields that I did not observe that the church was emptying until Solomon leaned over and touched me.

"We're to 'ave a talk wi' the bishop, Mr. Sargent, so best wait."

"Bishop?" I repeated, yet astonished at nothing after what I had seen. "Was that a bishop? Who governs this place?"

"That we don't know, sir. Miss Gairner 'as only been 'ere a week, like, while I got 'ere three days before you did, sir. I know werry little, sir, not 'aving seen 'is lordship yet myself. Werry reserved person, 'e seems to be."

The great church was emptied of its little crowd. I asked John where Omar ibn Kasim and Edith Gairner's Afghan were, and he was just telling me that they had disappeared somewhere in the castle when a man stepped up to us.

"Come," he said in that curious soft Arbi. "The council is waiting."

We rose and followed him through the rows of pews to the southern transept, where he told us to take candles from one of the holders and follow him. As we obeyed he opened a door and we went down a flight of steps into a dry, dust-ridden crypt. No sooner had we gained the flooring than Edith Gairner caught at my arm with a stifled cry.

All about us was a perfect maze of stone figures—all recumbent, all representing men clad in armor, with the crossed legs of the crusader, all eminently typical of Norman art. They were set in the walls, over tombs—everywhere, as if with the passage of years space had been set at a premium and the dead knights had been buried wherever possible. There must have been thousands of the images.

Our guide led us at a too rapid pace for us to examine them closely, however. In five minutes he flung open the door of a second passageway, through which we wound for a good ten minutes more. The corridor was low and wide; it was pierced through the solid rock, the marks of the hewing being plain to see. Then we came to our journey's end.

A large room—probably cut in a cliffside, for from the window I could see a wide expanse of the beautiful crater-valley—with many doorways, this council-chamber of the rulers of Themoud had been designed for many men, like the church, but there were only a half-dozen seated in the carven stone chairs. These chairs were ranked in semicircles around the open space before the window.

In the center, in the greatest and highest seat, sat a striking figure. He was a venerable man, with flowing white beard, clad in helm, chain-mail, golden spurs, and white mantle, and girded with a tremendously wide sword. The other five men were also armed, but only two of them had faces. These, with the old ruler, were over six feet in height; the other two were little more than five.

"Welcome, Christians," said the old man without rising. "Lady, be seated."

A stool was placed for Edith Gairner, while we remained standing.

"We have waited long for this day," went on the old man. "Now that all three of you have recovered your strength it is time that we reached an understanding. First I thank you in behalf of the council for your efforts."

I did not quite see the necessity for thanks, but John coughed apologetically and spoke out:

"I'd like to know where our two men are, your lordship."

"Your Saracens? They are safe, but it was not deemed advisable—"

"If you please, we'd like to have them quartered with us, just the same. They are Saracens, but they are faithful to us."

There was more in this than I caught. Solomon and the bishop gazed at each other, the blue eyes of each very determined; but it was the bishop who gave way.

"As you will, though it is scarce safe for infidels in Themoud."

"Safer than it will be for Christians before long, if our news is true."

John's curt reply brought every man leaning forward. The bishop sighed.

"Let us know each other. You are of noble birth?"

"Not I," returned John. "This lady is, and also my friend, Sir Frederick."

He glanced at me. I was standing astonished, to say the least.

"And I am Count Hugo of Antioch, Bishop of Themoud. Greetings, Sir Frederick; and you, Lady—"

"The Lady Edith," cut in Solomon hastily, at which Miss Gairner said nothing.

This sudden abundance of titles and countships in the midst of Arabia was something unexpected by us all save John.

"These are my sons, who succeed me ere long in my office,"

went on the count—"Sir Raymond, and Bertrand, as yet but an esquire."

The two who were taller than the rest rose and bowed. Both had huge swords like that of their father, both were fair-haired and clean-shaven, and both had an indescribable gloom in their handsome faces—a brooding darkness that sat in the eyes of every knight of Themoud.

The other members of the council, three knights, were named, and each bowed to Edith Gairner. Solomon, being asked his name, gave it.

"Your messenger, Count Hugo, reached the father of the Lady Edith, who was preaching the faith of the cross in Damascus, two years ago. He was called home unexpectedly, then communicated with me and through certain aid of mine started for this place.

"Hearing of a plot of the Osmanlis, who had in some way gained an inkling of what message you had sent out, I started with Sir Frederick here to warn you, but we were intercepted and had to fight our way through. Even now the Osmanlis are approaching with Arabs to wrest the writings concerning Mohammed and the secret of the Seal from you."

"Who are these Osmanlis?" asked Count Hugo. "Is Damascus, then, still a city?"

I began to wonder what manner of madhouse this was.

CHAPTER X

SONS OF THE CRUSADES

I HAVE SPOKEN of a peculiar brooding sadness in the faces of most of the men of Themoud, and I shall account for it in this place. Were I to explain the history as it came to me through many days of patient search and exploration the tale would be too long; as it is these pages seem to grow with marvelous rapidity, and I have so much to say of what happened later that I might best give Themoud's story here and have done.

As is well known, certain Norman nobles of Sicily founded the countship of Antioch in crusading days, holding it after the Norman fashion by the strength of sword. There was continual warring against the Saracen; on one occasion the then count conceived the startling idea of leading an expedition against Mecca and wiping out the Moslem religion in one blow.

Naturally, with the hazy notion of geography then prevalent, this idea appealed to the Normans, who had become half-Arab since their occupation of Sicily. A large force was organized in the strictest secrecy, a few French knights from Acre were enrolled, and under the leadership of Count Rainulf the journey was begun—a smashing charge straight across the hills to the east.

Taken by surprise, the Saracens were pierced, and the Syrian desert had been reached by about half the original force. Then the Saracens had clouded down in swarms and had pushed the remainder on to die of thirst. And most of them had done so.

Count Rainulf alone, with a dozen knights and a few Sicilian

Arab mercenaries, had struggled into this Themoud, where they found a few natives dwelling, unwarlike and knowing only the religion of fire-worship. Unable to face that awful desert again, and without camels or guides, the Normans perforce remained where they were; and from this mixed stock had sprung the people we found in Themoud.

I gained this largely from a great mass of parchments in the archives of Count Hugo. There also I found how in time the children of these crusaders had waxed mighty in numbers, how they had begun a systematic series of raids out over the desert, and how in the year 1347 these raids had culminated in a terrible defeat in which the flower of their knighthood was destroyed and from which only twenty men got home again.

This disaster had totally paralyzed what remained of the men, and it had been followed by a plague which had all but exterminated the race. Thereafter, though keeping their traditions, customs, knighthoods, and faith, the feeble remnant had never prospered. They seemed to have begun a slow descent into apathy, content to till their fields and care for their flocks and herds and to live in the dwellings of their fathers.

If by chance any wandering Arabs reached the place they were slain. The terrible desert lying around, the apathy of the inhabitants, and the ignorance of their presence here had all contributed to keeping Themoud unknown among the Arabs. The family of the counts almost alone had preserved its vigor.

Count Hugo a few years hence had realized that Themoud was doomed to degeneracy and extinction. So with the consent of the council he had sent his brother and ten men out into the world to reach some Christian nation and make an appeal for aid in the way of new blood and fighting men.

This brother had reached Damascus at the point of death, and there had come to the Rev. Uriel Gairner, who had cared for him. Gairner, hearing his story and receiving a certain message from Count Hugo, had in the end laid it before Solomon. Count

Hugo's brother had fallen into the hands of an Osmanli, who wheedled part of the story from him, and had died under torture.

Such, in brief, is the story of Themoud, as I have substantiated it before the Royal Society with documents and copies. Of its earlier history, when it was peopled by fire-worshipers as related in the Koran, I shall have more to say in another place, for this fire-worship was destined to have an awful and terrible sequence before I left the country.

To return. After Count Hugo had told me the tale of those messengers he had sent forth, John and I related our own story to the council, told who the Osmanlis were, and gave a brief description of the world's history.

"And when will these Osmanlis fall upon us?" asked Sir Raymond.

"Any time now," I made answer. "A man of Esmer Bey's character will force his way across that desert—but tell me, Count Hugo, what is there in all this that would menace Islam and provoke the Osmanlis to such outrageous efforts to reach you?"

Solomon coughed, but looking at the count I saw a little flame leap up into his face and brighten his old eyes.

"That, Sir Frederick, is the heritage left us by our fathers. Though they failed to destroy Mecca and Medina, yet they found certain proofs— However, you shall see this to-morrow, all of you. It is of the utmost importance that we decide on our measures of defense now. What are these strange weapons of which you said something to our men, sir?"

He addressed Solomon, but before John replied he checked him as one of the other knights leaned over and whispered. For a moment the count's blue eyes rested on John's face. Then he nodded, rose, and drew that mighty blade of his from its sheath.

"Kneel."

Solomon looked up at him, then obeyed. The flat of the blade touched his shoulder.

"You have earned your knighthood, Sir John; and by that Seal of Solomon which I now give you for your arms, as it is the arms of this land, I create you the equal of any of my men—a knight, though lands I cannot give."

It was a pathetic thing enough. This ruler of a handful of outworn people, whose extinction would create no ripple on the surface of history, harking back a thousand years and dubbing knight a little man who had before this held hands with destiny! I glanced at Edith Gairner, beside me, and in her eyes read the reflection of my thought—for which I began to like her.

"In the world but not of it," I murmured in English. "These men are fantoms of chivalry, shadows of another age."

"Yet they are men, Mr. Sargent."

That was both rebuke and answer. Yes! Despite the unreality of their shadow-existence, despite the doom that overhung them and looked forth from their eyes, these latter-day children of a dead civilization were still men; and it was not long before they were to prove their manhood and their blood, weak though it might be.

Often since then has it seemed to me that by no blind decree of Fate had this remnant of a once great people been permitted to linger in charge of a forgotten secret; but that through all the ages events had been shaping themselves toward that day when the lives of John Solomon and Esmer Bey and Count Hugo of Antioch should suddenly converge to decide the fate of Islam before that terrible Seal which an utterly forgotten people had fashioned in the bowels of the Man's Nose That Smokes. But I must not stray.

Now after John Solomon had been dubbed knight in simple fashion, for which the deep-eyed count apologized, we discussed arms and ammunition. All my effects had been carefully taken from my dead camel. Edith Gairner, who had reached the place with Akhbar Khan and three camels, had one revolver; John, of course, had nothing. Between us we could muster seven revolvers, something like a thousand rounds altogether, and four men who could use the weapons.

The council could not understand the nature of powder, but

accepted our explanations with grave acquiescence, though they
hardly credited the statement that bullets would pierce their
chain-armor like paper. These six men, the head of the whole
state—such as it was—would be obeyed with unquestioning
fidelity, Count Hugo assured me.

Thrashing out the whole situation, we found that they had
some eighty-odd fighting men, of whom fifty were knights
and the others esquires. It seemed that at the age of twenty-five
each man was dubbed knight by the count, in whose family the
bishopric and the temporal power alike were hereditary—a
strange jumble of fighting prelate and uncelibate baron! I think
the man was an atavism, a throwback to some grim Norman
of his line; certainly he was no doddering old man, as you shall
presently see.

These eighty men could garrison the great castle after a fashion. As to other defenses, Count Hugo said that he and Sir
Raymond would ride forth with us after luncheon and show
us the land. John Solomon balked at this, protesting that he
had never ridden a horse and never would—an assertion which
lowered him mightily in the esteem of all; however, he said that
I was a better fighting man than he ever could be, and advised
them to place such business in my hands.

For this I did not thank him, more especially as the old count
scanned me over critically, then unbuckled his sword and placed
it in my hand. At his direction I drew it forth—a tremendous,
murderous thing, two inches wide at the hilt and tapering little
to the end. Yet it was wonderful in its balance. I swung it up in
a manner that surprised them.

"Keep it," said the count quietly as I would have returned it.
"You shall have arms of the best, for we have great store, alas!
Now, may I conduct you, lady?"

And so we went back to the great hall of the castle, where a
score of us sat at one long table, while esquires, Bertrand among
them, served us. It was an oppressive meal, for these people were
silent, most of them, rarely talking among themselves except

when occasion required speech. That perhaps helped to account for their brooding look, together with the traces of degeneracy so prevalent among them.

Lady Edith, as Miss Gairner had now become, was given empty apartments in the castle, together with two women to attend to her wants. At dinner we met the wife of Sir Raymond—the old count's wife was long dead—who was a pleasant woman enough, with a baby boy. After the meal Miss Gairner went to rest for an hour before her ride, for she was going with Sir Raymond and me, while the rest of us sought the armory.

This was, in strict truth, a terrible place—like the whole castle, for that matter; since here were kept the arms of olden knights, each known by name. Here were bows and shields, lances and golden spurs, saddlery and mail and helms, equipment for hundreds of knights, and through the midst moved sturdy old Count Hugo, to me a keenly pathetic figure.

I was fitted with a light, link-woven mail coat, after some trouble because of my rather wide shoulders, and Solomon with another, which I must say gave him a ludicrous appearance. Other equipment I refused for the present.

When finally Sir Raymond and I left the castle to mount our horses I felt like a pageantry actor. When Miss Gairner came to meet us her first words confirmed this impression.

"Why, how crusadery you look, Mr. Sargent—or, pardon me, Sir Frederick!" she cried gaily. "And doesn't our friend look splendid?"

Sir Raymond did look splendid, for he sat his horse like a centaur, and in his gleaming mail he seemed like a picture from some old book of chivalry. We rode along the hewn way past the church, that mighty building which now housed so few people, and then paused at a cliff-turn of the road.

To our right was the valley; to our left, the defiles of the mountain and the desert beyond. Sir Raymond pointed out the road that led up to the castle—a wide causeway, incapable of defense, it seemed, except by men with rifles.

"Our best protection is the desert," he said gravely. "When the time comes that we see men approaching we can lead out our horsemen and see what can be done against the wondrous weapons you speak of, Sir Frederick."

I said nothing, for the temper of the man was gloomy, and I did not like him overmuch. So with an irritating air of finality he turned his horse, and we rode down into that crater-valley whose beauty never ceased to delight me.

In the old days, I found, the land hereabouts had been held in fief in true feudal fashion; but now, with so few of the people left, this custom was no more. Only enough land was under cultivation to supply the needs of the inhabitants; yet the stone farmhouses were beautiful—those that had not fallen into ruin—and the people who met us invariably proffered a greeting of grave courtesy.

We paused at the edge of the little river to water the horses. I found that the stream flowed on over the farther edge of the plain to the peaks that shut it in, whence the water was lost in the desert sands below. Looking back at the cliffs of the Man's Nose, I saw smoke ascending from the highest peak, above the castle, and asked Sir Raymond whence it came.

"There is a maze of underground passages through those peaks," he said carelessly, "hewn out by those people who dwelt here before my fathers came. Whence that smoke comes I cannot say, but it arises only at times. We never go down into the caverns, though my father knows them well, or used to."

That speech was typical of the shiftless, ambitionless character of this people.

The plain was crossed by good roads, or rather tracks, leading from farm to farm, crossing and crossing again. The entire country being about five miles long and as much in width, the knights could live each on his own farm, riding in to the castle when occasion required. A dozen of the esquires lived at the castle; their only recreation, so far as I could ever discover, was in exercises at arms.

In this the whole knighthood was undeniably skilful; they could ride, swing sword or ax, and handle their lances with marvelous dexterity—but their prowess had never been tested. Military practise was their only way of passing the time. They had no books; they could not read the Latin-writ parchments in the count's archives, and their only knowledge of the Bible was from a tenth-century vellum manuscript written in Arbi.

Yet there was a glimmer of romance over it all—over the unknown land, the knights with their shining mail, the massive castle and church. I asked Sir Raymond if crime had never entered Themoud.

"Sometimes," and he shrugged his shoulders. "For murder a man is given a horse and turned out in the desert to perish. For other offenses men are judged by my father or myself. But there are not many."

For the simple reason, perhaps, that none of them had ambition enough to be criminal, I thought. We rode to the farther side of the valley and then back home again.

On the return trip I learned something of Edith Gairner's story. Her father had been all his life a missionary; she herself had been born in Jerusalem, going home with her mother to America. There the mother had died a year since, upon which her father had come home and taken her out on this wild quest of his. She spoke Arbi nearly as perfectly as did John and I, and she was taking a keen interest in this new people which was foreign to me.

For, while I was interested enough, there was something about the place that frightened me after only a few hours of it. I think it was the realization of how those Crusaders had come from Syria, how they had settled down and grown mighty once again, how they had been again destroyed, how their descendants were enfeebled and spineless men—yet clung to their olden glories. Each time I passed that church, with its thousands below and its meager scores above, I shivered.

However, "Sentiment is all werry well in its place, but this ain't its place," as John said to this thought of mine. We reached home close to sunset, to find John and our two Moslems waiting. Omar ibn Kasim greeted me with a broad grin, and the Afghan Akhbar Khan, a bearded giant of a fellow, *salaam*ed gravely. Both wore mail coats and swords, but not the golden spurs of knighthood.

Solomon, Sir Raymond, the two men, and I were standing talking in the courtyard after Miss Gairner went to her rooms. Omar was telling Sir Raymond of certain customs of Arabia, and Akhbar Khan had drifted off to one side, when the sun sank. At this the two Moslems hesitated, then sank down in prayer.

The knight turned away, but three or four others who were passing Akhbar paused in evident anger. I paid no attention to what was passing until a fierce cry of anger roused me. I saw the Afghan spring up as one of the knights kicked him.

The next instant swords were out.

Akhbar Khan proved to have some skill with his weapon, but the swordcraft of the Themoud knight was a wonder to behold; before we could move his heavy blade had come down across the Afghan's helm, driving him reeling back, and all that saved him was the furious intervention of Sir Raymond, who had whipped out his blade and sprung between.

"How dare you?" he shouted, while tumult began to stir within the castle. "Shame, so to insult an ally, Sir Tancred!"

"Ally!" sneered the other. "Do we ally ourselves with infidels, then?"

No more passed, for here Count Hugo rushed out and closed the incident. Akhbar Khan laughed at it later, but it served to show the feelings of our hosts toward Moslems.

I should have said that the swords and armor and, in fact, all the metallic arms or utensils to be found in the place were very old. After the disastrous defeat and plague in 1347, all working in metal seemed to have been abandoned in that torpor of the people; my own sword-blade, as I discovered while cleaning it one day, bore an inscription showing it to have been made "in the fire of the Seal" by one Sir Gaimar, of Antioch, in the year 1228. All I can say is that Sir Gaimar, of Antioch, must have been a mighty man of his thews to forge a blade like that for himself.

Solomon and I, with the two Moslems, now took up our quarters together. We saw nothing more of Edith Gairner until that night after the evening meal, when she came down to the great hall. As the night was cold a huge fire had been lit in the fireplace, about which all of us sat, she and John and I a little apart.

There we told Count Hugo and his sons many things of the outside world, or rather she did, while I sat and listened and watched. The old count warmed to her remarkably. Bertrand, the younger son, even flashed into animation. But more and more I felt that this evenly poised girl, who with one Afghan had reached Themoud so much better than we, whose eyes gave no hint of her grief for that father who was lost, and whose very utterance of Arbi was sweet to hear—that this girl was subtly different from any woman I had ever met before.

And the difference, I should add, lay all in her favor.

CHAPTER XI

FOR THE LETTER OF SERGIUS

"**D**ANG IT, Mr. Sargent, why not?"

"It's impossible," I made dogged answer, staring down at the thing.

"Why, weren't half the Arab tribes either Jewish or Christian around Mecca? Dang it, sir, weren't it said as 'ow this 'ere werry monk Sergius, or Boheira, as they called 'im, taught Moham-med the Gospels?"

"Yes, I know all that—but, confound it, John, the thing's a forgery! It *has* to be a forgery! It couldn't last all these—"

"No, Mr. Sargent," broke in Edith Gairner quietly. "If you were familiar with the old uncial Greek, you would know that it is no forgery."

We stood in that hewn council-chamber, the six members of the council seated around us. Set on a stone table in the center by the window was that thing which had drawn Uriel Gairner and John Solomon and Esmer Bey to this awesome place.

It was a letter—no more—written in uncial Greek on a thick vellum, which had been taken from a small golden casket by Count Hugo and unrolled before us.

"If you remember, Mr. Sargent," went on the girl, "it was in 627, or the fifth year of the Hegira, that the Jewish tribes all but overthrew Mohammed and besieged Medina. Could it not be that he yielded to Sergius, hoping that the Christian tribes would help him, then recanted and killed Sergius when he over-came the enemy?"

Even in my heart I knew that the letter was no forgery. Yet it was incredible. Here is a translation:

FROM THE MONK SERGIUS, AT MEDINA, IN THE YEAR OF CHRIST 627, TO THE BISHOP OF NABATHAEA. IN THE NAME OF GOD, GREETING:

Know, O Epiphanios, that by the mercy of God a great blessing has been vouchsafed to the Church in these parts. As I wrote you last year, and previous to then, the man Mohammed, who in truth is inspired either of God or Satan, has shown no little interest in our Scriptures, even after he had set himself up for a false prophet before the Lord.

I received that epistle of the blessed Paul which you caused to be sent me from the bishop of Nejdran, and laid it before Mohammed. Now it has come about that the Jews of these parts, as well as they that do worship idols, have all but caused wreck to the ungodly enterprise of this man Mohammed, and do advance to lay siege to this our city. Thus is shown the mercy of God, my holy father, for two days since Mohammed came to me and made secret profession of the true faith.

O my father, even now I can scarce believe that I have been chosen for so great an instrument! Think—this Mohammed is a man of power, even as the blessed Paul, and will build up the church in Arabia Felix to a great height! An hour hence he comes to me in secret for the sacrament of water, and has promised that it shall later be openly made manifest to all his people.

He prays, my father, that you cause men to be sent from Nabathaea and Moabitis and Nejdran to his aid. Later I will write more freely of these things, for there are signs and wonders in the land without ceasing. With love and great thanks to God.

SERGIUS.

I forced myself to control the fever that raced through my blood at reading the Arbi transcription of this letter, made centuries since and placed with it in the casket that the knights of Themoud might read, for they knew naught of Greek.

Here was the explanation of all that had passed. Were this letter given to the world it would strike a deadly blow at Islam and shatter the Turkish Empire, for Arab would rise against

Osmanli, *Shiah* against *Sunni*, the Grand Senussi against the
Porte—and Heaven only knows what the end would be.

It was to the vital interest of the Osmanlis that the thing
be destroyed, for their only hold on the Islam world lay in the
reverence paid the Sultan as the head of the faith—this, and the
power they clung feebly to. Once that letter reached the outside
world, the result was staggering to conceive of. I shoved the
two papers into the casket again and put it hastily into Count
Hugo's hand.

"Take and hide it," I murmured, hardly knowing what I said.
"Better that this thing were destroyed—"

"Shame!" cried John Solomon, and I bowed my head knowing he was right.

So for a little we sat in silence, all of us. Then Count Hugo
began to speak, and that was the longest speech that ever I heard
from his lips:

"Of old time, Sir Frederick, our fathers came to this place as
you have heard, and found this letter among other things in the
keeping of the fire-worshipers who dwelt here. How it had first
come is not known, but it was here, and it is here. Until that
year of destruction when the better part of our race perished,
my forefathers intended that some day the whole people should
go forth, bearing that letter, and so rejoin their brethren of the
true faith in the outer world. Thus they have written. But afterward this thing was forgotten save by the men of my own family.

"My friends, let us speak freely. We are a weak and worthless
race, and our doom is heavy upon us, though how it shall come
I know not; yet God has left us this mission, to give that letter
to all nations that so Islam may be destroyed.

"By the emblem of the Seal of Solomon, which my brother
did bear forth and which is graven on your silver rings, swear to
me that if any of you shall reach the world again this letter shall
go with you. Each of us six has sworn it; now do you swear it,
and you, Lady Edith, with the other twain."

It came into my mind to ask him about this mysterious Seal

of which I knew nothing, and of which John Solomon knew nothing, for I had asked him of it; but I forgot the matter almost as quickly, since we took the oath which he gave us.

"Poor Sergius!" I thought to myself when we were on our way back to our own apartments in the palace. "His dream was soon spent and shattered, it seems."

"Well, sir, now you know what them there Osmanlis are after," said John as we three sat together before lunch. "I wish I 'ad more tobacco."

He whittled gloomily at the last remnants of his plug. Miss Gairner smiled.

"A little abstinence will do you good, Mr. Solomon—Sir John Solomon, I mean. Are you convinced that the letter was genuine, Mr. Sargent?"

"Yes," I said slowly. "Everything, historically and otherwise, points to such a conclusion. I wish we were out of here, however. There's madness in the eyes of the whole people, and I'm afraid of them."

"Quite right, sir," nodded John sagely. "But there's more than one kind o' madness, I says; and if so be as it comes to fighting, why, a madman with one o' these 'ere swords can do a mortal lot o' damage, says I. I'm done wi' the Orient, I am; if we gets out o' this 'ere bleedin' place wi' that there letter, why, we 'ands it over to the king—God bless 'im—and if 'e publishes it, well and good."

"Fighting, John? Why—think we'll have any trouble if Esmer gets here?"

"Not if, Mr. Sargent, sir—when! You listen 'ere," and John told me those things concerning Esmer Bey which I have set down in another place. "That's the kind o' man 'e is, sir and miss," he concluded. " 'E'll get 'ere with them Arabs if 'e kills 'alf of 'em first. 'E'll get 'ere, and then 'Eaven 'elp the poor women and children!"

"You seem pessimistic, to-day," smiled Miss Gairner.

But there was a little pallor in her cheeks as she spoke.

"Don't you think we'll be able to do anything at all?"

"No, miss; that I don't, and werry sorry I am to 'ave to say it.

Accordin' to Mr. Sargent, some o' them Osmanli soldiers 'ave rifles—modern rifles; the Ma'az men will 'ave muskets or may be rifles, too. Where'll we be then, I asks you? These 'ere knights and knightesses may be all werry fine to look at, but they're weak-faced, mortal weak-faced, and that's the werry worst kind o' stubborn, stiff-necked people to deal with, sir and miss. I knows, danged if I don't!"

John was very much in earnest, and very much shaken by his own words, as were we. He was perfectly right, for a weak man is hardest of all to argue with; and from what I already knew of the Themoud knights they would listen to no warnings until a few of them had fallen under Esmer's bullets.

However, there was time to give them a sample of our revolver-fire, which I determined to do that very day. Accordingly, after luncheon John and I and our two Moslems got every one in the castle down into the courtyard, where we hung up the carcass of a sheep that had been killed that morning.

Over this we draped one of the mail coats. Akhbar Khan stepped thirty paces away with my powerful automatic and sent a bullet at it. To our intense disgust the bullet struck a loose fold of the chain-mail and glanced off. I at once sent another which went through a double layer of the mail and through the sheep as well.

"A deadly thing enough in Christian hands," announced Count Hugo calmly as the knights crowded around to view the effects of the shot; "but in the hands of this Moslem the thing was harmless. Such is the power of God, Sir Frederick, though I blame you not for doubting it. When we ride forth against these Saracens their shots will be as harmless as was that first endeavor of your infidel."

"But can't you understand?" I protested. "The first shot failed only by accident. Here; I'll show you."

I motioned to the Afghan to fire again. His second bullet, of course, had the same effect as mine. But the mischief had been done.

"Ah!" the count commented. "Then the infidel can hit a mark which a Christian hits first. Verily these be wondrous weapons! But the Saracens which are to descend upon us, I understand, include no Christians. How, then, can their Christian weapons avail them?"

Who could argue against such a twisted conception as that? Not I, indeed. I put up my weapons with a few expressive words in English, and swore that I would have nothing more to do with the whole affair of defense.

"Don't take on so, Mr. Sargent," expostulated John afterward. "It ain't a thing to be 'elped, as the old gent said when 'e 'ad the gout, and cursing don't do no good. The fate o' man is wrote big on 'is forehead, sir, as the Koran says."

John was despondent. Of a sudden the whole situation made me angry.

"Well, if you think that I'm going to hang around here doing nothing, my friend, you're mistaken!" I snapped. "You've got a grouch, and you can nurse it and be hanged. Akhbar Khan! Go and ask your mistress if she'll go riding with me. Omar, find Count Hugo and ask him for four horses—you and Akhbar will come along."

The two departed, carrying revolvers, for after Akhbar's experience with the excitable and expert swordsman the day before we deemed it best to go armed. Half an hour later, leaving Solomon at home, the four of us rode out.

My anger was as much desperation as anything else. Two days had I been in Themoud, at least consciously, and so filled with wonders and unbelievable things had they been that my nerves were on edge. I felt that if another such thing as the letter of Sergius came to light I would promptly kick it over the nearest cliff. So it was just as well that the spectacle of Solomon's Seal was not thrust upon us at that time, or I think I would assuredly have gone mad.

On that ride across the fair plain several things took place. First and foremost I discovered that Edith Gairner had with her the most soothing way imaginable; after a half-hour's talk with her I was almost rid of my irritation and began to partake of her common-sense view of the situation.

"It's not a dream, and it's not incredible as it seems," she said calmly. "Count Hugo's brother probably gave away the secret to the Osmanlis after leaving my father, and you have seen that they do not regard it as incredible at all."

That was a sensible argument, I thought. I soon found, also, that this girl had not wasted her time. As we rode she outlined certain things which should be done at once. After a discussion that lasted until sunset we returned to the castle, and I was prepared to begin proceedings.

During the days that followed, Lady Edith was my active lieutenant in work and play. Poor Solomon seemed demoralized; his sufferings before reaching Themoud, the abrupt break-off of his old life and associations, the destruction of his company of devoted followers, and above all, the things we had found here at Themoud had all contributed to make him generally unstrung and nerveless. It was but a temporary condition, for later the first sign of danger seemed to tune him up to all his former alertness of spirit, yet at the time I was sorely impatient with his moodiness and general gloom.

Together with the two Moslems, Lady Edith, and Sir Raymond, and Bertrand—the only natives who had blood in their veins, save the old count—I visited every farmhouse and dwelling in the valley, ordering that horses should be kept in readiness to take all the people to the castle at the first sign of danger. This sign was to be a huge beacon on the highest tower of the castle, visible from all quarters, which would be lighted whenever any trace of the Osmanlis was sighted.

We wished to send men out into the desert each day, but this the shiftless crew absolutely refused to do, for they dreaded that desert, and small wonder. However, we made sure that every soul of the three hundred inhabitants would be in readiness to flock to the castle; Heaven knows we did everything in our power to insure their safety, and if they but had the spirit to heed our instructions the happenings that followed might have been averted.

They received the orders apathetically, promising to carry them out; but as we learned too late, not half the people paid any attention. Horses were not kept in readiness; no preparations were made to bring in the women and children; in short, these lifeless wrecks of a once mighty people brought their fate upon themselves.

None the less we accomplished a good deal at the castle. This, fortunately, had its own spring, so that in the event of a siege water would not be lacking. Getting wagons, we brought in a good supply of grain, and kept a flock of sheep on the mountainside where it could be brought in on short notice.

In the evenings Edith Gairner and I went over the archives, to the interest and keen appreciation of the old count and young Bertrand. We found that up to the "year of destruction," as it was locally termed, full records had been kept; then, as with all else, this had been abandoned. I thought then that there must be a curse upon this race; and long after, when I had brought the inscription under the great Seal to London, I found that I was not so far wrong.

So passed ten days, in a way the happiest and saddest and maddest and most foreboding of all my life. Each hour I was looking forward to the news of Esmer Bey's arrival; and after my tidings had spread abroad through all the people, that look in their eyes, as of brooding doom, seemed to grow and deepen. Indeed, so marked was it that Omar ibn Kasim gave them the name of "The People with Blasted Souls." But, amid the unreality of it all was the living presence of Edith Gairner, and I knew I was glad of those days of torture at Maan and all that had followed after—for so had I found her at the end.

I forgot that I still had Esmer Bey to reckon with on this point. And this was the manner of my remembering:

One evening—the same as that on which Lady Edith

and I had copied that Arbi transcription of the letter of the monk Sergius—I sat up late with John Solomon. He was more depressed than ever that night. Now that he had reached Themoud and found its great secret, it seemed to be a little thing to him after all. It is often so—we sacrifice a great deal to win some objective, then find we have risen above it in the very act of sacrifice.

Finally I ordered him to come for a stroll in the night air. He consented in listless fashion. Passing through the unguarded corridors, we came to the courtyard and gates, which were open, the drawbridge down. Here we met Sir Raymond, who for some whim of his own was keeping guard.

Suddenly, as we stood talking I descried a light in the sky over the valley. I took it for the moon, but Sir Raymond, puzzled, said that the moon did not rise for a good two hours yet. As the light grew we knew it for a fire, and watched anxiously. Then John gripped at my arm—and clear through the night we heard the mad hoof-beats of a horse pounding the rocky road past the chapel. I ran for a cresset, and as I fetched it the horse came.

"Death!" wailed out the voice of that same knight who had kicked Akhbar Khan at his prayers. "Death! Strange men be on the plain, riding giant beasts! Slaughter and fire! They have fired the grain—slain my wife and babe—God save—save—"

With a choking sob the knight crashed down from his saddle, and as he lay dead on the stones I saw a bullet-hole through his chain-mail. Esmer had come!

CHAPTER XII

HOW WE FOUGHT FOR THEMOUD

THAT WAS a night of untold horror. Foolishly enough, we had all taken it as a matter of course that Esmer Bey would reach Themoud as we had reached it, at the lower flanks of that mighty mountain called the Man's Nose. Instead he had circled around either with devilish cunning or else led by chance, and had struck through farther peaks, falling full upon the unprepared and unsuspecting valley.

At the castle there were a score of esquires, boys from eighteen to twenty-five, but no knights save Count Hugo and his elder son. As soon as the great beacon was lit I left John Solomon and Bertrand to care for the castle and Lady Edith with ten esquires, and rode forth with all the rest to help bring in fugitives. We did not know but that Esmer had divided his forces and might attack the castle also; this fortunately was not the case.

Once past the church and on the road leading down the valley, which we must now defend, I pushed on with Omar and Akhbar and Sir Raymond to do what we might with our revolvers, leaving the count to succor whom he could. The night was still, without a breath of wind. Across the plain the flaming fields were lighting the sky terribly.

Soon we met fugitives—first a woman on horseback, a babe in her arms, and a youth running gaspingly at the saddle-bow; then a horse galloping after, with something clad in clanking steel that dragged heavily from one stirrup. I figured that the

Arabs had spread out to do what damage they could, and that by shooting down a few in the darkness we would halt them and force them to collect until daybreak at least.

There was an awesome sound in the night as we advanced—a shrill, sobbing wail that went up from every soul in Themoud as the horror seized them and trembled back from the circling peaks. Now we passed others and in the gathering light began to see things more clearly.

There was one sight that has always stuck in my memory. Two steeds thundered up to us and stopped, whinnying. On one sat a girl of five, who greeted us with a smile; on the other, a beautiful white stallion, sat a woman shot through the back and dying, her blood staining all the horse's withers. In one hand she still gripped her husband's sword; his shield was hung about her neck, while from the reek of the weapon I knew that she had proved her Norman Stock that night. She died as we came up. I sent the child galloping on toward the rear without pause.

I became aware that our little company was growing. Twisting about in my saddle I saw that half a dozen knights had joined us, silently, as was their custom. Calling one of these, Sir Raymond found that the enemy had apparently struck at a dozen different points, slaying all without discrimination and scattering widely. We rode on again and soon, without any warning whatsoever, found ourselves in the thick of the murderous work.

A scream darted out from ahead. I spurred forward, a horrible thirst for vengeance in my heart, a frenzied lust for the blood of these demons. A moment later I reached a farmhouse, around which I dimly saw a dozen gaunt shapes that I knew to be camels.

Another scream from the house—and as I spurred to the doorway a flame leaped up and the scene flashed upon me. About the door stood a group of *burnoosed* Arabs, while a half-dressed knight held them at bay, sword in hand. A shot rang out and he staggered back, but before they could enter I was at their shoulders and my automatic spoke.

There had been twelve Arabs there, but one got away. The knight, wounded in the shoulder, and his wife we sent back to the castle, spurring on to the next house. It is not nice to write in cold blood of all that we did in the next hour. We came upon party after party, while Omar rode at my left and Akhbar Khan at my right, we three doing all that was done, for I refused to let Sir Raymond take chances. We were like to need every sword that could be saved to Themoud.

We could usually find the Arabs by the shouts of *"Allahu, akhbar!"* they sent up whenever they caught a fugitive, and we did bloody work among them. However, we did make one prisoner, and this was the manner of it.

I had been about to order a return, fearing to strike on the whole band of Esmer, when Sir Raymond urged me on to the next stead, where dwelt a cousin of his. We had not yet reached it when we knew that the Arabs had been before us, by the shouting; fire sprang into the standing grain, and as the light jumped up and we rode down upon the place there came a tattoo of hoofs from the opposite quarter.

Five Arabs only were emerging from the house, having done their work, when into the light rode old Count Hugo, his beard flying over his shoulders, a bloody blade in his hand, and a goodly company behind him. The Arabs leaped to their camels, but we also rode in on them; then they delivered a rifle volley pointblank that sent two knights reeling to the ground, and we came together.

I had no chance to shoot in the mêlée. Count Hugo, rising in his stirrups, delivered one terrible cut that sheared clean through an Arab's body and sent the camel off screaming and snorting with pain, for the blade had bitten him; another Arab was neatly run through with a lance, and Omar shot another. The remaining two, seeing they were surrounded, dropped from their camels, squirmed through the mass of horses and, simitars in hand, gained the doorway of the house, where they turned at bay.

The maddened knights were closing in, when I saw by the

splendid arms and clothing of one Arab that he was a person of some weight, and I stopped the onrush. Riding out, I called to the two and asked who they were.

"I am *Sheik* Zohri of the Ma'az tribe," answered he whom I had picked out.

At my assurance that his life would be spared he yielded readily. The other refused; and when Zohri was bound and taken behind the saddle of a knight, Sir Raymond dismounted and went at the other with his sword. The Arab was skilful enough, but Sir Raymond was well-nigh crazed by his fury for vengeance. At the third blow he stepped back a pace, drawing the Arab from the doorway; then his great blade flashed up in the ruddy glare and came down like a bolt. We saw the Arab's head suddenly fly asunder—his neck and shoulders parted likewise—and before the thud of the blow had ceased he was cloven in two from head to groin.

After that sight I was glad to ride again into the darkness.

Posting sentries and scattering a few scouts as we went, we rode back to the castle, a mournful company. Here, as might be expected, we found all in wildest confusion, out of which John Solomon and Edith Gairner were slowly bringing some order. With great cressets lighting the courtyard, old Count Hugo took his stand in the doorways above and called before him the head of each household.

It goes to my heart to think of what followed. Out of those three hundred and some odd people there were ninety-five who stood around us, and of these seventy-two were men. The terrible disparity of numbers was accounted for by the fact that at one of the inlying farms that afternoon there had been an informal joust followed by a feast. At this some two-score knights had been present, and most of them had been drunk when the alarm came. Count Hugo had gathered them into his band, to find that their families had doubtless been among the first slain.

Think of it! Out of them all only a score of women and children saved! Good Heaven, what horrible silence hung on that courtyard when the numbers had been taken! I can see the figure of old Count Hugo yet, standing there with the tears streaming over his white beard, but with never a sound of weeping rising up.

Fifty knights and twenty-two esquires, every man of them with a desolate horror stamped into his face—that ring of faces was too much for me. I turned and passed inside the castle, not hiding my tears. I wanted to leave these men alone with their grief and remorse; I could not bear to stand and watch them, and this feeling was shared by the others, even to the two Moslems.

"Inshallah!" I heard Omar mutter as we came to our own rooms. "Of a truth, Akhbar Khan, Eblis has let loose his devils this night! How many did you slay?"

"Twelve that I know of," came the grim reply. "And—"

"Silence!"

Solomon's voice rang out as of old, and I knew he was himself again.

"A light, and less talk, fools! Here is a seat, miss."

A light was made in a cresset. John, his face twitching oddly, fell into English as he addressed us.

"This is a werry bad business, sir and miss, a werry bad business—just like that. I—I— Dang it, ain't there no 'ope for some o' them women, Mr. Sargent?"

"None," I replied, looking down at Edith Gairner's pale features. "Before Heaven, we did all men could do, John."

"I knows that, sir; I knows that. Now, if you please, let's forget it for a bit. What are we a going to do next?"

"Fight, John."

"Did you get the guns o' them as you done for, sir?"

Fool that I was, I had never thought of it. Coincidentally with his words a heartrending groan swelled up through all the castle from that stricken crowd down below. As we sat listening, frozen into silence, there came to us the sound of singing. Now, whether it was some national chant of this strange people, or whether, as I am more inclined to think, it was some ancient form of litany and battle-hymn together, handed down from the olden days, it swelled and died and swelled again in a most moving and terrible fashion—changing from meter to meter, mournful and utterly desolate at first, but rising to a great crescendo that swept up and up until I saw Akhbar Khan clutch at his sword and felt my own fingers creeping to my swordbelt.

I give here a version of that ominous litany, which was in Arbi. To realize all it brought to us, recall our position: we, crouching alone in that upper room, and they singing down there in the courtyard, men and women together who had seen their doom and knew it was upon them:

> "God of old, who rules the sounding years,
> Alike our God of battle and of tears—
>   Hear us, O God!
> The darkness falls; deep doom is on the land,
> Thy people perish; where is now Thy hand?
>   Hear us, O God!

> "O Death! Death! Death! Thou hast come to us here.
> Help us, O God! Our valleys are stricken and sear;
> Gone are our bravest, our best-born and noblest and dear;
> Our strongest lie low in the dust—
>   God! God! Be Thou near!
> Hark to us desolate; list to us sorrowing! Hear!
> God of aforetime! God of the aftertime! Rear
> A bulwark to shelter us! Put forth Thy sheltering spear,
> For death and destruction have come to the hearts of us here!

> "Unto us whose skies are gray
>   In the east a light is spread;
> Hearts of us, be strong to-day!
>   Fear and failure both be fled!
>   With the past our past is sped.
> Up and at the foe who wait!
>   Gone be our despair and dread—
> God and Courage keep the gate!

> "Lances gleam in brave array;

Christmen, Crossmen, look ahead!
Smite the infidel and slay—
    Drown his crescent moon in red!
    Knights are we and knightly bred;
What have we to do with fate?
    Up and strike! Mahound is dead!
God and Courage keep the gate!

"God heareth! God heareth! The shadows upsteal!
Ride! Ride to the call of His trumpet-peal,
To the snarl and the swirl and the sheen of steel!
    Up and strike! Up and strike!
Christ rides with our vanguard; Death thunders behind!
Spur! Spur! For our Cross-flame hath smitten them blind!
Spur! Spur! Strike their ranks like a flame on the wind!
    Up and strike! Up and strike!
There's a flame on the wind and a flame in the sedge,
And the flame of our faith flares from windrow and hedge;
Sword-flame and Cross-flame! Up! Up! With the edge!
    Up and strike! Up and strike!

"Up and strike! Up and strike!" reechoed the roaring shout. I caught Omar ibn Kasim, the battle-lust in his wild eyes, yelling the words. He fell silent suddenly and shrank back into a dark corner; Akhbar Khan smiled grimly at nothing. Out of the ensuing silence a single low, welling groan came faintly. Those who had sung had realized their impotency.

I could imagine what it had been in other days, when knights by the hundred crowded the great church on the crag-side, and swelled forth that deep, final chorus amid their banners and blazonry, their mail and clashing swords. But now we heard the sonorous voice of old Count Hugo sounding, and though we could not make out the words, there was no need. After that Edith Gairner, pale and shaken, sought her own chambers, and we slept.

Two hours of rest, and we were up with the sun to find all reported quiet. A dense cloud of smoke hung on the valley below us, and as this would presently lift with the morning breeze, I left John to assist the old count in getting things straightened up as regarded food and arrangement of the people, while with Sir Raymond I went to examine our captive, *Sheik* Zohri, who was brought to the courtyard before us.

He was a lordly, insolent fellow—a typical desert outlaw—with no trace of fear or decency in him. To our questions he replied only with taunts as to those he had slain during the darkness before we caught him; so that in the end we had much ado to restrain the blood-mad knights from ending him then and there. When he saw that, he changed.

"Give me my sword again," he said sullenly, "and one of you *kafirs* meet me in fair combat, or else slay me here. I will tell you naught, and Esmer Bey will not ransom me. If I win, I go free; if I fall or am overcome, I serve you."

At that a roar of assent went up. I saw that argument was useless. Young Bertrand pushed forward to his brother's side, his eyes aflame with eagerness.

"Oh, my brother!" he cried. "Let me earn my spurs by this combat!"

Sir Raymond eyed him a moment sadly and nodded. With a great laugh Bertrand flung up his sword so that it spun in the sunshine and fell again into his hand.

"Give him a mail-coat some one!" he exclaimed, discarding his shield and taking his huge Norman blade in both hands. It was done; and, simitar in hand, the swarthy, powerful Arab faced the boy.

I had no great fear for Bertrand, but I was sorry to lose *Sheik* Zohri, who, despite his words, would have been a valuable captive. And lose him I did, for as he came at Bertrand with a deadly rush, the boy heaved up his sword. Laughing a little, he leaped lightly to one side; there was a whirl of white fire, and the Arab's arm dropped off, smitten clean through mail and bone at the shoulder. And that, as you may guess, was the end of *Sheik* Zohri of the Ma'az tribe—yet, indeed, not quite the end.

By a touch of sheer cruelty Sir Raymond put the body on the

steps of the church in the attitude of prayer, intending that it
should be found by the Arabs thus. Meanwhile, finding that the
smoke-pall was lifting, I sent for Omar and Akhbar and asked
for a score of knights. With these I rode out to see what might
be seen of Esmer Bey.

The count and his sons I refused to take, for there would be
bullets flying, and I wished them to be safe. The others mattered
nothing; they were brave with the courage of cornered rats, and
something more, but I had small love for them, seeing that their
sottishness had brought such disaster upon their womenfolk. To
do them justice their remorse was very keen and bitter indeed,
but remorse does not repair what is done.

Once past the church I halted. The rocky road down to the
plain might be defended for some while, and it occurred to me
that with a few rifles we might do something there. Not daring
to trust the two Moslems alone with the knights, I sent Akhbar
Khan and Oman ibn Kasim off together, to try to pick up a rifle
or two from the slain Arabs.

Slowly the smoke-clouds drove away before the breeze, and
finally disclosed the farther half of the valley blackened and
desolate, though the flames had died out. We rode onward at a
brisk trot, ascertaining from a weary scout that Esmer's camp
lay by the river-outlet of the lake. Presently, indeed, we saw this
for ourselves.

Esmer Bey had reached Themoud with ninety-odd men and
two hundred camels. We could see the animals herded under
the trees. Still a half-mile from the lake and camp I saw a party
equal in numbers to my own riding forth with a white flag.

Now after the things which had been done the last night I
had small mind to honor any rules of war toward these men, but
I halted my knights and rode on alone, my automatics ready. The
party of Arabs were mounted on horses, doubtless taken from
the farmsteads. They halted likewise, and one of them rode out
to meet me in the space between; even from afar I recognized
the powerful figure of Esmer Bey. He, with certain of his men,
had discarded their *burnooses* and taken to the chain-mail of

slaughtered knights. This sight had drawn a mutter from my men, but no more.

"So! It is my Egyptian again!" cried Esmer as we rode up to each other.

He was the same powerful, incisive, dominant man, deadly cold despite the flaming devils of cruelty that now glared unchecked from his black eyes. He was handsome, too, for he had taken a knight's helm and wore it with the mail-coat.

Revolver-holsters were slung about his waist and a carbine hung at his stirrup, but touched with some spirit of ironic romance, I think, he had also appropriated one of the Norman swords. Save for Count Hugo or his sons there was not a man in all the knighthood to compare with Esmer Bey in either body or mind, shame that it is to say it!

"Well, Mr. Sargent, this is quite a surprise! So you have reached the far-famed Themoud, only to find it a place of theatricals, eh? Neat costume, this."

"I see you still have my mark on your cheek," I taunted, for I could not repress my virulent hatred of the man.

His face darkened and his fingers flew to the burn-scar.

"Allah curse you!" He reverted to Arbi. "It was you who slew my men last night!"

"What did you expect? Your Ma'az men can come to the castle if they want Zohri."

"I thought as much. Well, I'll give you the Rev. Gairner for the *sheik*. I meant to shoot the fool, but we might better trade him. Time enough for killing."

I agreed to that exchange. There came into my mind an old tale of the Moorish wars in Spain—or was it the tale of the Cid? In any case the main incident stood out clearly.

So we arranged to send ten men with *Sheik* Zohri to meet ten men with Gairner, who, it seemed, had wandered into Esmer's party after having lost himself. Esmer had brought him along as a prisoner. We made a truce for the rest of the day. To my great satisfaction I learned that some thirty of Esmer's men had fallen the night before.

Esmer Bey made no bones of his determination to massacre every soul in Themoud except Edith Gairner, and to get the letter of Sergius. I told him I had seen it.

"Then so much the worse for you," he replied coolly. "I ought to have finished you there at Maan, Sargent. However, castle or no castle, you'll pay, by Allah!"

"One to a bargain makes a poor price."

As I flung the proverb at him I turned to my own men, with his evil laugh mocking me, and so for that time we parted.

Riding swiftly home again, leaving a few scouts by the way, we met Omar and Akhbar Khan, who had found no rifles. Telling them something of my plan, I picked out seven knights and sent the rest on to the castle, halting at the church.

I make no excuse for what followed. I had agreed to deliver *Sheik* Zohri in exchange for Gairner, and there had been no word of life or death. We strapped a board to a saddle and set up the body, muffled in its *burnoose* again, so that it looked life-like enough.

Then we rode down to the plain once more, I and Omar ibn Kasim and Akhbar Khan a little ahead of the rest with Zohri, our automatics ready for use. Soon we saw the ten Arabs coming toward us with a bound man in their midst.

In this matter, at least, I tricked Esmer neatly. Nor has the matter troubled my conscience overmuch since then. Indeed it has always surprised me that Esmer did not slay Gairner before sending him back to us.

Our parties met, and the two prisoners were exchanged. Then as I fully expected the Ma'az men let out a howl of fury, and bullets began to sing. Two of our knights fell, Omar got a bullet through his arm, and I lost my horse; but after we had shot their leader and four others the rest gave over their objection and took their dead *sheik* home.

As for me, I shook hands with Gairner and then with great

joy picked up five very good Snider rifles, plucked the bando-leers from the slain men, and so led my party home again. Two knights were an excellent exchange for five rifles, to my mind.

CHAPTER XIII

JOHN SOLOMON WANTS A SMOKE

URIEL GAIRNER was a very pleasant surprise to me, being not at all as I had conceived him from the description of the consul at Port Saïd. Underneath his beard he was a keen-faced, hard-jawed man of a deadly earnestness—open-minded enough in all things, with a saving trace of humor, and with an eye to trust at the first glance. What was more just then, he also had the ability and the will to handle one of our five rifles against Esmer.

"I tell you, gentlemen," he said to us that noon after all the introductions were done with and he had greeted Edith, "I saw things last night that drove me frantic. Those men out there are human fiends—no less! I am obedient to your orders, Mr. Sargent, and I think you'll find me quite a fair shot."

"Beggin' your pardon, sir," spoke up John, "but 'ave you that there *firman?*"

Gairner had not. Esmer had promptly appropriated it. Also, the Afghan, Yar Hussein, who was a cousin of Akhbar Khan, and who had left with the missionary in search of his mutinied men, had been made a prisoner by Esmer, but had in some manner slipped away the same night and by now he was probably safe in Damascus or Maan.

This news for some esoteric reason seemed to please John mightily. Several times I caught him eying the big Akhbar speculatively as if he were figuring out a problem in his own mind.

That afternoon was peaceful. Mr. Gairner inspected the letter of Sergius; I give him credit for displaying no more emotion than a stone. He merely declared that we had more important things to consider, and so handed back the casket to Count Hugo. After that we held a council of war.

The fortress had been provisioned, and I, who by general consent, took command of the forces, sent Bertrand with ten men to camp on guard at the foot of the road down to the plain. Also, I gave him command of the scouts. There was no danger of *his* going to sleep! That boy, like his father, was a Norman.

At the first sign of an advance from Esmer we arranged to go down with our rifles and hold the road, to the church, with the valley between church and castle. Gairner had great respect from all in Themoud, partly because he was a clergyman and partly because he asked for an outfit of hardware and swung a sword with the best of them. At this time I abandoned that big sword temporarily, taking instead a very fine, long ax of Damascene work which I found in the armory. Sir Raymond could not swing it, but perhaps I had the knack, for it fitted me exactly.

Then, having appointed officers to see that the watches were changed regularly and that scouts were kept out, Solomon, Gairner, and I returned to our rooms where we found Akhbar Khan relating tales of Afghanistan to Edith and Omar. Then it was that John betrayed his "reversal to form."

"Dang it!" he broke out abruptly. "You ain't got any tobacco, Mr. Gairner, sir?"

"Sorry, Solomon—I don't use it."

"All werry well, sir; a man as don't smoke, why he goes off on a spree like every time 'e refuses a cigar. But it's main different with me, sir. I 'as to ave me bit o' baccy, and it ain't 'ome without it, just like that."

John looked so doleful that Edith Gairner laughed and we with her.

"Oh, you can laugh!" he said, sucking at his empty clay. "See 'ere, Omar ibn Kasim! You come along o' me into this next room.

If me and a Hazramaut man can't find a way to get some baccy, why we'd best give in to Esmer Bey and 'ave done, I says."

The two of them went by themselves into the other room, where we heard them talking, but thought little more of it. Gairner told how he had been lost and found by Esmer; he had been well enough treated, but he was very bitter against the Osmanli for the earlier treachery, and small wonder.

"We don't know what may happen, Mr. Sargent," and he turned to me earnestly. "I take it that you are aware of Esmer's plans. Now if anything should happen to me I want you to promise that Edith does not fall into his hands alive—that's all."

Taken aback for a moment I looked at the girl. She had gone pale on a sudden, but though her eyes were wide, they looked very steadily into mine. She put out a hand and clasped mine.

"I would feel safer, Mr. Sargent, if—if you—would promise father."

So, though with no very good grace, I promised. But to myself I vowed that when I got another such chance at Esmer as I had had that morning no white flag would hold my hand. And *that* was a vow I intended to keep faithfully!

Just then John called Akhbar into the other room. Presently, after a little hum of talk, all three of them came back. John was rubbing his hands quite contentedly, while Omar was grinning widely—which was a sign of huge excitement. Stately and grave as ever, Akhbar merely fingered his prayer-beads.

"Well, Solomon, what have you been hatching up?" asked Gairner, smiling as if he had not been in deadly earnest a moment before.

He never said very much; he was one of those quiet, steady-spoken men whom one can bank on from Hull to Halifax and back again.

"Why, sir, about that 'ere tobacco," returned John quite complacently. "You see, sir, them Ma'az men, as I 'appens to know, ain't used to be a living far from their camels, in a manner o' speaking. What's more, they're smokers, which all the tribes ain't."

"You're right there, Solomon," broke in Gairner, nodding. "They all have marrowbone pipes with a hole drilled in one end."

"Yes, sir."

John looked at me. Now, knowing him as I did, knowing his little ways of hiding an inner thought with true Arab subtlety, I began to wonder if he was really thinking of tobacco. But it seemed that he was—at least, just then.

"Now, Mr. Sargent, sir, you know as 'ow them Ma'az men would be keepin' of their camel-bags close by their camels like. Also,'ow they'd be keepin' of their worldly goods in their camel-bags. Werry good. Now, sir, if so be as you'd let me give orders just this once, I'll prowide 'baccy for us all, and do it shipshape and proper by sun-up."

I looked at John, and John looked at me, tapping his empty clay pipe. I was hankering after a good smoke myself, and said so.

"Go ahead, John. You're as much boss of this outfit as I am, and more."

"Werry good, and thank you kindly, sir. I'd like to speak wi' the count, sir."

Leaving the puzzled Gairner behind, John, the two Moslems, and I sought Count Hugo. There John requested twenty men who should be ready to ride two hours before dawn, unarmed and without their clanking mail. We explained nothing, but the old count assented without asking any questions. He even offered to accompany us, but we refused.

"And now what?" I asked when we were back again.

"Why, sir, a bit o' sleep might be a good thing—a werry good thing, I says."

So we packed Edith Gairner off to her own quarters and turned in. John, as usual, kept a tight mouth about what he proposed to do, so I knew that his plans were all ready.

Some time during the early hours Solomon awoke me.

We put on our white mantles with the golden Seal on the

breasts, leaving our mail-coats behind. John handed me a rifle and bandoleer, and gave others to Gairner and the Moslems.

"Now, sirs, if so be as you'll pay 'eed to what I say! Mr. Sargent, you'd best take one o' them knights to guide you. As soon as we get to the plain you and Mr. Gairner and Akhbar and Omar cut off wi' that 'ere guide and circle around to the opposite side o' the Osmanli camp. The camels, Omar said, are on this side?"

"Yes—under those tamarisks. They're close to camp, though, John."

"That's all right, sir. You get on the opposite side, just like that, across the bank o' that river. Then let loose wi' them guns. If you meets with sentries, why finish 'em off quiet, 'cause why, you've got to surprise that 'ere Esmer Bey, dang 'im! Then pull off gradual like back toward 'ome."

"And you'll cut out the camel-bags, eh?"

I smiled, understanding his plot now.

"Mebbe, sir; mebbe. But mind you 'old 'em till dawn—draw 'em away from camp if so be as it can be done."

"All right; I have the idea."

John took the fifth rifle himself, and the five of us went down to the courtyard where twenty white-clad knights were waiting with the horses. I did not see why John was taking so many men, but finding Sir Raymond in command, I chose him for my guide and left the rest to John.

At the foot of the road we found Bertrand and his men wide awake, a circumstance of which I was glad. With them we left John. For the rest we had a stiff breeze to rustle the grain and drown our hoof-beats. By the time we got within the danger zone the moon was hanging low over the rimming peaks. It was a moral certainty that Esmer would have sentries, and so when Sir Raymond showed us the little lake just ahead we left the horses with him to be brought up at the first alarm and slipped ahead on foot.

We stole around the shore of the lake toward the mass of

tamarisks which marked the river and camp. Suddenly I caught star-glint on steel ahead, and a low voice asked in Osmanli:

"Who goes?"

It was one of Esmer's regulars.

"Less noise, fool!" I answered in Osmanli as we separated to steal in on him. "Is it not written that a man may plunder the unbelievers?"

A low chuckle answered me, for naturally the man would never suspect that any but his comrades could speak that tongue. Soon I glimpsed him, rifle at the ready, peering forward to see me; a white shape uprose behind him and there was a thud as Akhbar brought down his gun-butt.

"Take his cartridges," I ordered softly. "We may have need of them."

And so we did, for it was a sinful waste of precious ammunition that followed—at least, considering the outcome of that night it was a waste. I think Omar put a knife into the man as he lay, but I am not sure of that.

We gained the bank of the river, across from the camp, which had been made around one of the stone farmhouses. Here we met a second sentry. As there was no further need of concealment I answered his challenge with a bullet, and with that we opened fire on the camp, pumping those ancient Sniders as fast as we could work a breech-bolt.

Whether we did much damage I cannot say, but at all events we brought a hornets' nest about our ears. Omar, who had been wounded slightly in the arm that morning, got a bullet across the brow that stunned him. Esmer's men began to splash across the shallow stream, yelling as they came.

Luckily Sir Raymond came up with the horses. We flung Omar over a saddle and beat a hasty retreat, then stopped a hundred yards farther on to deliver another volley or two. I am bound to say that the ruse worked to John's utter satisfaction, but not to mine, by any means. Though we spread out through the grain the Arabs could tell our position fairly well and sent lead hailing all around us.

Fortunately we escaped serious hurt and managed to stop their rush until we could get away again. Then a bullet plumped through my leg and horse together, and we went down in a heap. Akhbar was close enough to make out what had happened, and he got me up behind him and off again.

They were after us now—and on horseback. Things were unpleasantly warm, so I concluded that we had done enough for honor and John Solomon's tobacco, and incontinently put for home at our best speed—Omar reviving as we galloped. Had they followed us things might have turned out otherwise, but Esmer was afraid of a trap. I could hear his vibrant voice piercing the night as he recalled his men. They sent a last defiant *"Allahu Akhbar!"* after us, together with a volley, and we rode back to Bertrand's camp just as the light began to spring up in the east. I hoped John had his tobacco, for I had paid for it with a hole through the calf of my leg—and it hurt.

As it happened, John had his tobacco—and something more. With the sunrise I knew suddenly what he had really been after all along—for looming up against the eastern horizon sending Bertrand's poor scouts into wild alarm, was Esmer Bey's entire herd of camels!

John, mopping his brow, got stiffly off his horse, groaned, and stood beside me watching the ungainly beasts driven past us up toward the castle.

"Dang it!" he said, puffing with great satisfaction at his pipe. "S'elp me, Mr. Sargent, I'll never ride one o' them there 'orses again! I'm that stiff and sore—"

"Bully for you, Solomon!" cried Gairner, delighted.

He had just finished binding up my leg.

"Anybody hurt?"

"No, sir—not as I knows on. 'Ow about you?"

"All safe, John," I laughed. "I've got a hole through my leg, but I guess I'll not limp very long. Omar got a crease across his head and we lost a horse—that's all. Did our demonstration satisfy you?"

"Werry good, sir." And with that he brought out one of those ungainly marrowbone pipes and some tobacco, which I took without demur. "All I can say is that we did werry much better than what I looked for. And now let's get up and see that 'ere count again; better throw out more scouts, Mr. Sargent. Esmer Bey might be feeling like chasing them camels in a 'urry."

John took the two Moslems, and I saw that he still had something up his sleeve. So, arranging for a few men to work back toward Esmer's camp and keep an eye on him, I followed with Gairner, and we came to the castle; the camels were herded into the valley between church and castle, and we had some trouble getting through.

As might be expected, there was great exultation in Themoud over our coup, though I could not see how the camels were to be of any advantage. John did, however.

We had barely reached the courtyard when we were summoned to the great hall by Count Hugo. There we found all who were not below with Bertrand. I saw John whispering with Akhbar Khan. In the high seat sat the old count, fully armed, Sir Raymond beside him and Edith Gairner on his left. He motioned us up to him, and I dropped into a seat, for my leg was throbbing a bit. The other knights stood down the length of the hall, along the tables on which the morning meal was set out.

"Sir John," began Count Hugo, "you desired speech with me and with the Council of Themoud. This is the council; speak."

John, embarrassed and coughing apologetically, knocked out his pipe, started to fill it, stopped, put it away, and finally spoke in his fluent Arbi.

"It is an important matter, Count Hugo. As you know, those Osmanlis out there have no mercy, and they want that letter concerning Mohammed the prophet. More than that, they intend to destroy every man who knows about that letter. But we have their camels, and whoever has camels can get away from here across the desert."

I started. Like a flash John's whole plan came to me. I think it came to Count Hugo also, for he ceased pulling his white beard and sat like a statue through all that was said thereafter.

We have enough camels here, Count Hugo, to carry off our whole people and to spare. I can see no reason why we should not do this; once across the desert and you would all be in comparative safety, for at Damascus we can get protection. Esmer would not be able to follow us with horses alone.

"If we stay here there will be bloodshed, and more than likely we will lose. We outnumber the Osmanlis a little, but they have weapons which will speedily lose us that advantage. There you are, sir, and if you'll take my advice you'll load those camels with people and food and water and be off out of here before sundown."

John nervously pulled out his pipe, and this time filled and lighted it, which composed him mightily. There was a dead hush over the hall. I knew that John had solved the whole problem by his master-stroke. It was as he said. We could leave without danger of pursuit, carry off the letter with us, and let Esmer stay here or perish out in the salt desert, just as he chose.

"I thank you, Sir John," began Count Hugo, his sonorous, manly voice ringing deep and clear through the hall. "I thank you in the name of my people for your efforts in our behalf and for the deeds you have done for us. But this matter concerns the whole people, and not me alone. First, Sir Frederick, what is your mind on this?"

"I think Sir John has been inspired," was my swift answer. "He has cut the knot, and all that remains is for us to do as he says. Esmer has sworn to slay us all."

"And you, sir?"

Count Hugo turned to Gairner.

"Yes. I also. I can see no question in the matter, for my part."

Neither could I. But as I looked about me there was a queer

something in the faces of those knights which disquieted me—
why, I knew not. Instead of being brightened up by John's really
brilliant plan, the brooding darkness had deepened in their eyes.

All looked up at Count Hugo as if at a spokesman. He,
however, uttered no hint of any emotion, but called on one of
the knights to give an opinion. The man stepped out, his harness
clanking a little in the silence.

"I, too, thank Sir John," he said, his voice coming more
strongly and firmly than his degenerate features warranted. "But
my family has been slain. Why should I go, who desire only to
kill before I, too, am killed? Let the others go, and let me stay."

A hum of approval passed up from some at this speech. John
stopped smoking very abruptly, and looked fixedly at Akhbar.

"As you will," replied Count Hugo, "and well spoken. You,
Sir Gaimar, whose wife and child were saved—do you speak
for yourself?"

This Sir Gaimar was one of the very few who had something of the count's strength of features. He smiled slightly as
he spoke.

"Why, my lord count, I see no choice in this affair. My
knightly brethren have been murdered basely; my trust lies in
the cross, not in camels; and my sword is sharp. As for my wife
and child, I had sooner have them slain knowing me worthy of
my spurs than have them live knowing me a coward."

Count Hugo stilled a murmur of approval with his uplifted
hand. As you may imagine, I heard this in stark dismay. These
people were fools, rank fools; yet who could but admire their
folly? None the less, dismay and astonishment sat heavily upon
me, so that I could hardly believe what I heard. Poor Solomon
seemed unmoved, deep as his disappointment must have been.

Before the count could speak again there was a little rush of
steel on steel, and Sir Raymond, heaving out his great blade,
leaped down, turned, and faced his father.

"Count Hugo of Antioch, I, the head of the knightly Order

of the Seal of Solomon, do claim right to speak here before all men, as the laws of this land do give me."

Now I caught a strange gleam of pride in the keen blue eyes of Count Hugo as he motioned assent. Sir Raymond spoke, holding out his sword before him, its point touching the stone floor and both hands clasped on the shoulder-high pommel. I never saw him look so knightly save on the day he died.

"Know this, O count! My wife and my child also are safe, but they are not in my mind. Long ages ago my fathers came to this place, and builded here, and lived and died here; they lie, most of them, beneath the church where they worshiped God. I also have thought to lie there; but it has come to me, I know not how, that I shall lie elsewhere.

"Now, this is my mind, Count Hugo, my father. Let these Christians who have come to us go hence, bearing with them the letter of Sergius and this lady, Edith. Let them take the beasts and go whither they will in safety, for this quarrel is none of theirs.

"But for us there is no place on this earth save Themoud.

"Here lies my sword," and he brought it up and flung it down with a great clang. "In your hand, O count, is the fate of this knighthood! Bid us leave this land of our fathers like whipped curs, or bid us stay and fight and die, if need be, like men and knights!"

At that the old count sprang to life indeed. With a single bound he was out of his high seat and pressing the great blade back into his son's hands, while roar upon roar filled the hall. It died away suddenly, and I looked up to see Edith Gairner standing, tears in her eyes. But her voice came firm and strong.

"I am proud of you, knights of Themoud! But do not think that we would run from you, heavy though the odds be. I and mine are not cowards—and I stay!"

At that I caught myself shouting with the rest; then subsided as I realized the mad folly of it and groaned. The count turned to John Solomon, who spoke out before the question came.

"No need to ask, Count Hugo. If you want to know, I think that you and your people are fools. But I am here, and here I stay."

Gairner nodded likewise, unable to speak for the ringing shouts that were like to have shaken the rafters. Then I found myself on my feet amid silence, and my voice sounded strange in my own ears.

"I stay, and I fight for and with you, Count Hugo! I agree with Sir John in that you are fools; but—well, I will be a fool also, and if it is for the last time, I think that I will die in good company."

So with that I sat down and filled my marrowbone pipe, for I was aching to smoke, and the scene had unnerved me somewhat. Count Hugo smiled and turned to Omar ibn Kasim, who merely fingered the bullet-crease on his brow, grinned, and clapped a hand on his rifle. That was answer enough. But Akhbar Khan stepped forward stolidly, shaking his head.

"I would go hence, lord," he said slowly.

I glanced at Solomon, astounded; but John sat quietly filling his pipe anew and did not so much as look up. That the stalwart Afghan should thus prove himself a coward was a startling thing. The Gairners, father and daughter, showed their amazement. The old count, however, only smiled.

"Sand is of many colors," he said quietly. "Sir Raymond, see that this man be given all that he will, and furthered on his way in all manner possible."

The knight nodded, touched Akhbar Khan on the arm, and together they passed down the hall and out, the crowd shrinking back from the tall Afghan, who strode along with his head high, as if he saw none of them. I was struck speechless, but when we were alone again, we all rained questions on John Solomon. I suspected then that it was his work, but he would say nothing.

"Them as asks questions gets less'n they asks, I says, sirs and miss. Akhbar, 'e wanted for to go, so I says to him, 'Go,' just like that."

So the Afghan went. From the castle we watched him and

his ten camels wind off into the salt desert that afternoon without a word more. Neither he nor Omar knew of what was in the letter of Sergius, naturally. After giving Akhbar a long head start, we drove the rest of the camels back into the valley again for Esmer to find if he wanted them. It was bad military tactics, I admit, to restore the camels to our enemies; but as we did not have enough pasturage to maintain the animals within our own lines, I had the choice of either sending them back or of ordering them killed; and I had not the heart to countenance an order for the butchery of the unoffending brutes. Also I had a selfish motive as well, for if ever John and I and our party were to defeat or circumvent Esmer Bey and attempt a journey home, these camels would be the only living things capable of transporting us. In a manner of speaking, then, I tempered tactics with mercy and mercy with foresight by making Esmer Bey custodian of camels which I myself hoped to use in good season.

That night I went down to Bertrand's camp with Gairner and John and Omar, for here would be the first battle. And I must say that sorry as I was to remain, my pipe and tobacco were a great comfort.

CHAPTER XIV

"FROM BATTLE, MURDER"

I CANNOT BUT admire Esmer Bey's generalship. Immediately after that council of which I have just told, I went forth to find his men moving upon Bertrand's position; but no sooner had the camels wound down into the plain again than the Arabs collected them without a shot being fired, and moved back to their camp.

Esmer had plainly feared that we would decamp as John Solomon had planned; now that he had the camels again he knew that we lay practically at his mercy. And we got no further chance to change our minds about leaving. That same afternoon he moved the camels back to the far line of hills, and scattered his men in a series of outposts over the whole stretch of valley.

In one way he had the advantage of us, for from every point in the plain either the church or the castle could be descried, with the road leading down from the former to the valley. Thus, except by night, we would have no chance or riding down and cutting off an outpost or two, for by the time we were there the other Arabs could have assembled. And at night, as I found, scouts were spread out toward our camp very thoroughly.

After two days of inaction, during which the Arabs did no more than ride from farm to farm, burning the bodies of the slain for fear of pestilence and collecting horses and food on all sides, I began to wonder what Esmer's plans were, and took counsel with my helpers.

"He's in no hurry, evidently," said Gairner thoughtfully. "He may be trying to throw us off our guard so that he can surprise us some night."

"Hardly. He could no more surprise us than we him. How would it be if we sent a party around the mountains, through the desert, to catch him behind, entering through the hills as he did?"

"That's just what 'e wants, Mr. Sargent."

"How so, John? How do you make that out?"

"Why, 'e knows as we've got rifles. But if so as 'e gets these 'ere knights down in the open to give battle, there'll be a' perishin' slaughter then and there. 'E's a waiting for that, 'e is. If 'e 'as to come up 'ere to fight, why 'e's a going to lose some o' them Arabs, and knows it. And right now men's precious to 'im. 'E's a werry careful man, as the 'ousekeeper said when the old gent 'ad the gardener up for kissing of 'er.

" 'Old off, I says, Mr. Sargent—just like that; 'old off. If so be as 'e comes at us, then go for 'im: but if 'e don't, then 'old off and let 'im be."

That was good advice, for Solomon had evidently pierced Esmer Bey's intention. It was hard to hold the knights in, however; they had lost their fool idea about rifles been harmless in Saracen hands, but they were wild to be at the men who were destroying and looting on every hand.

"What's this Seal they talk about and wear on their garments?" asked Gairner one day. "The man who found me in Damascus, Count Hugo's brother, had the same thing on his clothes, and while I know it is called the Seal of Solomon, why on earth do these men venerate it, as they plainly do?"

"Search me."

I shrugged my shoulders.

"John doesn't know, and it'd be foolish to bother them about trivial things just now. Every man of them is on edge, and we have to hold them in as much as possible."

I was glad of the respite, for we had a number of wounded, and every man would count. My own wound was a mere trifle;

after a few days I was walking around as well as ever, save for a slight soreness. Indeed, I was doing more than walk, for when it became plain that for the present Esmer was content with lying still and trying to draw us out, Edith Gairner and I went for long climbs about the Man's Nose, accompanied by Omar or Uriel Gairner, for John would not climb.

Sometimes we were not accompanied at all, for Gairner was busy with the count's archives on his own book. We found out many interesting things about the Man's Nose That Smokes on these trips. One was that men with rifles could sit on the crags above and drop bullets into the castle as they wished; but they would first have to gain the road up, past the church.

Another was that the curious smoke rising at times from the northern end of the mountain did not come from the peak at all, but from some point half-way up a tremendous precipice. The rock, like that desert outside, was the most outlandish jumble that ever I saw in all my life—a mad mixture of granite, lava, and gneiss.

It was undoubtedly of volcanic origin. Perhaps this explained the great ruins lying in the desert at the foot of the crags. These were visited, riding down one day; and the moment we issued from the shadow of the mountain the heat smote us terrifically. By now I had become used to the cool air of the plateau, and could hardly stand it; but we made out before we left that the ruins must have been covered over thousands of years ago, and gradually blown clear of volcanic dust and sand. Indeed a great part of them were still sunk in solid lava, which seemed to have flowed down from the ancient crater above.

This was doubtless the great city Themoud, of whose destruction Mohammed has so much to say in the Koran, and which at one time was very powerful, being on the ancient trade routes. Even before Mohammed's time these had been long abandoned, however; but from the nature of the carvings and friezes we found, I believe, that the city had been built either by the Macedonian Greeks, like the Indian cities, or else by some more ancient and utterly forgotten peoples.

Little by little, during those days of semitruce, I came to know
Edith Gairner better, and she me. I was not so glad about this
last, either—but I suppose no man ever is glad to have himself
known down to the ground by a woman of infinite sense and
great attractiveness. He always wants to know her, because the
more you know some women the more it uplifts you; but taking
it the other way around, a man is pretty cognizant of traits about
him that aren't a bit pretty. Anyway, I was. You would have been,
too, if it had been Edith Gairner.

However, all things must have an end. Nearly two weeks had
passed thus, happily enough for me, but wearily for Count Hugo
and his son, when Esmer developed his knowledge of human
nature quite unexpectedly. One day I rode down to Bertrand's
camp to find Sir Raymond in tremendous excitement; the cause
was not far to seek.

I have said that Esmer's men had donned some of the armor
of the slain knights. Now there were twenty of them fully clad,
moving toward us from Esmer's headquarters at the lake. They
carried the long Norman swords, but so far as we could see were
not armed otherwise. As they came closer they began to spread
out and ride back and forth as if daring my men to go at them.

For that time I managed to hold back the knights, but the
next morning the score of Arabs sallied forth again, keeping just
out of fair rifle-shot. To see these men, clad in the arms of their
friends and brethren, and not to go out and take revenge, was
next to impossible for these knights of mine. I held them in for
a bit, until finally Sir Raymond flashed out at me:

"By the cross, Sir Frederick, either let me lead twenty of my
brethren at these dogs, or else look for another captain of them!"

"Have it your own way," I replied helplessly. "After you've
fallen into the trap, though, don't blame me."

That sobered him a little, but we could see no trap in evidence.
The majority of Esmer's men were in camp by the lake, for we
could see the glint of rifles; and while I knew perfectly well that

he was not risking twenty men in the mere effort to draw blood, I was unable to see where the danger lay.

The twenty might have arms concealed about them; it was ridiculous to suppose that they were trusting to those huge Norman swords, which they had never used before. Since Sir Raymond was unable to keep himself or his men in hand longer, I made him relieve me of all responsibility in the matter in Bertrand's presence, told him to keep out of range of Esmer's camp at all costs, and bade him god-speed.

His twenty picked knights were saddling up just as John Solomon came down to find me. He heard what was forward and groaned, shaking his head despairingly.

"Dang it! I could feel it a coming, sir. Well, I'd best go back for Omar and Mr. Gairner, for I 'ave a werry good idea as summat is due to 'appen. No good arguing wi' this 'ere stiff-necked generation; let 'em go and learn a lesson, sir, and much good may it do 'em, says I."

I prevailed on him to remain, however, sending a man for Gairner and Omar. I, too, had an uneasy feeling. It seemed natural enough to Sir Raymond that these Arabs should come forth to challenge him, but I knew better.

Now I am bound to say that if I had enough downright courage—which I have not—and had nothing else in the world to live for—which I have—I would like nothing better than to make just such an ending as Sir Raymond of Antioch made that morning. I have never seen anything more inspiring in all my life, nor anything more terrible except the Seal of Solomon; but at the moment I forgot the sadness of it in the mad excitement that carried me away.

As his knights formed up behind him Sir Raymond started that noble battle-chant which I had first heard on the morning of the massacre. Every voice joined in with his, the horses stepping forward slowly. The lances had been abandoned, but every knight had his naked sword in hand and carried his shield slung about his neck. As they moved farther down into the plain itself and the horses gradually swept up into a gallop, still that chorus came back to us, faint and more faintly:

> "Christ rides with our vanguard;
> Death thunders behind!
> Spur! Spur! For our Cross-flame hath smitten them blind!
> Spur! Spur! Strike their ranks like a flame on the wind!
>   Up and strike! Up and strike!
> There's a flame on the wind and a flame in the sedge.
> And the flame of our faith flares from windrow and hedge;
> Sword-flame and Cross-flame! Up!
> Up! With the edge!
>   Up and strike! Up and strike!

Sir Raymond alone of all his company carried out that word, however. Splendid he looked as he led them, but the Arabs did not wait his coming. Solomon groaned once at the sight.

Carried away by their mad charge, the knights paid no heed to the matter of rifle-range. A little puff of smoke darted from the grain at one side and another on the other side, where men had lain hidden; then more. A knight pitched out of the saddle and lay still as the others went over him; a horse went down—another knight. But the rest paused not. Sir Raymond, far in the lead, thundered down on the score of Arabs who were now in flight.

More puffs of flame and smoke darted out. Now the men at Esmer's camp rode out and joined in at long distance. But Sir John Raymond, untouched, gained swiftly on the Arabs. Even from where I stood I could see him rise in his stirrups and could catch the flame of his sword as he swung it and whirled it in both hands.

Down it flashed—and the hindmost Arab seemed to lose his helm suddenly, and his head with it. An instant more and the knight was in the midst of them, while his men dropped by ones and twos on the way behind him, but made no halt nor swerve.

Again and again I saw that great blade flame in the morning sun. Vainly the Arabs strove to turn on him, for they could hardly swing the huge swords; for a moment I thought he would cut them all down one by one. He took a bloody vengeance on them indeed! But of a sudden he whirled his steed and made for those Arabs coming from camp.

Still the puffs of white spat out from the grain. Now there were but two left of his twenty, and they far behind.

Whether that shield slung before him saved his life during that mad ride I know not, but at all events Sir Raymond rode straight for the Arabs, though they fired hot and fast as he came up to them. Once his horse stumbled badly, doubtless hit. Then with that tiny sword-flame darting around his head once more he struck them.

What happened there I never knew. We saw a great swirl of men for an instant. Then it straightened out, and the Arabs came on at a gallop, leaving behind them something that glinted in the sun. Bertrand, who had stood at my side, turned to me with burning eyes.

"By Heaven, if I might die like that!" he gasped out.

Then Solomon gripped me, and I found Gairner shoving a rifle into my trembling hands.

"They're coming!"

And coming they were. Perhaps Esmer Bey thought that the twenty were our sole force, or perhaps the blood of the Arabs had been maddened by that brief conflict, but they rode on, over the last two knights, spread out, and came for our camp at the gallop.

"Pick off Esmer if you can," I ordered quietly, and told Bertrand to keep back the rest of the knights, with Sir Gairner. The Arabs still had a good half-mile to cover and more. Looking back at the steep road and the church above us, I saw the tall figure of old Count Hugo standing there motionless and knew that he had witnessed all. I felt a pang of pity for him in that moment.

Our camp here was sheltered by a small grove of trees, and the thirty knights who were left to us drew up behind these.

Twenty of them I sent back to the castle, sorely against their will, with Bertrand; then, grimly telling the others that they had best prepare for death, I rode out with Gairner and John and Omar.

A hundred yards from camp we left our horses and spread out behind some scattered boulders. By this time the Arabs were not more than three hundred yards away, but that is a long distance for good shooting. Moreover, I did not want to open fire till I could see the lordly figure of Esmer Bey, of whom there was as yet no sign. So I waited until their rifles began to spit bullets—wildly enough—before I pulled trigger.

I flatter myself that we did good work there with our rifles and automatics. We dropped man after man, and that was too much for the Arabs to stomach; they slipped from their steeds and began to open a dropping fire on us, at which we mounted and rode back to camp unscathed. For the moment the rush was checked.

The Arabs, however, had not won fame as the most desperate of desert outlaws for nothing, and they were well within range of us. My mailcoat saved me that morning from two bullets.

I knew that for my knights to try to stem the tide was useless. Enough lives had already been flung away. So I ordered the men up the hill to the church. At this Sir Gaimar came near to mutiny, and so proved that John had been right; no man on earth could argue against such people.

"Die if you want to, then!" I exclaimed savagely. "But at least effect something by it. Come up there to the church and let them think we've retreated; then go down at them with your ten men. We'll give you a little help, and with luck you can strike a deadly blow and get back to us."

They gave a grunt of satisfaction at that, and obeyed. We covered their retreat, then gradually drew up the hill ourselves, while the Arabs yelled like demons and used up an unconscionable lot of ammunition, but did no damage.

The church stood at the very crest of that hill-road, as I have said before. I sent the knights around behind it, bidding them

ride out and down at the Arabs when I gave the word. The four
of us with our rifles and revolvers stood together at one side
out of sight from below. Looking down, I saw the Arabs, a full
thirty of them, ride into our abandoned camp. We fired no shot,
however.

For a moment they looked up at the silent church on the crag
and talked furiously, plainly debating as to whether it was a ruse
or not. Had Esmer been there they never would have tried it,
but he was safe in camp; and indeed they had clean run away
from him that morning. Then one furious voice rose clearly to us:

"By Allah, I say they have gone! That is their mosque up
yonder, and they are hiding in the castle; up, and plunder the
mosque before Esmer Bey comes! *Allahu akhbar!*"

"Allahu akhbar! Slay! Slay!"

The wild shout reechoed again from the cliffs. With one
accord the Arabs pushed their horses at the road, rifles ready.

I motioned Omar down and sank out of sight myself. Looking forth from between the rocks, I waited until the foremost
Arabs got squarely abreast of me, on the level space leading to
the massive church, and not thirty feet from it. Then—

"Up and strike!" I roared out.

With the words I rose and pumped my Snider into them,
the others with me, and followed that with my two automatics.

Instantly the whole roadway jumped into an inextricable
confusion of rearing horses and yelling men, who tried in vain
to get their steeds in hand so that they might use their rifles.
And in the midst of it all Sir Gaimar and his ten struck them
like a thunderbolt.

Perforce we had to stop shooting, save at the hindmost. Say
what you may, those knights knew how to fight at close quarters.
Here and there rifles spoke out, or pistols, but the fighting was
too mad and furious for much gun-play. Even I lost my head. I
know I dropped my rifle and ran back to my horse; mounting
him and getting that splay-bladed ax in the air, I rode down into
the midst, absolutely crazed by the battle-lust.

John Solomon called me a fool for my pains afterward, but no matter; I have never been so frankly drunk in my life, and drunk is the only name for it. I sent that ax into an Arab who had just pistoled a knight in the face, and felt him crash down beneath it. Then another Arab reared his horse at me, and I put the spike of the ax into the breast of the poor beast with a yell, so that he toppled back and crushed his rider—and after that I do not remember exactly what happened, except that I rode beside Sir Gaimar down the hill, putting all my strength into that ax until something clipped me on the helmet and I slid down from my horse to the body of another knight unconscious.

The grinning face of Omar was the first thing I saw as Gairner pulled me up. Sir Gaimar and two others stood by me, both wounded, while across the plain four Arabs were riding, and on the hill above John Solomon was pumping good bullets after them and yelling like mad. I hated to see John wasting lead, and leaped up with a ringing head.

"Stop that!" I roared at him. "Hey, John! Stop wasting cartridges!"

"Good Lord, man!" half-laughed and half-sobbed Gairner, catching me. "You're a perfect giant for strength! Hold him up there, Omar!"

Smiling grimly, Sir Gaimar got off his horse and picked up my helmet, which had a tremendous split clear across the skull. The sword that had made it had given me a light scalp-wound beneath. However, I was soon myself again, though strangely weak with the passing of the excitement.

"Now, John," I said when I gained the top of the hill again, having found three or four Arabs living—Omar despatched them with his knife—"what'll we do next?"

"Get inside that there castle, sir and stay there. Lud! It fair give me a bad turn when you went down, sir."

"It gave me a worse," I grinned. We all saw plainly, however, that to hold that road further was impossible; we had won a victory, but it had cost us men, and we had all too few left.

Esmer had fewer still, and things were looking more hopeful for us, but when he came up in person I knew well enough that we would never get such a chance to slay again. Nor did we, as it turned out.

Leaving Omar on keep-guard and to collect the rifles and cartridges of the fallen Arabs, the rest of us went back to the castle—six in all, out of thirty-odd who had been knights that morning. As we went John and I figured up Esmer's losses.

He had started in with something over a hundred men. Thirty of these had fallen in the massacre-night; we had shot five over the matter of *Sheik* Zohri, and we might reasonably allow another five to the getting of John's tobacco; while that morning we and Sir Raymond had disposed of, say, thirty-five more. That would leave Esmer about twenty-five men.

I own that all this talk of slaying is a terrible thing to go over in cold blood; yet at the time it did not seem so terrible to us who had passed through the awful night of massacre. I have met men who talk of killing five or a dozen or twenty men in the Philippines, some by torture; others who have told of shooting with their own hand scores of black men in central Africa; others who jest about the things they did in China—and these, mind you, men of my own faith and color.

Now I am not boasting of such things; it is a part of a tale that must be told, and no more. By my faith I, Frederick Sargent, who write this, firmly believe that there is no blood upon my conscience; those men of Esmer's, and Esmer himself, were not human beings, but wild beasts, and nothing but wild beasts.

As for John Solomon, I honestly believe that he never thought twice about it!

CHAPTER XV

"AND FROM SUDDEN DEATH"

THERE WAS great sadness in the castle when our decision was set before Count Hugo and made known to the others. We still had twenty esquires and as many knights left—forty in all—to set against Esmer's twenty-five; but the happenings of that morning had brought home to them all how bitterly useless their weapons were against Esmer's rifles.

The aged count himself was the first to admit that we were right, and that the church could not be defended. I remember the wail of anguish that went up from every throat as he declared himself, but he faced us all, calm and noble and stern.

"My people," he said with unmoved voice, "I have seen terrible things this morning; I have seen my eldest-born and my knights go down into death, almost without a blow. Yet there is no sorrow in my heart; rather I am proud of those who so died and of those who fought for us.

"My people, God has whispered to me in the night that we are not utterly to perish, and that this visitation has come upon us for our sins. How this may be I know not, but let there be no more weeping. Look on this woman, and think that we still have swords to swing."

He turned to Sir Raymond's widow, who stood erect and firm behind him, her babe on her arm. I heard Edith Gairner, beside me, sob in her throat.

"Bertrand," went on the old count, "ride forth with your esquires and bring in the bodies of as many as may be found, but take no risks—I your father so order you. Let the bodies be brought back into the church, and there let all my people gather for the last time. After that the crypt and passages shall be sealed up until these times be past."

I had no mind to be present at that burial, and besides my head was swimming with my wound. So while Gairner, at the express wish of the count, went to attend him in his priestly office, Edith and I and John sat in our own chambers; and after a little John went out to see that Omar brought in the rifles and ammunition. Thus we were alone.

And we were silent, too, for a long while.

"I wish," I said, looking out across the desert—"I wish I had a little house up in Maine, close to the sea and not very far from a trolley line to town, so that I could just settle down there with some books and learn about the things I've missed in life. I don't—"

"And what would you do there in your little house?" she asked swiftly. "What would you do? Dream your life away after—this?"

"No! I want to go back to my own people for good. I'm tired of it all. I think I'd like to teach oriental languages somewhere— Lord knows I have enough of 'em at my tongue's end! Or I might write some of the things I've seen and done."

"You queer man! You—a college professor with spectacles! Why did you make that wish, Frederick Sargent?"

I looked at her, but I did not smile.

"I only wish I knew, Edith Gairner."

Well, she gazed square at me for a minute, and right there I knew that *she* knew. Did you ever have a woman throw out her soul at you—not saying a word, but just letting you see what she thought? Perhaps you never had a chance, though it never does come to a man very often—it never had happened to me before, at least. Of course, I'd talked with plenty of women before then, but either they were playing the game or I was, and that's a very different kind of thing.

"Perhaps I can guess why," she said finally, her eyes shining.

I caught up her hand and brought it to my lips for a minute, wondering if I'd mistaken her meaning after all.

"This is no place for talk such as I have to say," I stated, fighting down my first impulse. "When this affair has been settled one way or the other, Edith, then I want to ask you something. If Esmer wins—"

"How can Esmer win?" she asked quietly.

I stared for an instant, then laughed.

"He couldn't if all of us had you to give them heart, dear lady! I care not except for your sake; after this I will do my best, and if we win—"

"*When* we win," she broke in again softly.

"When we win—" I repeated, and laughed once more. "But here's John back again; so that's an end of our talk, Edith, for this time."

And with one thing and another intervening there was no next time for a great while to come. During the days that followed I often remembered her quiet confidence. For a space it cheered me mightily indeed, though later it brought little except bitterness to my mind, when Esmer had won to the great Seal and mocked us there.

John Solomon had attended to provisioning the castle, and, as usual, his work left nothing to be desired. I half hoped that Esmer would try a flag of truce again, in which case I would certainly have done for him; but he knew better than to trust us.

What took place at the church I do not know, for Gairner would never say a word in regard to it. Count Hugo sent back word by Bertrand that he would be absent for some little time, and that I was to be in absolute command of the castle until his return. The boy himself did not know the reason for this; but I conjectured rightly enough that the old count was taking his time about sealing up the crypt below the church, and that he had secret ways of entering the castle. Sir Gaimar alone had gone with him.

Several days passed with affairs in this condition, but I had little idleness. In the first place the Arabs had occupied the church. Though I do not think they found much plunder there, it served them well as a fortress. Esmer had tried out the mettle of our men, and was not quite sure what madness they might attempt; so for the time he lay quiet. We could see his Arabs occasionally exploring the cliffs around us.

Esmer was too good a strategist to overlook the chance to fire straight down at the castle, I knew. The place had not been built with a view to bullets, and when I pointed this out to Bertrand he saw the hopelessness of it at once. Still, there was nothing gloomy about him. He often joined us in our own rooms—a splendid fellow, serious-minded, and yet at the same time vibrant with youth and strength.

He and I went all over the castle, Gairner sometimes accompanying us; and on one exploring trip we found an immense banner of black, with white cross and the golden Seal over all. There was no flagstaff, but fastening it to a long lance we made shift to fly it from the topmost tower, where it still flies for all I know to the contrary.

The castle, built on the brink of a tall crag, was open to attack on only two sides, which was one good thing. John and Omar had brought in some twenty rifles, with a good supply of cartridges; but try as I would I could not make those Themoud men even attempt to use the weapons. Bertrand alone did so, used a handful of cartridges in practise at a mark, and thereafter was considerable help to us.

After five days of this quiet, during which we arranged a number of dummy figures on the wall the better to fool Esmer as to our numbers, Count Hugo came back to us, appearing at the noonday meal without any explanation. Simultaneously with this Esmer began his offensive operations.

He had undoubtedly been waiting in patience until he could get his men posted in the most advantageous positions, for while we were greeting Count Hugo a number of knights went out to the walls; a few moments later I heard a sudden crackle of rifle-fire, which rolled up in volleying echoes and brought us all to the courtyard.

Four knights and seven squires had been swept from the walls by that one murderous fire. From the cliffs above half a dozen men were dropping bullets into the courtyard, but with small effect. It is hard to fire from a height and keep any aim, especially with Sniders.

The best we could do was to man the corner towers, whose rooms were loop-holed and inaccessible to the fire from overhead. Bertrand, who was now a knight, was put in command of these defenses, and, with John, Gairner, and Omar, and our score of rifles, managed to keep the Arabs at a distance. I had other things to think of that afternoon, for no sooner had he been made to realize the danger than Count Hugo commandeered my services and those of Edith Gairner.

"Even were the castle taken," he said quietly, "all is not lost. Lady Edith, will you gather the women and children here in the great hall? I think it were best to place them in safety at once, and if need be we can follow them later."

I asked no questions, but I recalled having heard something of underground passages. And there was the mystery of the Seal of Solomon. Therefore, I reasoned, Count Hugo's place of safety had something to do with these, and in that I was not far wrong.

Edith assembled the women quietly there were a scant half-dozen children, some of them orphaned. These Edith herself took in charge. The count sat calmly stroking his white beard, while I smoked, for now we had plenty of tobacco and to spare. When all were before us and the last farewells had been said the count rose and stepped to the wide fireplace.

There he pressed heavily upon one of the carvings, and the whole fireplace, fire and all, swung out into the hall, smoking up the place considerably. He beckoned me, and I followed him into a passageway, the women after me. This was lighted by immense lamps hung from the ten-foot roof; I think they were of bronze, for they gleamed dull yellow. No doubt the count and

Sir Gaimar had prepared all things for our coming during those long days of absence, though I never ascertained this positively.

The passage continued for a long distance. Then came a flight of steps and a second and wider passage, which gradually shelved downward. At times I heard the trickle of water, though none was to be seen. The air was cool and sweet.

"These lamps," said the old count abruptly, "will burn for about two weeks, and there is a good store of oil. In case aught happens to me, Sir Frederick, Lady Godwitha knows the secrets of all these passages—she and none other."

This Lady Godwitha, I might say, was the widow of Sir Raymond; she, however, does not enter into this tale.

The passage was very wide all its way. It turned only twice, with no side entrances or windings, a circumstance which would seem to indicate that it had been originally intended for another purpose than that of defense. It was dry and dustless. As my feet felt an irregular floor, I looked down and saw a stone flagging, worn in smooth ridges by the feet which had passed that way.

There was a strange and peculiar comfort in that, because that continual downward slope of the cavern had begun to terrify me. But at thought of the thousands and thousands of feet whose passing must have worn the stones below me, and the untold centuries which it must have required, I felt rather better again.

Abruptly the passage swerved upward and ended in a door near one of the lamps. This door was very wide and large, made to fit the passage, and of deeply rusted iron. I touched it and cried out in astonishment, for it was actually warm! Count Hugo called to the women to stop where they were; but, instead of turning to the door, he stamped twice on one of the stone flags and waited.

After a moment, during which Edith Gairner stepped beside me and took my hand in hers, a massy section of the passage-wall slowly rolled back on itself, and Sir Gaimar stood before us. What was more, there was a blaze of daylight ahead of us, which I was very glad to see.

By what I saw then and afterward of the rock strata, I am inclined to think that the passageway from the castle had been developed from a natural cavity, running through a stratum of some softer rock, while this place in which we now were was roughly hewed from the granite, as had been that council-chamber under the church.

There was a long series of chambers, eight or ten of them, all very large and all carven in the cliffside, so that the windows looked out over the desert. I was puzzled to know our position at first, until Edith Gairner pointed out, in the waste below, a huge black basaltic column, which we had often remarked from the cliffs. Then we realized that we must be in the very peak of the Man's Nose, as indeed we were.

Taking Edith and Lady Godwitha, Count Hugo led us through the rock-chambers, and showed us stores of grain and corn and honey and wine, with firewood and a fireplace set in the outer wall for cooking.

"Then—you want us to stay here?" asked Edith, rather pale.

"Yes, my daughter. Here there is safety for you, since the Saracens will never find this place, even though they find all else. That opening in the passage-wall can be laid bare only from the inside; Lady Godwitha knows the secret of the levers, and will show you it later, for we dare not trust every one with it."

"But what about water?" I asked anxiously.

The count smiled and beckoned us to another room, where a good-sized trickle of water came down through an opening in the roof, collected in a pool, and ran off in a deep hollow cut in the stone floor to the outside wall.

"It is from the same spring which supplies the castle itself," he said. "There is no lack of either food or water, Sir Frederick, so have no fear."

He turned to Lady Godwitha.

"Open to none save to those who stamp twice, my daughter. That particular flagstone is made hollow so that the sound rings loudly in the first chamber. Best keep one or two women always there on watch. And now farewell, for we must be going."

I bowed to those of the women I knew and shook hands for a long instant with Edith Gairner.

"Bring my father safe," was all she said.

I answered that I would, and so we went forth into the passageway again, Count Hugo and Sir Gaimar and I. The wall rolled up after us; when I looked for jointure in the rock I could see none.

"Our fathers did good work here," the count smiled sadly. "They cut out those chambers, and it was here that they did those mail-coats and weapons and other things."

"Did they work without forges, then?" I asked.

"Nay; but the forges are in another place. The people who were here before them had fashioned this passage and others which wind through other cliffs of the mountain, but it was our fathers who made those chambers as a refuge."

"And what did the others make this passage for, then?"

I turned and touched that curious iron door, which was so rusted that it shook under my hand.

"And what lies behind this door?"

"This passage was made for the worship of idolators."

Count Hugo spoke somewhat stiffly, and turned away as if he disliked my questioning.

"As for the door, there lies behind it what is known as the Seal of Solomon, the very heart and core of Themoud, wrought here of Satan as I verily believe. Take care that you open not that door, Sir Frederick, unless I or Sir Gaimar or Bertrand be with you, or it may well be that you will find other things than you dream of inside there!"

There was that in his voice which caused my hand to drop from the door. I turned away after him and Sir Gaimar, wondering much. I confess freely that it went very much against the grain to turn my back on that door; for, despite all the vexation and danger and responsibility which oppressed my mind, I was strong in curiosity concerning what this Seal of Solomon really was.

It was the device of Themoud and of the knighthood; the sword Count Hugo had given me had been made "in the fire of the Seal" six hundred and eighty-six years ago; I had seen that device on a village wizard's robes in a little Persian town across the Euphrates, and on Luristan rugs; it was known through Moslem Countries as the Seal of Solomon, exactly as Count Hugo called it; and Hugo's brother had brought it to Damascus, whence it had come to John Solomon, to be used as his own proper seal.

But all this explained nothing. What did it mean? What *was* it?

Well, I got no answer to that question for some little time, because when I asked Bertrand about it he only looked a bit frightened and said that he would show me some day. If those people had had a little more sense on the spot, I would have been saved an experience which nearly ended my reason and life together.

When we got back to the castle, not entering by the hall fireplace but through a side passage into one of the other rooms, we found Uriel Gairner demanding to know where his daughter was—and quite naturally, for we had been gone something like three hours in those underground passages. That was easily understood, for the castle was on a crag at the southern end of the Man's Nose, and the peak of the mountain, rising gradually to the north above us, was easily a mile away. The upper portions of the entire mountain were serrated and dissected by valleys, but the whole stood on a solid base, which, I suppose, was pierced by those hidden ways.

We soon satisfied Gairner that Edith was safer than she was like to be in the castle, judging by the events that had transpired in our absence. The church was not in sight from the castle, though a portion of the valley beyond was. Some of the Arabs had stationed themselves just out of rifle-shot before the castle, with a number of the ancient banners taken from the church.

It was the same old story. The Arabs had proceeded to show what they thought of Themoud and its knights by defiling the banners in every way possible, and a dozen of those fool knights had promptly gone out to rescue them.

The result, as might have been expected, was that our force had been decreased by a third, while Esmer had lost not a man. Count Hugo tried to drum a little sense into their heads, lashing them bitterly for their lack of self-control, but he had not the heart to say very much. Solomon, ensconced in a tower, had known nothing of it until too late.

"Dang it!" he said that night when we were alone. "I've never met such people in all me life, never! When so be as a man don't learn by experience, I says, it's a sign as 'ow 'e ain't werry much of a man, says I. A banner's a banner, just like that, and a life's a life; but it's werry easy to get another banner, I says, and werry 'ard to get another life, just like that."

A truism which the Knights of the Seal did not seem to realize. I told all three of them where we had been that day and what we had found, and it interested them no little.

"And you didn't open that door?" queried Gairner, smiling. "Well, I'm going to see what's behind it some day, and what this Seal thing is."

And he did, too; but I am not altogether sure that he got much joy out of the seeing.

After that things went fairly quietly for two days. Esmer tried to tempt us out again; but with my presence and that of the count to restrain them, the remaining knights and esquires betrayed some glimmerings of sense.

We settled down into a state of siege finally, Esmer's men taking pot-shots at us and we at them, and neither side doing any damage to speak of. We dared not go out on the walls except at night, but a guard in the towers was sufficient to keep good watch. Unfortunately, I had only one clip of cartridges left for my automatics.

Solomon, who rarely betrayed his genius except in times of stress, began to grow moody again. He said that this relaxation on Esmer's part was by no means natural, and I was inclined to agree with him, though Gairner, who had not enough imagination to hurt him greatly, pooh-poohed our anxiety altogether.

However, it was well placed enough. On the third night after our visit to the rock-chambers below I was on guard from midnight to dawn. About two in the morning John came out, protesting that he was unable to sleep. Having seen that my five guards were wakeful and posted along the walls, John and I stretched out on the battlements, lighted our pipes, and settled down in comfort.

Now, being fairly proud of my general proficiency, I protest that I kept a good watch that night and heard not a sound. Once, indeed, by the light of the courtyard cresset below, which we kept burning all night, I saw two or three mail-clad men sauntering along the opposite wall, but thought nothing of it, nor did John. It was not unusual for our knights to sit on the battlements and chat, even in the small hours.

After a bit John got up, and went off to the nearest guard, to ask about some trivial matter which had occurred to him. Then his voice came back to me:

"Mr. Sargent! Mr. Sargent! For the love o' Heaven, come 'ere!"

I jumped up, and as I approached saw the form of my guard lying prone on the battlements, John leaning over him. An instant later a rifle spat out from the darkness ten feet away, and John went forward and lay still without a sound. Then a yell pealed up:

"Allahu Akhbar! Slay! Slay!"

CHAPTER XVI

"GOOD LORD, DELIVER US!"

UNTIL THAT wild yell shrilled up I did not fully know what had happened; then I saw the knife-haft in the back of the knight who had been on guard, and with that pulled out my automatic and gave the man who had shot John his death.

We had a bad ten minutes of it; indeed, had it not been that Solomon had found out what was going on a little before Esmer's men had their ladders up, the castle would have been taken then and there.

To my vast relief John scrambled up, blood running down his neck, but I could not see what came next, for the mailed Arabs who poured on me from the darkness. A dozen of them had got up by means of a rope and a rude form of grapnel, and more were coming with ladders. The guards had been stabbed, every man of them. Before that whirl of assailants I was driven back and saw no more of John Solomon.

Bertrand in one tower and Omar in the other began to speak out with their rifles. Gairner had slept inside the castle, but I heard his voice piercing the din as the knights poured out. And they arrived just in time, for with my last cartridge gone I had jerked out that sword of mine—which, fortunately, I had worn that night—and was trying to hold off an Osmanli soldier who stabbed at me with his bayonet between shots.

I finished *him* just as three knights swept up and Gairner located a crowd below who were raising ladders. It was no long time before they perceived that this was a losing game for them, and drew off with a last volley that sent two overeager esquires toppling over the battlements and ending with a crash on the stones below.

Except that we repelled the attack, we came off second-best, for I had wasted the greater portion of my bullets in the uncertain light. As that had been my own salvation, however, I had no cause to grumble. A good part of the original attackers got off scot-free because we did not find their rope and grapnel at once; had Esmer's whole force come by the rope we should have been lost. I never did understand why he made such a mistake, unless he was willing to gamble with ten men or so, but not with his whole party.

I looked around for John, but he was not in evidence; and by the time I got those fool knights off the wall, where Esmer could pick them off, into the comparative safety of the courtyard, I began to count up losses. Three knights and four esquires had gone the way of all flesh, and we could locate only three dead Arabs on the premises. Omar ibn Kasim and Gairner came up to me as I was setting out new guards.

"Where is our master, Suleiman?" asked the former, staring around.

"Inside, I suppose. He got knocked over at the start of the scrimmage, and is probably tying up his wound."

"He's not inside, Sargent," said Gairner.

The missionary looked worried.

"He didn't drop over the wall along here, did he?"

"If he did he'll lie there till morning," I replied, nettled. "Do you suppose I'm going to take a look now and get a bullet through me for my pains?"

If Gairner didn't Omar certainly did, and with a sigh I knew that it was up to me. So, taking a few torches of the resinous wood they used, I let a couple get started and flung them over the battlements, taking a look down.

The two esquires who had gone overboard lay down there, huddled up, but there was no sign of John Solomon. Naturally, the bullets came spatting all about me, unpleasantly near. After I had inspected the second wall with the same vain result I got down to the courtyard in a hurry, safe but badly scared.

"No Solomon," I said briefly, and sent a dozen men to search for him throughout the castle.

By this time I was alarmed. I knew that John had got a rake across the head from a bullet, and such things are likely to work injury.

He had not gone over the walls, that was sure. When the men had made certain that he was not in the castle I called Gairner and Omar to a council of war, which Count Hugo also attended.

"He didn't fly that I know of," I said helplessly. "Otherwise how and where did he go?"

"Those Osmanlis didn't fly, either," retorted Gairner dryly. "They came up by a rope and got away by a rope, and, if I'm not very much mistaken, they took Solomon with them when they went."

I felt sorry for John if this was so. We could reach no other conclusion, try as we would, and finally had blankly to face the realization that John must be in the hands of Esmer.

It was a hard thing to realize—a hard thing to face. John, in his quiet way, was a singularly dominant personality. Not alone Gairner and I, who knew him of old, but the old count and his men as well, spent that night in grievous anxiety; all had come to appreciate John's qualities, especially since that affair of the tobacco, which had made a deep impression on Count Hugo at least. As for Omar, he sat all that night out on the battlements, looking toward the camp-fire of Esmer on the hill and rubbing his sword-edge on the stones.

"They won't spare him, Sargent," declared Gairner gloomily. "Esmer will have to cover up his tracks after this terrible work in Themoud. Islam would not stand for it."

"But that letter of Sergius would disrupt—" I began.

"Not a bit of it. It would, I grant you, knock over the Osmanlis, for it is the Osmanlis who foster the anti-Christian sentiment among certain sects. That is a selfish fostering, of course; but you and I know, Sargent, how terribly sincere the average Moslem is, and how easily that letter would be assimilated and turned to profit. It would not hurt Islam as a religion, for Islam accepts Christ and His teachings, as we know.

"Politically, however, it would have a big effect, and the Osmanlis realize it to the full. With all the harking back to early ways that is going on now, there would be a great upheaval that would sweep the Turk out of Arabia and Syria and put an Arab into power at Medina. The *Shiahs* are waiting for just such a chance. If one of us gets out of here to tell what has been done Esmer would pay heavily for it."

I nodded, realizing the force of his words, for Gairner knew the present situation better than did I, after my absence. Esmer, in fact, could hardly have impressed any other than the Ma'az men to go with him, and these only because their *sheik* was a captive. The Osmanlis are not loved in Arabia.

If Esmer had really captured John Solomon, he would be sure to make use of his prisoner. And with the dawn we made out an Arab coming toward the walls, unarmed and bearing a white flag. I could see that there was no treachery intended, so lowered the drawbridge and let him in.

"*Salaam aleikum,*" I said ironically.

He smiled and made formal response.

"And on you, peace. Our lord Esmer offers you safe conduct to his camp. We have taken a prisoner, and Esmer Bey would deal with you."

"How know you who I am?" I made answer.

"It is written that to ask a man's lineage is useless when you may read it in his face," came the polite and somewhat flattering response.

"Also," I retorted, "it is written that some men are locks unto good and keys unto evil, and I think Esmer is one of such. Wait."

The Arab sat down on the stones, staring around, while I withdrew to where Count Hugo and Gairner waited with Omar.

"Well, what do, you think? Is it some trap?"

"Of a surety," growled Omar ibn Kasim. "Does a lion seek a gazel in order to ask a blessing upon him?"

Gairner looked troubled.

"There might be some scheme of accommodation in Esmer's mind, Sargent. Still, I doubt it. If it were not for Solomon—"

Now I did not want to go out to see Esmer. I felt instinctively that Esmer would like nothing better than to get me into his power again. In this I was perfectly right, though I did not guess his reasons. So, hoping that Count Hugo would add his word of dissent, I turned to him.

"It is hard to decide, Sir Frederick," he answered, eying the Arab and stroking his beard. "One man may not tell another the right in such things. Yet if you go not, then I will, since Sir John has suffered much for us."

That was a foolish and a knightly answer, and for the second time within twelve hours I was forced into doing something which I disliked intensely through nothing more than self-respect. If our positions were reversed, however, I knew that John would not hesitate to put his head into the lion's mouth if it would help me.

So with a sigh I consented. At the Arab's suggestion I left my arms behind and went out clad in my white woolen cloak. It was not at all a pleasant thing to see that Arab's grin and to hear the drawbridge clash up behind me, I can tell you. Nor was Esmer taking any chances, because as we went ahead a couple of Osmanlis—all he had left, I believe—rose up from among the rocks and searched me very thoroughly for weapons. After that, while I cursed myself for a fool and looked down a rifle-barrel, they bound my arms behind me, and in this fashion I joined John Solomon a few moments later.

In order to give a better comprehension of what followed then and later, I should explain that Esmer's camp was placed on a shelf of the hillside overlooking the castle, and consisted merely of a fire among the rocks. The Arabs were grouped nonchalantly about Esmer and John, the latter being tied up. Esmer looked up with his evil grin as I was led into the circle.

"All ready for the consultation, eh?" he said in English.

John looked at me as if he were sorry that I had been such a fool, and I merely grunted at him. There was not a bit of use reproaching Esmer, so I kept silent.

"I did not think you would come," went on the Osmanli in Arbi. "And how do you like our little *jehad*, Frank?"

It was John who made answer.

"*Jehad?* A holy war without the consent of the *padishah?* Was not this war unprovoked?"

"I have the *firman* of the Sultan," shot back Esmer pleasantly, the Arabs grinning. "And what if this war was unprovoked, my fat *imam?*"

"Why," rejoined John stoutly, "the Koran does not mention *jehad* as one of the five pillars of religion: neither does it enjoin an unprovoked attack on any one. If you knew Arbi as well as you know Osmanli, Esmer Bey, you would know that the very word means something else."

"Ah, a very *imam*, in truth!" sneered Esmer, though I caught a quick look passed among the Arabs. "Surely it is written that God loveth not injustice; yet this Frank killed Yelniz Pasha unjustly, and we have but fought for the cause of Allah."

"And in the same *Sura* of the Cow it is written to kill the unbelievers," added one of the Arabs boldly, "wherever they may be found."

Solomon laughed.

"Fools, to let a Christian interpret your own writings! That verse referred to the idolaters of Mecca—bethink you! 'Until the only worship be that of God,' so runs the text.

"Do we not worship God, also?

"Have we not been willing to make peace?

"Fools! To let an Osmanli thus trample on the word of the Prophet!"

Only then did I see his intent. Esmer saw it, also. His dark face sprang into anger, swift and terrible, as the Arabs laughed at their fellow speaker.

"Careful, Suleiman! I am master here—"

"It is written in the *Sura* of the Story that those who seek to exalt themselves upon the earth shall lose paradise," went on John calmly. "You have done wrong, Esmer Bey, and out of the mouth of Mohammed will I prove it."

Now Solomon's words were having their effect, for it was evident that he knew his Koran far better than did Esmer. Also, every Arab knows that not only is war not enjoined against Christians, but that Mohammed and his followers always numbered Christians among their friends. While Esmer looked blacker and blacker John proceeded to push his argument home.

"You have done wrong, Moslems, in thus attacking a peaceful Christian people. The Sultan's *firman* was intended otherwise.

"Did not Mohammed give religious freedom to the monks of Mount Sinai?

"Did not Omar ride into Jerusalem by the side of Christian priests?

"Did not Arab and Christian worship in the same church at Damascus?

"Is it not written in the *Sura* of the Bee—"

"Silence!" roared out Esmer, suddenly perceiving the astonishment depicted on the faces of his men. "Gag the fool!" he commanded in Osmanli. His two remaining Turkish soldiers obeyed, trussing up poor John until all he could do was roll his eyes.

"You're a nice nest of dog-brothers," I told him in the same tongue.

He only darted me a swift but deadly vicious glance and waited until his men had done.

"I got you here for a purpose, Mr. Sargent," he said in English. "In fact, the only object of that attack last night was to get hold of you or Solomon here. Strange that a fat little fool like that should have become so well known among Moslems!"

"Not very strange," I told him hotly. "Though he is a Christian, if you were half so much versed in your own religion as he is it would be a good thing for you."

"Well, well! Enough vituperation!" and he waved my words aside as if putting away some tangible thing.

His cold yet flame-lit black eyes rested on me quite calmly and chilled the anger out of me, strange as it seems to say it.

Yet that was exactly my feeling, so powerful was that man's brain. He forgot, and he made me forget for a moment, any personal score between us, until I felt that I was standing before some inflexible, unswerving machine that would drive to its end through or over any weak opposition of mine.

"Now, listen, Mr. Sargent—and you, too, Solomon. We'll have no more of this petty stage-acting, if you please. The facts are that I'm here for just one end, and mean to carry that end to its fulfillment. You are blocking me. Why?"

"For the same reason that you are here, Esmer. A matter of sentiment—of religion, if you call it that."

"That is a lie," he stated quite dispassionately. "You simply blundered into the thing, Sargent. But why is Solomon here? Answer for him."

"Because he's a Christian, and because he was appealed to by the same man you Osmanlis killed under torture—a knight of Themoud, who came to Damascus—"

"I know; I know! But you Christians don't strike into such things for your religion. You don't believe in it sincerely enough. When you do a thing like this, it's for some ulterior reason."

John had been contorting his head violently for a minute, and now his words came through the muffling cloths; what could be seen of his features was purple:

"That's a lie, Esmer Bey!"

Esmer looked at him judicially, met the wide blue eyes

squarely, and for half a minute seemed to be trying to pierce to their depths. Then he nodded slowly.

"Yes. You are right, Mr. Solomon—and I was wrong. You, I am willing to admit, went into this game for disinterested motives, and you have certainly lost by it."

With that Esmer turned his back squarely on John, as if dismissing him altogether from his mind, and eyed me cynically.

"Well, what did you keep on at this for after you had blundered into and out of my hands at Maan? What do *you* gain, Mr. Sargent?"

"Since you don't seem to take much stock in my high purity of ideals," I answered dryly, "I might say that I've kept on largely to defeat you, and so far you've been pretty well blocked."

"Oh, no—no; hardly that.... Well, you approximate the truth, I think. Lay this personal prejudice aside, Mr. Sargent. It is unworthy you. Now you admit that you gain nothing even by defeating me—which you cannot do. In that impossible case you might carry the letter of Sergius to the world and do a great deal of damage—or you might dispose of it to the Ottoman government, sir.

"Would not money measure all your gain? You are evidently a man who has spent years in the Orient. You tricked Yelniz, who was a fool, and you tricked me, who am not a fool. Just now you are helpless in my hands and may be killed without danger. Instead of killing you, I set aside all personality and offer you three things. First, any sum of money you may name; second, the Order of the Mejidieh of the first rank—you may appreciate what *that* means—and thirdly, any place of honor or power within the gift of the Sultan."

"You offer this—for what?" I asked as he paused.

"For the letter of Sergius, or for your active cooperation in getting that letter by joining my men openly. I do not make the offer because I am afraid of you, Mr. Sargent; I make it because I honestly admire you, and because, working together, we could do some great things in the future."

"You flatter me," and I laughed at the thought. "But I must decline. I have sworn service to the ruler of that castle, Esmer, and in any case I do not think I would greatly care to be associated with you. You smell of evil as an Arab smells of musk on Friday."

I seriously think that he had been in earnest in his offer—which showed how much power he held at Constantinople, by the way. He looked steadily at me, then rose and stalked away, plucking at his pointed beard. I could see him walking among the rocks, the Arabs watching him half fearfully, half in doubt. I heard one of them mutter:

"The fat *kafir* was right, brother. This Osmanli is a friend of Eblis, and Satan has whispered to him. But we must keep on—for death lies behind!"

And death lay ahead, also, if he had but known it.

Presently Esmer Bey sat down, smoking a cigarette and still deep in thought. After a time he came back to us. I saw that he held a long, cylindrical affair of some grayish substance, which his thin fingers tapped nervously. I happened to glance at John, propped against a rock, and was surprised to see his eyes bulging out. Esmer saw it, too, and smiled—his old, cruel, purposeful smile.

"Ah! You recognize the specimen, Solomon? Well, well! Strange how such a thing could be found here in the heart of Arabia, is it not? Yet here it is; and if you, or whoever it was pillaged our saddle-bags, had but extended your search a few weeks ago, you would have overcome me, indeed. As it is, Allah willed that the fate of the letter of Sergius should turn upon just such a thing—the failure to make a good job of raiding our camp, for example."

I wondered what this thing was, but did not intend to make a fool of myself by asking questions. So I said nothing. The Arabs looked indifferent, but Solomon's eyes bulged a little more, and the two Osmanlis darted furtive glances as Esmer's fingers continued to tap the cylinder. The explanation came suddenly, smilingly.

"Dynamite, Mr. Sargent; some very fine stuff, too, for which I had to wait at Maan, as you know. Well, it seems that my waiting was to some purpose, for without this dynamite I could not get into the castle down there, and without getting in I could not very well get the letter—eh?"

I thought for a little that he was trying to bluff me.

"You've made a pretty good waste of time since you've been sitting down before our castle then," I remarked with what I fondly imagined was scathing irony.

Esmer cocked his head on one side and smiled at me.

"Well, what's the answer, Esmer?" I went on. "Are you trying to run a little bluff?"

"Bluff?"

He frowned at the word, which was evidently new to his supply of English good though it was. However, he caught the sense of it and laughed.

"No—no, I am not trying to trick you, if that is what you mean. No, Mr. Sargent.

"Now I have this and some others like it—very fine dynamite, too. How easily it could be tossed over the walls down there, or simply placed against them some night and set off by a bullet in the dawn. What of your fortress then, Mr. Sargent?"

"If that's dynamite you could blow the wall in, all right."

I scrutinized the cylinder, wishing that Esmer would stop tapping it in that irritating fashion.

"But why the deuce haven't you done it before?"

"Ah—think, my dear sir! Think!"

I thought, but to no purpose. I could see no reason on earth why, if I was in Esmer's position, I should not have mastered that castle a week ago and more. His men had dribbled away, but once he blew in the gates or the walls their rifles would easily dispose of the knights who were left. In fact, a determined attack would probably have done so in any case; but he did not know just how many men we had.

Esmer continued to smile, enjoying my perplexity; then handed the dynamite to an Osmanli, who with evident relief carried it off among the rocks, away from those tapping fingers of his masters.

"I must confess I don't see your object, Esmer. Either you have recently located a remarkable dislike to taking human life or else you're losing your grip. And I must say you don't show any evidence of the latter."

"Thank you, Mr. Sargent. Coming from you, I appreciate the compliment. No; your first premise was quite correct. My sole reason for not using this dynamite before now was a merciful one."

"So you wanted to spare our lives?" I retorted sarcastically.

"Exactly. I wanted to spare human life, to phrase it more correctly."

There was that in his voice which bespoke sincerity, in spite of his half mocking air. It puzzled me, for I knew quite certainly that the man had no more mercy or pity in him than the black stone of the *Kaaba*—nor as much.

Furthermore, as Gairner had said, it was directly to his interest to destroy every tongue which might spread abroad reports of what had taken place in Themoud. He had declared a *jehad*, or holy war, against an unoffending people, Christians; were it known, every law-doctor in Islam would arise against him, and he would perforce be sacrificed upon the altar of the Osmanlis' safety. The Ma'az men—what remained of them—would have to keep silence for their own sakes.

And yet he had undoubtedly meant his last words. After watching me amusedly for a long moment he proceeded to explain the inconsistency.

"As regards yourself and the others, Mr. Sargent, I regret that I do not find it advisable to offer clemency; yet I will make you one more offer, and the last. Because I knew Miss Gairner was in that castle I have spared it. Go back and bring her here, where she may remain uninjured, and then go where you will.

"If you choose to fight against me and remain alive when the castle falls, I promise you life. Otherwise, I can wait no longer. Refuse, and we use our weapons—and she must take her chance with the rest.

"Her safety lies in your hands, Mr. Sargent; so bethink you well. You gain nothing by refusing to bring her out here to safety, and you lose all, for I will certainly kill you. Accept and save your life, and hers with it."

CHAPTER XVII

ESMER'S NEW WEAPON

F ROM THAT night when Esmer and Yelniz talked in
their tent I had absolutely forgotten the former's benevolent intentions toward Edith Gairner, except for that one time
when I had promised Gairner not to let her fall into Esmer's
hands alive; and then it had only been a fleeting memory.

Now, however, it came upon me in full force, slowly but surely,
as he spoke, until it sickened my mind. For an instant I could
absolutely feel the bottom drop out of things. It's hard to explain
that feeling. If you have ever forgotten an important thing, had it
swept entirely out of your mind, and then had it jump out at you
most abruptly, you may get a faint inkling of how I felt just then.

I did not know how Esmer intended using that dynamite, and
he came nearer to shaking me than he knew with that subtle
temptation. I could go inside and fetch Edith out, well enough,
I was confident, and Gairner along with her; and after that it
would go hard, but I could manage to dispose of Esmer in some
fashion, even with my bare hands, as I had so nearly done before.

Now came my bitter regret that I had not done so; for no man
other than Esmer would ever have forced other men across that
horrible desert. If he flung that dynamite into the castle, as his
ingenuity would soon enable him to do, and the great hall was
destroyed, how would Edith Gairner and the other women get
out of those underground chambers?

I glanced at Solomon, writhing under the thought, and
caught his gaze fixed clear and full upon me. Now, he said after-

ward that he really tried to convey an idea into my mind, and if
so he certainly succeeded; for my whole indecision was borne
away in the recollection of Count Hugo.

The women and children were in safety, whatever befell. If the
carven fireplace were destroyed—and I remembered the exact
pressure-point which would open the secret door—there were
others, of which Lady Godwitha, Hugo, or Bertrand would have
the secret, besides Sir Gaimar. I was a fool to doubt.

"Not I!" was my laughing answer, while Esmer Bey stood
and wondered. "If you kill me with John Solomon, you lose two
hostages whom you may need. And as for hurting Edith Gairner,
why—she does not fall into your hands alive, my friend, in any
case. But neither does she fall into your hands."

"So," rejoined Esmer slowly, "you are very confident, Mr.
Sargent—I wonder why? Perhaps you will explain?"

"You bet I'll explain!"

I could not help my old hatred of him flashing out.

"To revert to Osmanli, Esmer, you are a dog-brother—you
murderer! Murderer of women and children!

"Do you think for a minute we would take any chances on a
man like you? Not much!

"All you will find in that castle will be men with weapons, and
you won't find the letter of Sergius, either.

"So that was your game, eh? You're not after that letter so
much as you are trying to get hold of Miss Gairner—and you
with your fine talk of Osmanlis!"

That was a bit unjust but as the flame leaped up into his savage
eyes I went on:

"Now I'll give you a proposition in my turn, Esmer. You go
ahead and take that castle if you can, and when you're all through
then you come back to me, and if you've found Edith Gairner
I'll give you the letter of Sergius for her. How is that?"

Esmer found it not to his liking. He did not lose his grip on
himself; but as he stood and plucked at his beard, that devil of

rage dancing in his black eyes, I knew that he was struggling as he had made me struggle.

"You are clever," he finally answered coldly; "but you mistake. I want Miss Gairner—yes; but first I want the letter. If I find her—Yes; I accept your offer, but I mean to find the letter, also. So you know where they both are—and they are not in the castle? Now I think that you might be made to tell, Mr. Sargent."

"Oh, you do?"

I laughed at him, but my laugh came from anger and nothing else.

"In that case go ahead, Esmer Bey. You know how much you got out of me there at Maan, don't you? *Keupek!* Village dog without a bite—go ahead and waste time!"

It is not nice to be a *bey* of some power and to have your men hear you called a dog by a prisoner. I thought Esmer would strike me down as I stood; but, though his face snarled and quivered, he kept his self-control. And I felt a little admiration for him in his readiness to give up Edith Gairner for the letter. He was sincere in that, and he was equally sincere in wanting her.

"Still, I repeat that you might be made to tell, Mr. Sargent. However, I have no time to waste on you, as you so rightly remind me."

He stood considering for a little, when it occurred to me that I might do some good by backing up John in his attempt to stir the Arabs.

"What about that *firman* of the Sultan which you stole from Mr. Gairner?" I asked in Arbi and turned to the men. *"Aslahek Allah!* May God set you right, brethren, for this man has led you far astray. He—"

Esmer's fist caught me on the cheek. I went down and lay there, looking up at him as he stood over me, lashed almost beside himself with his fury. I laughed a little, and that made him more angry still.

"Allah blast you!" he roared in that sonorous, vibrant voice of his. "You would tempt me to shoot you like a dog, eh? But I will

not, my friend! No! I will hold you, both of you, till you wish
that I had shot you!

"As for the letter, it may take its course; but I swear by the
Koran and the holy tombs of Medina that I will hold that girl
before I have done."

With which he launched out into a furious description of
what would then take place, which will not bear reproduction
here, but which drove flame into my soul. Had I been a mighty
man such as is told of in stories I would have burst my bonds
asunder and fallen on him where he stood; but this was not in
my power, for all my madness.

Moreover, his words lashed me into cold, not hot, rage—cold,
iron determination that he and I should one day have a settling,
and that if ever my fingers got his throat a second time there
would be no sparing. When he had finished, panting and word-
less, I laughed again; then spoke slowly:

"Though you slew me here and fled, Esmer Bey, you would
not escape. For the blood you have shed in this place there comes
an atonement, and if man does not punish you then God will.
Remember this."

Esmer looked down into my face, commanding himself. For
a fleeting instant I caught a flicker of something like fear in his
eyes. Then it had passed into swift scorn; he laughed.

"Good! And now carry these two off and guard them—or,
stay! Leave them here, and if they talk, well. But if they talk in
Arbi, take a whip to them."

His commands were given to the two Osmanlis, who carried
us near the fire, into the rock-shadow, set us there and loosened
John's gag. Esmer called the Arabs, and they went off together
in the direction of the church, leaving us under the Osmanlis'
guard. I saw that Esmer feared John's tongue, hence his orders
that we were not to speak Arbi. If John had been given half an
hour with those Arabs I verily believe he would have detached
them from Esmer.

"Dang it!" he said when his gag was gone. "This 'ere's a werry bad fix for you to be in, Mr. Sargent."

"Very bad for you, also, John," and I told him how I had come and why.

There had been no prohibition against Osmanli, for Esmer did not know that John spoke it; so before answering me Solomon called one of the guards and asked him to get out his pipe, fill and light it for him. The fellow obeyed, all agrin at the coolness of the little man.

"Yes, sir, werry bad," he went on, when his clay was comfortably reposing in its accustomed corner of his mouth and he was puffing satisfactorily. "To use a bit of Amurican talk, sir, I should say as 'ow we was up against it, in a manner of speaking. That dynamite, sir, makes things look mortal uncertain."

"That's a little way dynamite has, John. I would be inclined to say that it makes things look mortally certain for somebody. I'd like to be unbound and have ten minutes with Esmer."

"Yes, sir; I'd like for you to 'ave that same better than meself. When it's a matter o' fighting, sir, why, you like it and I don't. I'm werry unselfish, as the old gent said when 'e give the 'ousemaid three kisses, and I likes to give others pleasure, so to speak. It ain't every man as can fight, I says, only it ain't every man as knows 'e can't fight neither, says I."

"Quite right, John, as usual. Now, what's your advice as to our present situation? Can we do anything?"

"Yes, sir. I ain't slept since I was 'auled and 'ove over them there walls like a bag o' meal and given the scare o' me life, Mr. Sargent; so I says sleep while we can, just like that."

This being John's invariable and favorite advice when there was nothing better in prospect, I accepted it. It was now nearly noon, and as I had not slept the night before I had little difficulty in finding slumber, and indeed in sleeping until night.

I wakened to find a couple of cakes thrust into my hand, together with a jar of water, and managed to make a good enough campaign meal. Esmer and his Arabs had returned, and after guards were sent out I saw there was to be no attack that night. Esmer sat near us in silence.

"What said that letter of Sergius, Mr. Sargent?" he asked abruptly, staring down into the fire and with no trace of animosity in his face.

I told him, inwardly wondering at the man. In spite of all his evil and cruelty, there was something lofty about him, about the manner in which he could absolutely disassociate himself from his deeds and surroundings, as if he were but an instrument and were not responsible for his doings. He had none of that humility which is the most cherished possession of the true Moslem, but was proud—a man of adamant, unbending and unbreakable.

"So Mohammed was a Christian!" he mused in English. "And the story of the man at Damascus was true, then! A pity—a pity that Parrish Bey was destroyed!"

"Eh?" exclaimed John suddenly, starting. "You knew Captain Parrish, Esmer?"

"Why, yes, Solomon."

Esmer laughed slightly, but bitterly.

"We fought together for Adrianople against the Bulgars, and had I been in Constantinople at the time you would never have obtained that *firman* which brought about his death."

John looked troubled, and small wonder. I recalled his story of how he had effected the destruction of Parrish, a renegade American who was building a stronghold for the Senussiyeh in Arabia, and it seemed to me that if Esmer had been a brother-in-arms of Parrish there was little hope for John Solomon. At the present moment Esmer was not thinking of animosity.

"You're a strange man, Solomon," he said still musingly. "And you, Sargent, a stranger. Do you know, you almost made me afraid this morning with your prophecy! If I believed in a God—" and he paused.

"What of the Koran?" I asked, feeling out his mood.

"The Koran?"

Again came his bitter laugh.

"Was not the Prophet a Christian by this letter? So the letter must be destroyed, Mr. Sargent, lest we Osmanlis lose our grip on Islam. To the Arabs it would matter little, since the Christian writings are sacred to them, also, the cross itself being revered of many tribes; but to us— Well, I think you know what would happen. The race of Osman would be no more, for we must fight hard against you Christians. We might hold Constantinople, but the rest would break away from us forever. No; we have outraged the Koran, we Osmanlis, and I, Esmer Bey, must fight a fight for all my people lest we perish."

There was something almost sad in his bitter voice. I think, given his own way, he would have preferred to send out that letter of Sergius and then to conquer Islam once more if need be, for such was his nature. He lit a cigarette, the firebrand he used bringing out the gloom that sat upon his cruel, insolent, handsome face.

"Well, no matter! 'Do it!' they said. 'Do it, Esmer Bey! Destroy this letter and this people of Themoud.'

"So I have destroyed, and will destroy; but I think that I shall feel fate upon me in the doing. Well, at least I am no coward."

And with that he passed up and away from us, walking off into the night. I looked at John and caught the amazement upon his face. It was the only time that either of us ever knew this terrible man to soften. Perhaps some foreshadow of his end had come to him, though none of us dreamed how awful and yet how glorious that doom was to be, for as yet we knew nothing of the Seal of Solomon. That knowledge was not far from us, however.

That night and the next day passed quietly. Looking down at the castle, we could distinctly see the glitter of arms from the knights and from the dummies we had placed here and there on the walls. Once I saw Count Hugo, recognizable from his great height and flowing beard, standing on a tower and looking up as if searching for some trace of us.

Esmer made no offensive movement, though he and the Arabs were gone for most of the day—where we knew not. John

and I were unbound only to eat and drink, and at these times
the two Osmanlis stood over us with rifles ready. However, our
hands were too helpless from the bonds to attempt any escape,
though by means of brisk rubbing we could get the circulation
going again.

I must say that things looked pretty gloomy for us. I had no
doubt that Esmer was preparing for a final attack. To get away
was a physical impossibility. A good deal of baggage had been
brought up to the camp, the church no longer being headquarters; and when Esmer and his men came in that night they
started active preparations.

These consisted of measuring out the remaining ammunition,
which was only about ten rounds per man. Their occupation
became evident. They also had been utilizing and searching for
the ammunition of their slain comrades; Esmer's supply must
have been exhausted sooner than anticipated, or else it had not
been overlarge.

"Dang it!" ejaculated John in my ear. "If I 'adn't been and made
a perishin' fool out o' meself over them camels, we could 'a' looted
their dynamite and cartridges all shipshape and proper, sir!"

I nodded, but there was no use in crying over spilled milk. As
many of the Arabs still bore the huge Norman swords, Esmer
commanded these to be laid off, and they were piled up not
far from us. The Arabs, however, including Esmer himself,
donned chainmail and helmets with the darkness. Although
we could not catch his orders, we had no doubt that the crisis
was approaching.

About midnight—for I had kept awake purposely—I nudged
John in the side. We saw Esmer and five Arabs standing talking
together across the fire in low tones. Then they moved out into
the darkness and vanished, but not so soon that I had not seen
their loads. They bore the dynamite; and remembering Esmer's
statement about setting it off at dawn, I concluded that nothing
would happen immediately.

In this I was correct. For perhaps an hour I stared down at

the dull glow which denoted the castle, but heard no outcry, no alarm. Then, just as the moon was searching out the darker valleys, Esmer and the five drifted silently into camp and flung themselves down. Evidently the charge had been placed.

I gained some few snatches of sleep that night, though my bound wrists and ankles hurt too intolerably to allow of much repose. Toward dawn Esmer rose, spoke to the man on guard, came over, and made sure that we were too tightly bound to escape.

"Well, you may lie and watch what happens," he said gruffly.

As he evidently had need of all his men, I knew that we would be unwatched; but the thought brought me little comfort, because there was no possibility of escape. The Arabs rose and made a hasty meal, after which they each took his rifle and slipped away into the grayness. Esmer alone remained.

Slowly the dim outlines of the castle took firmer shape, until at length the sky was all ablaze with the dawn-spears. Then, as I made out folk moving about the castle walls and courtyard, Esmer picked up his own rifle and carefully adjusted the sights.

"I give you one last chance to change your mind, Mr. Sargent," he said, looking at me coolly. "You can still save Miss Gairner if you say the word."

"She's where all your dynamite wouldn't reach her," I smiled as pleasantly as possible, under the circumstances. "Shoot away."

"So I expected. Then adieu for the present, gentlemen. When next we meet I trust that you will have company of the best."

He bowed ironically.

"A werry pleasant companion, but 'e's a bit too anxious to 'ave 'is own way, as the 'ousemaid said about the 'ead butler."

John looked after our retreating captor, who was making his way down the hillside. The Arabs had vanished.

"Is 'e really a going to set off that 'ere dynamite, Mr. Sargent?"

"It looks as if he intended to, John."

"Then all I can say is good-by to them knights down yonder! What's 'e been and done with it, sir?"

"Probably put it up against the walls out of sight from above. They are pretty old, and you can trust him to pick out the weakest place."

"Then if 'e sets it off by firing of 'is rifle, 'e'll 'ave to go within shot o' the walls?"

"Evidently."

"Then you watch Omar, sir. 'E's a werry fine shot, is Omar."

Though the same idea must have occurred to Esmer, he displayed no hesitancy whatever about putting himself in danger. As he had said, he was no coward. He had deliberately chosen the hour of sunrise to set off the charge; so slowly but steadily he walked down toward the castle, picking his way delicately and leaving a blue thread of cigarette-smoke behind him.

When he was within about three hundred yards of the castle I saw a spat of white shoot out from one of the corner towers, the knights having got under cover. This was followed by others, showing that Omar, Gairner, and Bertrand were wide-awake. But Esmer never slackened his pace, nor hastened it.

He paused at two hundred yards, as nearly as I could judge, and, lifting his rifle, took a cool and careful aim, though we could distinctly see the bullets hitting up the dust around him. Then his rifle spoke out. And again. And again....

From the central space of the front wall, between the corner tower and the gates, a great cloud of white puffed up, followed by another cloud of dun smoke, which hid all the castle from us except for the banner waving from the highest tower.

Then came an appalling concussion that welled up and set all the mountain thundering with its echoes, while I distinctly felt the vibration of the ground. Following this was a moment of intense silence, broken only by the rolling echoes, and then came puny rifle-cracks.

As the dust-cloud settled I heard a groan from Solomon. The castle stood, of course, but the whole front side, from the gates to one corner, was a great mass of ruins, and in one spot even these were blasted away to the bare rock. And toward this point the Arabs, hidden until now, were rushing, firing as they came, while Esmer led them. And with that the sun rose.

The scene that followed made a dread spectacle, viewed from where we lay helpless on the cragside. From the unshattered tower on the left rifles spoke out. I felt huge relief because Gairner and Omar had evidently escaped. From the inner castle-gates a number of figures rushed out across the courtyard to the breach. There Esmer paused as the two forces came together.

The Arab rifles must have taken terrible toll in that first minute or two, but from the corner tower others answered. Then Esmer's men rolled up the breach, though not because the knights wavered; knight and esquire fell side by side that morning. Soon shining points glimmered here and there among the stones, where men lay.

"Mr. Sargent! Mr. Sargent!"

I turned impatiently at John's shouts. He had dragged himself to the pile of swords, and was paying no heed to what went on below.

"Get this 'ere sword out, sir!" he cried, kicking one of the huge sheathed blades toward me. "Get this 'ere sword out and cut these blasted ropes, sir!"

CHAPTER XVIII

UNDERGROUND

WELL, WITH John's cry the terrible scene below passed clean out of my mind. I flung myself upon the big blade. Holding it down with my body and shoulders, I made shift to catch the cross-hilt between my teeth and so draw it forth, a fraction of an inch at a time, as I could hitch my head forward.

It is little to tell of, but with bound wrists and ankles it was a hard thing to do. When I had a foot of the blade bared I got myself up so that I was sitting on the sheath, then managed to kick at the hilt with my feet until the sword came away.

That much done, it remained only to cut the ropes, which I did clumsily enough and at the expense of a goodly bit of wrist-skin. So stiff and bloodless were my hands that I could not move my fingers for a long minute, but finally I got the sword between my wrists and hacked at the rope about my ankles till it fell away. Then I managed to do the same for John.

For a space we sat there rubbing madly at our wrists and ankles, pounding the blood into circulation. I bethought me to glance down, hearing another crackle of rifles.

There was a swirl of men in the breach, though much less numerous, and I caught a star-bright flashing of sword-blades. Then all swept into the courtyard, and one or two bright specks darted across it to that tower still held by Omar and Gairner; the others rolled on to the inner gate of the great-hall itself, where one great figure glittered out—old Count Hugo.

They went at him like a pack of dogs at a deer. Even in the midst of it all I was startled by the fewness of them, and thought that if we could but get there in time we might yet turn the tide. The count's sword flared and flared again, but more redly. Then I saw Esmer, also recognizable because of his figure, standing out at one side. A fleck of white broke from him, and at the shot Count Hugo's sword went down and did not rise again.

But still the old man held the doorway, fighting with a murderous dagger, as we discovered later. Again Esmer shot and yet again, and now the tall figure reeled back and out of our sight. The Arabs fought for entrance until Esmer roughly pushed his way among them. We saw a few break off and begin shooting at the tower. Esmer and the others vanished inside the castle.

"They've been and done it, sir." John almost sobbed the words as we rose and took a few trembling steps. "They've killed 'im— the old man!"

"One minute, John," I said and picked up the naked sword that had freed us, for other weapons there were none. "Best take one of these."

I was rather surprised that he did so, for John was firmly opposed to fighting—where his own skin was concerned. However, swords in hand, we began the descent of the hill.

On my part, I was not so much eager for vengeance as I was eager to get inside that hall, and so into the secret passageway. If I could get Bertrand, Omar, and Gairner out of the tower, we might yet turn the tables on Esmer, for he certainly had only a few men left.

So, anxiously we hastened down the hillside until at length I broke into a run, heard John wheeze along behind me for a bit, and finally left him far in the rear. It was a hard task to keep up speed and carry that heavy sword, but I managed it well enough, and finally panted up to the terrific breach in the wall.

Here the first reality of that hand-to-hand struggle smote me, for a dozen bodies, Arab and Christian, lay among the still smoking stones. A shrill yell came from the courtyard: and as

I struggled over the barricade I was just in time to see a man, streaming with blood but not yet spent, rise from the ground and spring at one of the two Arabs who were firing on the tower. It was no other than Sir Gaimar.

His sword came down, and the Arab rattled out his life as I came wearily up and took the other Arab in the rear before he had a chance to whirl about and fire. Leaning heavily on his sword, Sir Gaimar wiped the blood from his eyes and looked at me.

"Greeting, Sir Frederick!" he gasped out. "Greeting in an evil hour!"

"That remains to be seen," I answered and sprang to the tower-entrance with a shout to Gaimar.

The next moment Gairner, Omar, and young Bertrand were with us, and John came heaving his slow way over the strewn stones.

That all opposition was not yet over was made evident by the yells and shots which came to us from within. I conjectured that Esmer was spreading what men he had in the endeavor to finish off the defenders and make search for the letter and Edith Gairner. However, I lost no time.

"Come!" I cried, turning. "We must make that passage before Esmer gets back to the hall. If his men are there, or he himself, we'll have to fight them off and reach it."

Still carrying that bloody sword of mine, I led the way up to the entrance, where lay old Count Hugo with two Arabs beneath him. I could hear the sob that broke from Bertrand; then I was inside the hall.

By some fortunate chance it was empty save for the bodies of two or three knights. With a bound I had reached the fireplace and set my fist to the carving. I knew the place, and the stone gave to my hand, but it seemed an age before that huge stonework began to swing out into the room. Now but for an act of utter folly on my part we should have got away.

Bertrand cried out that he would bring the body of his father, and Sir Gaimar, all but spent as he was, seconded the idea.

"No time to talk of bodies!" I exclaimed.

But Bertrand's face stopped the words on my tongue. For an instant I hesitated; then, cursing myself for a fool, I turned and ran back to the entrance with him.

There, as luck would have it, we met two Arabs who had come around the courtyard from some other exit. Bertrand whipped up his rifle and made a clean miss, then staggered back with a bullet in his shoulder as both Arabs fired.

The double blast drove me back, blinded; but I remained unhurt, and managed to fetch my sword down once and felt it quench the life in one man. The other turned and fled before the smoke rolled off; and now, supporting Bertrand, I gained the outswung fireplace.

"In with you, Sir Gaimar!" I cried.

"Nay; I would support Count Bertrand," he replied gallantly.

"You have hard work enough to support yourself," I answered impatiently.

But John Solomon had already skipped into the hole, with Omar and Gairner after him. Bidding Sir Gaimar close the place up—for I did not know how to do it myself—I lifted Bertrand inside and turned to hear a shot and a terrific yell. Esmer himself was coming across the hall.

Well, that massive door slammed shut before his face, while he tore wildly at the carvings. The last thing I saw was his foaming, furious countenance. Then, catching at Sir Gaimar for guidance, I laughed harshly.

"The fox is holed now, sure enough!"

"How mean you, Sir Frederick?"

"I mean, Sir Gaimar, that, now Esmer knows where we are, he will have that fireplace down stone by stone, but he will find us! How many men has he left?"

"I know not; but I think not more than five or six."

At that I gave a whistle of astonishment. That must have been a bloody battle, and desperate. But now Sir Gaimar coolly sat down beneath the first hanging lamp and described to me the particular stone on which I must stamp to have the rock-chambers in which the women were sheltered opened to me.

"Do you go on with Count Bertrand," he said, "for he is sorely wounded, I fear, and must have care. I will hold this passage until you return. Go—with God!"

So, with something like a lump in my throat, I wrung his hand and passed on to the others. Omar was holding up young Bertrand, but a hasty look showed that his wound was not serious, though the loss of blood might well prove so. At any rate, he was out of the fighting.

Bidding Omar return to help Sir Gaimar, I caught up Bertrand and went on with the other two. That big fireplace, solidly as it was built, would soon be torn down, and then we would have Esmer with us. I suddenly thought of the letter of Sergius, and shook the half-conscious Bertrand into life—roughly, I fear.

"It is with the Seal of Suleiman," he answered vaguely to my query; and so I knew that it was behind that mysterious door which Count Hugo had omitted to open to me. After that I gave little thought to the letter, being occupied in other matters.

We came to the rusted iron door, and while Solomon and Gairner held up Bertrand, I found the flagstone and stamped twice. Almost at once the section of wall swung back, and I saw Lady Godwitha and Edith Gairner, pale and anxious-eyed, standing to receive us.

There was no time for talk. Gairner took his daughter in his arms for a moment—poor man, it was his last kiss on this earth!—and I pushed Bertrand forward, with a hasty injunction to Lady Godwitha to care for him and not to let him come forth. I wished to be no teller of bad tidings, and knew he would tell the tale once he was conscious. A swift touch of hands with Edith Gairner, and once more we stood alone in the passage.

"Now, what shall we do?" I asked. "I'd better go back and help hold that passage, I suppose. John, you and Gairner had better break down that iron door and get hold of the letter. Then wait for me here, and as soon as we check Esmer I'll bring the others along. The only way to do is for us all to get in there with the women and let the storm blow over."

Since there was no chance whatever of Esmer's finding us there—especially as he had used all his dynamite on the castle-wall—this advice was counted good. Here I found another mistake to correct; for had we brought Omar and Sir Gaimar along, by now we would all have been safe inside the rock-chambers. But I had to go back after these two, and so gave John the excuse for which he was itching to break down that door.

I set off at a run while they started the work; but as I ran the thunderous clang of blows from behind began to merge curiously with other sounds ahead, through which pierced suddenly the sharper crack of a shot. I had gone all the way to the entrance, nearly, when I stumbled into Omar and Sir Gaimar, where they had dashed out a lamp.

"They broke through, and now they are around the corner behind us," whispered Omar. "I just fired—"

A flash, and a bullet sang past us. Omar answered it with two quick shots, and a scream came down to us. But this sort of thing could not endure forever, and I knew it full well.

"We must run for it!" I said. "Start off, Sir Gaimar, and we'll follow."

He vanished with a great clanking of harness, while I recovered breath.

Now we were in a bad plight. Esmer had lost no time getting into the passage; and, since it was straight and well lit, he had had no difficulty in following us. If we could delay him we might get into the rock-chambers safely; if that section of the passage-wall were seen by Esmer, even though he did not get in, he would know where we were.

So Omar and I started off, and as we went we put out those

hanging lamps which lighted the caverns. Unless Esmer had fetched lights his advance would be checked; he could use some of the hanging lamps from behind, but he would be fearful of surprises, and would necessarily go slowly.

We soon caught up with Sir Gaimar, and I saw that he was in much worse shape than Bertrand had been. He must have been in the thick of the whole combat, for his mail-coat was literally ripped to pieces by bullets, though he had no mortal wound. He stripped away his harness wearily, retaining only his sword.

Suddenly, without any warning, he seemed to stumble and fell prostrate. I tried to help him up, but saw that he was sense-less, and called to Omar in an agony of fear. But as I have said, Sir Gaimar was a large man. Though we managed to lift him between us, it was soon evident that at this rate we would never make headway on Esmer. Omar dropped Sir Gaimar's legs with a grunt.

"No use," he said shortly. "Here; I have water."

We got the knight to his feet again after no little difficulty. I must confess that I began to despair of shaking off the misfor-tune which seemed to have dogged us ever since Bertrand insisted on bringing his father's body. Once we passed by that flagstone we could not get admittance to the rock-chambers; otherwise we might have gained the iron door and held it indef-initely.

On the other hand, there was the danger of delaying—a terribly vital danger, too, for we already had a sample of Esmer's iron determination and swiftness of action in the way he had smashed an entrance into the secret passage from the hall. If we signaled to Edith to open to us Edith might come in time to—

Well, the honest truth is that I was afraid of the man, and my fear sapped my resolution, much as I hated him. Face to face, hatred overleaped fear; but with my imagination given a chance to work, it was the other way around. I am no coward, mind; but the unreal life in this place, the terrible things which had happened since Esmer's coming, all had rather unsettled me, and I would defy any man to go through the same unmoved.

So while Gaimar sobbed air into his lungs I stood indecisively for a little, then caught him by the arm and led him on, Omar putting out the lights as we went. For any of us to stop and check Esmer's advance while the rest gained safety was out of the question; not one of us would have consented to any other man's death in such wise. Wherefore we came near all dying together.

I was watching behind for lights, and sent Omar back to fire a shot or two and run, while I led, or rather carried Sir Gaimar, who reeled like a drunken man. So, in my intentness on what lay behind, I did not catch the faint sound that came from ahead of us. Omar fired two shots after a moment, showing that he had sighted Esmer, and presently he dashed up to us, breathless.

"I hit him!" he gasped.

"Who—Esmer?"

He nodded and held out his hand.

"Yes, for I saw him stagger. If the bullet went through I do not know. It was my last. Give me cartridges, *sidi*."

"Are yours gone? I have none."

Omar flung down his rifle without a word and caught Sir Gaimar on the other side, accepting the dictum of fate with his usual *"ma'alesh"*—which carries more meaning than the rarely used *"kismet."*

Then I heard the sound from ahead.

It was a shriek or scream, faint, but coming regularly. As it echoed along the passageway it lost all meaning to my ears. Nevertheless, Omar ibn Kasim uttered a grunt of surprise.

"Inshallah! It is the voice of Suleiman!"

So it was, and quick fear leaped into my heart, together with a sob of despair. Solomon and Gairner had gone at that iron door hammer and tongs, intent, despite the danger around us, on seeing what lay behind. I recalled the order of Count Hugo not to open the door unless we had a guide—and I ran ahead, leaving Omar to follow with Sir Gaimar. Then I caught the scream more clearly.

"Mr. Sargent! Help! Help! Mr. Sargent!"

It was more than a mere scream—it was a shriek of heart-wrung agony, ringing with fear and horror and utterly impossible to describe. Dreading I knew not what, I ran on until the door, shattered and spent, came into sight. Then a blast of warm air smote me, and as I gained the door and saw what lay beyond, for an instant my heart froze within me.

CHAPTER XIX

THE SEAL OF SOLOMON

I SUPPOSE I must describe the place before telling what happened there, but it is a hard task and one that I shrink from. In all my life I have never seen a place that was more awe-inspiring and terrible than this, nor do I think any other man has.

It was a vast cavern, occupying nearly the whole peak of the Man's Nose, as I found later. And it was lit not from above, but from below—by just such light as I saw once before, one night when I was lowered into Ætna. By daylight the horrifying beauty of that light would perhaps vanish, but there was no daylight in this cavern.

Shimmering not in one color, but in a play of all colors, lighting all the gloom of the place with a weird and ghastly radiance, the light literally bubbled up from the central pit of this cavern-amphitheater. So far as I noticed then, this pit was merely a depression in the center of the place, the source of the light being out of sight.

The heat, more than the light itself, halted me. Bottled up within this cavern for years, save for an exit it had found below, it now rushed past me with the draft into the passageway, stopping Esmer and his men for a little through fear of the unknown.

Although instinctively and without any tangible reason I felt a swift fright of that central pit which seemed to be the source of light and heat at once, it was not this which absolutely unmanned me for that first instant, nor was it the huge carven figures which leered from the high walls around and stretched grotesquely upward to the unseen roof-dome. Instead, it was the floor.

From what I knew of the place already, I was certain that it had once served as a place of worship for those unknown people whose city lay desolate in the sands below, and who, according to tradition, had been fire-worshipers. Also, though the cavern was partly natural, it had undoubtedly been improved upon by man. In no other way could that floor have stretched in a steep descent from the walls to the central pit, all around.

It really was an amphitheater, although the seats were not built, but were merely depressions hollowed out in the rock. None the less they were plainly visible, and here and there among them were grotesque statues, or idols, each about ten feet high and with a little level of rock all about them.

"Help, Mr. Sargent! Be careful—for Heaven's sake, be careful!"

By one of these statues, some thirty feet ahead of me, I made out the recumbent figure of John Solomon, and sent him back a reassuring cry which waved up in dizzy echoes overhead. Then with my first step forward I perceived why that appalling horror rang through his voice.

For not only were the floor and seats highly polished—as only centuries can polish basalt or lava, until they absolutely shone like mirrors—but weaving about through all the seats, crossing and recrossing as far as I could see, shooting up and down and across, was a groove in the solid stone.

As yet there was no definite reason why I should stand aghast at that sight, unless it was a premonition, a sense of the tremendous perversion of humanity that lay behind this whole place. That groove in the rock was more than three feet across and a little less at the top; the sides of it curved concavely, and it glittered about through the seats in a perfect maze of light-lines, so highly was it polished. Perhaps I should properly speak of it as "grooves"; yet there was but one continuous line, after all.

A ridge of rock like an aisle ran from the doorway to that statue near which John Solomon lay. The ridge was unbroken, though on either side of it ran one of those grooves, doubling about the statue and darting somewhere into the maze. I ran forward on the ridge, and as I did so I made out that Gairner must have fallen into the groove and been unable to get out for some unknown reason.

Just as I reached the rock-platform about the statue, Omar and Sir Gaimar came to the doorway behind, and the knight cried out something that I did not catch. I had small time to waste, however.

Solomon, with one foot hitched about a carven foot of the statue, lay with most of his body down in that groove. To his outstretched hand clung Uriel Gairner. I never want to see such a look of fear on a man's face again as I saw on his in that weird light. I gripped John and pulled him up, throwing out all my strength in the effort.

Slowly I reached Gairner's hand, and saw that with his other he was trying to cling to the edges of the groove; but so highly was the rock polished that he could get no hold—which was precisely the intent of the hewers. I got John out, and was pulling up Gairner when, to get a better grip, I jumped across the groove.

Gaimar's quick shout came too late. As my foot struck the rock it slipped away, and I had only a brief view of Gairner pulling himself up as I went down. Then everything closed out from my sight except the roof overhead, and I found myself looking up through the groove-top. I had fallen into the thing.

And then—

I began to move!

No words can tell the horror that fell upon me. I tried to dig my feet, knees, hands, into the smooth sides of that tunnel-like groove, but could catch on nothing. Moist though they were with the cold sweat of fear, my hands could not clutch and hold even on the edge overhead. Then I felt the thing dip under me, and I shot downward with fearful velocity.

Thinking I was going down into that central pit to some unknown revolting fate, I screamed—twisted about. But still I shot down. Then up—and up, feet first, gradually slowing my pace, until I writhed upward to try and fling myself out of the groove. Instantly I darted down again—and caught one glimpse of my friends, standing on the far side of that ghastly cavern. I had gone clear across the place!

It all came upon me suddenly as I sank back and slid faster and faster, turning sharp curves and slower ones. This was a place of fire-worshipers indeed, and there must be some horrible kind of fire in that central pit. By a devilish ingenuity this recrossing groove had been run around and around the whole floor among the seats, and when a victim was chosen to die he was simply slipped in a groove and started off. After that he would not stop, for so cleverly were the ascents and descents graduated that upon reaching a rise he would shoot on again before he could get out.

Petrified with the sheer terror of my position I lay and looked ahead, down the glimmering rock-groove that stretched beyond me. Now I knew why Gairner's face had worn that look of unutterable fear. A few more turns, a little more of that helpless sliding, and I would shoot down and down—to what?

I could imagine how that place must have been in ages past, with all those seats occupied—the victim shooting and darting around underneath, absolutely beyond all help, with that sea of people around enjoying the spectacle! I have read of horrible things—aye, and have seen some in my time; but nothing to equal this.

Again there came a long rise. As I felt myself slowing I writhed up and tried to throw out my hands over the rim of the groove. I managed to sit erect indeed, but slid along in the same manner; there was nothing to hold to, and after another sharp dip I swept around a turn, doubling one of those great statues, and up to the crest of the rise again. Looking out I saw that I had come half-way back to the others, and that Omar was leaping across a row of seats, Sir Gaimar's huge sword flaming out radiance in his hand.

Then I swept down and was flung prostrate with the rush. Down and down I went until I saw the groove growing lighter ahead; abruptly I took a turn, and a great blaze of light and heat struck me so powerfully that I groaned and shut my eyes, thinking the end had come. But no! Another quick turn, and shooting now with frightful speed I began a long climb.

Looking ahead with fear-strained eyes, I caught something that smote a new light down my path—something gleaming that touched the bottom of the groove. A little nearer, and wild hope sprang up in my breast as I knew it for the sword of Gaimar, and saw Omar standing by the groove, waiting till I came.

No need to cry advice to me. As I gradually slowed I could see that he was waiting on the very crest of the rise where my speed would be least; the sword-point came down with a crash of sparks and bit into the smooth rock a little. Then I struck it.

So great was the shock of it that the sword was swept out of Omar's hand, and I saw it clatter into the groove ahead of me, and so spin away and away. But the instant of pause was enough. Omar's hand swept down to mine; John Solomon reached his side at the same instant. As they laid me out on one of the rock-aisles I fainted dead away.

My weakness lasted only for a minute or so. I came to myself as the two were lifting me to one of the platforms, where stood Gairner and Sir Gaimar. John gripped my hand, tears coming from his eyes; but before he could speak Gaimar touched me:

"Look!"

We turned, and when I saw his object I could not repress a shudder. It was the sword—darting like a flame of light around the opposite crest of the floor-space, for we could see every movement of it, so cunningly had those grooves been fashioned and angled. Half around the vast circle ran the blade, then vanished with a swoop downward; and as a great coruscation of sparks leaped up for full thirty feet from the central pit I looked down and saw—the Seal of Solomon.

Now, this was what that pit contained, being visible from the statue platforms only, and not from the seats.* The pit itself was some twenty feet across, and round; it was full of molten lava, which bubbled up and down, but never rose above a certain height by reason of a vent, probably natural, in shape of a cleft in the rockside. When too high the lava trickled down through this cleft and so to the outside of the Man's Nose, thus forming the thread of smoke which at times ascended from the mountain.

Set down a little from the top of the pit was the Seal of Solomon—that strange diagram, its corners touching the sides of the pit for support. Whether it was of rock or of some strange unmeltable substance I do not know, but at all events it was there; and when the storm of sparks caused by the fall of the sword, which came out at the side of the pit, had died away the Seal of Solomon glowed still with the lava that stuck to it.

The Seal alone was within sight of those rows of seats. In the ancient days it must have been a weird and wonderful sight indeed to watch the victim plunge here and there, take the last awful swoop, and then, after the spark-shower, to see that wondrous Seal struck out white-hot and glowing! Whatever forgotten genius invented such an infernal place, it was certainly worthy of awe and fear.

For my part, I could only grasp Gaimar's hand and babble out something. Poor Gairner was, I think, in hysterics, for he was laughing horribly. Omar was sitting on the platform, hands across his knees, staring about quite unconcernedly, while John fumbled at his clay pipe, tears of sheer horror streaming still from his eyes. I laid a hand on his arm, and he jumped.

"Brace up, John; brace up!" I said, making a desperate effort to command my own faculties, for I was sorely shattered mentally

---

* *No doubt the seats were for the people, the platforms for the priests, who would know the nature of the seeming miracle.—H.B.-J.*

and somewhat skin-scraped in body. "There's nothing super-natural about this."

"No, sir; but—but it's main 'orrid! It's downright devilish, Mr. Sargent; that it is!"

"You had a close escape, Sir Frederick," spoke Gaimar weakly, for his wounds and exertions had told heavily on his remaining strength. "Had you slipped away from Omar there, nothing could have saved you—"

"Never mind," I broke in with a shudder. "I saw the sword; it was enough."

All of us had forgotten Esmer absolutely. Looking down at the Seal of Solomon, still glowing redly and gradually cooling off, I saw that the Seal and the edges of the pit were thickly overhung with lava.

I suppose that in the old days the fire-worshipers had had some way of scraping off the accumulations that formed; and since there had been little sacrifice after the coming of the knights and the Norman settlement, no one had cared to risk the work. So in course of time I assume that the Seal will be covered more and more, until in the end it will be a solid mass of lava, closing the pit.

In any case it was a marvelous piece of work, as was the entire place. Diabolic, yes; but displaying in its every line what wonderful science and engineering skill those ancient people of Themoud must have had. With such a place of worship as this, it was small wonder that their fame had spread abroad and that Mohammed spoke of them as utterly accursed. Well, according to legend and to the ruins we had found, their own god had in his good time destroyed them, which I think is the finest example of poetic justice I ever came across in real life.

"But what if I had stopped and begun to go backward?" I asked Gaimar.

He shook his head wearily.

"I do not know. There are ancient writings in the archives

about this place, but I have been here only a few times, with Count Hugo."

"That is not a hard thing to try," exclaimed Omar, his teeth flashing.

As he still wore his steel helm, though not a man of us was now armed since Gaimar's sword had gone—for Gairner had lost his rifle, either when he fell in or before—the Hazrami took it off and calmly dropped it into the groove that doubled the platform on which we were, so that it slid backward.

We watched it for a little, but in the end lost interest. I think that it merely stopped after a space. Started in the right direction, nothing could stop, for the builders had naturally enough not figured on starting a victim in any other way. The start was at the top, by the door where we had entered, and with the initial speed of the first descent the victim, whether man or animal, must almost have been afire with friction before he went into the lava.

I am inclined to think, after talking it over with John in cold second thought, that human sacrifices were not made here, indeed. This for the reason that the groove was so large, being a good yard across on the inside. Either an animal was used, or else the original inhabitants must have been men of great size and girth—which may have been the case, for all I know to the contrary.

What wakened me to the reality of our situation was a whiff of John's pipe, which he had managed to get going. Though I was still weakened, the feeling of horror fell away from me abruptly. I turned to Sir Gaimar, who had sunk down against the feet of the statue, his head in his hands.

"Where is that casket with the letter of Sergius? I don't know where Esmer Bey is, but we may still have time to get out of here."

"The casket?"

Gaimar pulled himself up and looked around.

"I do not know, Sir Frederick. Count Bertrand said it was

here, however— Ah, is that not it yonder, on the third platform from here?"

I looked where he pointed and saw something glimmering yellow. John nodded.

"There it is, Mr. Sargent, and there let it lie, I says. It ain't fetched us any good as I knows on; it ain't fetched Count Hugo any luck, nor Esmer neither. I'm done with it, I am. I've 'ad me fill o' this place, sir, and I says we'd best get out of 'ere as soon as may be."

"Well, John," spoke up Gairner unexpectedly, "we took an oath in the matter of that casket, I believe, and I for one intend to keep it. Still, I'd be glad to get out of here myself. It's oppressive, to say the least."

So I suggested to Sir Gaimar that he show me the best means of getting the letter and then take us out of the place.

"I will get it," he said, nodding. "Let me go alone, Sir Frederick, for there are places to step of which I know, and I think my strength will carry me that far and back again. As for getting out, walk along this ridge from the statue to the door. It is safe."

He motioned to the aisle of rock, which was unbroken by the groove, but slippery enough, and more than enough, to suit my fancy. As he still wore a tattered mantle of the order, he drew in his sword-belt and so stepped away from us over the groove.

It must have been a ticklish task, walking in those seats of dead Themoudians, and with that winding groove cutting here and there and on every side, with a slip possible at any instant; but Sir Gaimar never wavered. Once, indeed, he stopped— through weakness, I fancy; and John groaned as the knight wavered and all but fell. A moment after, however, he passed on and made the first and second platforms, on which he rested.

As he started out for the third, which was a quarter of the way around the amphitheater, I saw that he was failing. None of us said a word as he slipped: but he recovered himself and then plunged desperately on, running in a way that made me feel sick, leaping and slipping and staggering. None the less he made the third platform; but as he did so we saw him reel, clutch at the statue for support, and go down in a mass, unconscious.

"Well!" John heaved a tremulous sigh. "Now we're in a pretty pickle, dang it! We can't go off and leave 'im 'ere, that's certain."

"Let me go after him, Sargent!" exclaimed Gairner.

He was pale, but that hard jaw of his was set and he even took a step forward. At that I caught his shoulder.

"For Heaven's sake, be quiet, Gairner! Wait—I can't think! Omar, you haven't heard anything from Esmer Bey?"

"I have heard nothing," responded the Hazrami stolidly, glancing back at the dark doorway. "But I do not think that Esmer stands waiting for the camels to milk themselves."

Neither did I. We had no weapons, and could put up no kind of a fight if we met Esmer. To apply for entrance to the rock-chambers was impossible with Sir Gaimar lying unconscious on that platform for Esmer to find. Besides, I could not tell how long we had been in this horrible place, whether it had been the hours it seemed or only a matter of minutes. John, as usual, came to the rescue.

"If it 'as to be done, why, we'd better be a doin' of it, I says. Mr. Gairner, sir, if so be as you'd get that 'ere Sir Gaimar? And Omar, you go to 'elp. Mr. Sargent, you and me, we'll go back on scout, like, to see—"

But just then Esmer arrived.

CHAPTER XX

VICTORY AND DEATH

"**H**ANDS UP, gentlemen—you make a pretty target!" I turned with a curse as the clear, vibrant voice pierced to us. In the doorway behind and above stood Esmer, revolver in hand, and behind him two mail-clad Arabs.

"Go down and bind those men," he ordered. We had put up our hands helplessly.

It was plain that the Arabs had small liking for their task, and I half hoped and half dreaded that they would go over the ridge into the horror of the groove. But they did not, for the aisle was fair walking enough, and they were doubly scared—frightened of the unknown place about them, but more frightened of the devil whom they served.

As for Esmer himself, I honestly think that he gave neither attention nor thought to anything around. He was a man of one purpose, indomitable and absolute. He had been driving through those passages in search of us; now he had found us, and he kept his gaze steadily upon us, while the two Arabs bound us with strips torn from our own clothes. With that he ordered them back, and they obeyed speedily.

Whether he had more men left I know not, but imagine he had, for he was no man to leave his rear unguarded. Sending these back into the passage to keep watch, he put up his revolver, cynically held a match to the wall, and lit a cigarette. Then, and not until then, did he look around him.

I think that all of us had the same feeling of doom as we stood bound around that great statue and looked up at this man or devil above us, in whose hands we were. If I had not known him so well I would have admired him intensely in that moment for he was, I think, the most handsome man I ever saw, the noblest-looking and blackest-hearted man I ever knew.

He stood motionless, and his cigarette went out in his fingers as he gazed. The weird light danced on his mail-coat and helm, and lit up the strong, large-boned lines of his face and his magnificent physique. A wonderful figure he made as he stood there, gaining a slow but perfect comprehension of what the place was.

Then he lit his cigarette a second time and started toward us. Half-way along the stone aisle he paused and for a full moment scanned the interweaving tracery of that groove, a puzzled wonder in his eyes. Small reason that he could not understand its import, inasmuch as he had not seen what we had seen! I do not think that he noticed the huddled figure of Sir Gaimar at all; and when at length he stood before us on the platform he was his usual cool, assured, masterful self, as if the wonders of that place had made no impression on him.

"Well, well! My old friend Mr. Sargent, and the Rev. Uriel Gairner, and poor old John Solomon and his man!"

Esmer spoke with mock surprise.

"And down yonder the Seal of Solomon, eh? Then I take it that we are all gathered here to worship. What god, please, Mr. Gairner?"

"Satan, if you had your way," spoke up Gairner bitterly.

He was beside me, John on the other side, Omar behind.

"Yet I doubt if he wants the worship of a treacherous dog such as you, Esmer Bey."

That, for some reason, lashed Esmer deeply. I could see the little flaming devils of anger spring up in his black eyes, and I have always thought that what came afterward was through revenge for Gairner's bitter words.

At any rate, he looked at us fixedly for a space, then turned away. I was suddenly anxious lest he see Sir Gaimar and guess at the nature of that golden casket; from his quick glances around the place I knew that he was seeking for some trace of the letter of Sergius. He could see nothing suspicious, for the form of Sir Gaimar was partly hidden by the statue on his platform, and he turned back to us again.

"Well, Mr. Sargent, I have destroyed Themoud. But there are two things I have not found, and if you recall our conversation on the hillside you will remember that I am very anxious indeed to have them."

"There's no use going over it all again," I said wearily. "If you want to kill us, go ahead and do it, for we have no weapons. But as for telling you where Edith Gairner is, never!"

Now, until this Uriel Gairner was not aware that Esmer had any special intent other than to gain the letter of Sergius. I had not told the missionary of the conversation between Esmer and Yelniz as touching his daughter, and the promise I had given him had been asked for on general principles.

Now Esmer turned his vindictiveness full upon Gairner, who was looking from the one to the other of us with wide-eyed horror.

"You were not aware of the honor in store for you, eh?" mocked the Osmanli as he fingered his revolver. "Once, indeed, I had thought to make you marry us, Nazarene, but now there will be no need of that. No, indeed!"

For my own part I had so piled horror upon horror within the past few hours that I listened quite unmoved, merely wishing that I had my fingers on his throat. Not so with Gairner, however. A deadly serious man cannot stand overmuch of such things; and when added to that he hears such words as those of Esmer anything is like to happen. I myself believe that he was out of his head from then on, though John says otherwise.

"Dog!" he spat at Esmer, the cords standing out on his head and neck as he strove with his bonds. "Dog!"

That word lashed the Osmanli as before.

"So! I am a dog? Cursed Nazarene, what good has your God been to you when a dog barked at Him, then? I think your God must be a coward, indeed, when a dog's bite can so tear through His protection!"

"Dog!"

And the word came with more venom than ever.

"What—again?"

Esmer's laugh was forced and not nice to hear.

"So, after I have blown down your walls and sent your knights to Eblis and torn my way into your secret passages in the very bowels of the earth, you name me dog? You fool of a Nazarene! Well, then, since I have torn like a dog and dug like a dog and conquered like a dog, be careful that I do not snap like a dog suddenly!"

As Gairner repeated the epithet the Osmanli's rage flashed out. With a stride at us he struck Gairner heavily in the face, knocking him back across the flank of the statue, and jerked Omar from behind us, his revolver keeping us all quiet.

"So! An Arab consorting with unbelievers!" he sneered, all his innate cruelty surging up in every line of his face and every accent of his sonorous voice.

Omar only grinned at him.

"My men said that there was a cry of *'Allahu Akhbar'* rising against us, but I did not believe them. So, friend of infidels, what is your name? Of what tribe?"

Omar told his name and whence he came, while beside me Gairner straightened up, his face streaming with blood. I pitied him, but could do nothing.

"Ah, a Hazramaut man!" Esmer laughed out. "Say, Omar ibn Kasim, do you know where this infidel girl is placed?"

"Allah alone knows all things," grinned Omar. "If I knew, *sidi*, it would be for my master, Suleiman, to order me to tell."

"A Hazrami, of a truth!"

Esmer seemed not ill pleased. Then he turned back to us.

"Listen, Mr. Gairner! Either tell where the letter of Sergius may be found, or tell where your daughter may be found—and choose quickly! For either I will give you life and the life of any other man here you may wish. For both, the lives of all."

Gairner's face contorted spasmodically. Perhaps he saw what was at hand.

"Dog!" he mumbled, his eyes steady.

"And yet again?"

Esmer paused and took a step back.

"There is a proverb, Omar ibn Kasim which says, 'If you meet a viper and a Hazrami, spare the viper!' But I, Esmer Bey, do not believe in proverbs, so—"

Absolutely without warning, he flicked up his revolver and a shot crashed out, the flame of it searing past me. I saw poor Gairner shudder. A terrible look swept into and out of his eyes. Then he pitched forward, dead, and rolled off the platform.

That was too much for me. Though my hands were helpless, my feet were not. I took one leap forward and kicked Esmer full in the stomach, so that he dropped his revolver and doubled up with a gasp. It had been in my mind so to send him back, to go slipping and slithering into the groove, but something warned him; before I could reach him again he turned and ran along the aisle, where he whipped out another revolver and faced me.

I thought that he would surely slay the rest of us in that moment, and so, perhaps, he intended. But as the weapon came up I saw him suddenly freeze into startled amazement. Then an awestruck look passed into his face and his arm fell. Following his gaze I saw that which had happened.

The body of Mr. Gairner had rolled, as I said, from the plat-form. Thence it had fallen into the groove which doubled around the end and sides of the platform. It was this which Esmer had seen. For by some chance the body had fallen so that it started in the right or downward direction, gaining just enough impetus to take the first rise. After that there was no stopping.

With horrified silence upon us all, we watched. Down the

body swept, glinting and glistening—for its mailcoat shed back the light radiantly—and then up to the rise opposite us. Doubling and curving, down it came and then back again, twisting along past statue after statue, shooting back down to circle the pit of flame at terrific speed. But I could watch it no longer, and sank down against the rock, fearing the awful madness that tugged at my brain.

Only at the wondrous shower of sparks, leaping up in a veritable pillar, I looked up again and saw the Seal whiten and redden and glow and die. Then I glanced up at Esmer, at a clatter of sound.

It was his revolver, which had fallen unheeded and rushed away to follow upon the groove-path; but as no sparks came that I remember, it must have been of too little weight. Esmer himself was standing facing us, a terrible fear stamped into his face. After a moment he raised his hand and wiped the sweat from him. I could see him trembling, nor did I blame him.

Then he sat down and for a little watched the Seal fade out into a black tracery against the red glow beneath. I suppose he could not trust his feet for a bit. At last he rose and made a somewhat unsteady path to us, displaying no animosity for my kick; indeed, he had probably forgotten it altogether.

"What place of devils is this?" he said, slowly getting himself in hand. "By Allah— Well, there is one of you gone. How now, Omar ibn Kasim! Would you like to follow the same road? But I forgot: you probably know nothing of the letter. Come, Mr. Sargent! How about you?"

"I have traveled the road once this day," I responded, pulling myself together. "I would sooner travel it again than tell what you want to know."

He gazed at me curiously, then nodded as if at something he had expected. And so he came to John.

"Suleiman! Suleiman the mysterious! Now I think that your devious ways are like to end in a still more devious way, Suleiman!" he said in Arbi. "What have you to say?"

John was ghastly pale, and his round face was all seamed and aged, so that I thought he would weaken. But not he. His jaw shoved out defiantly.

"There is nothing to say, Esmer Bey. I am a Christian, though no gentleman; that should be answer enough."

Esmer merely looked him in the eye for a minute, then turned without a word more and went back to where the revolver lay—the one I had kicked from his hand. He picked it up and twirled the cylinder, looking at it thoughtfully. What he intended cannot be said, for at this moment a great shout rang out eerily, and we all turned.

Sir Gaimar had come to his feet, and was holding aloft the golden casket as he cried to us. He could have known nothing of what had been passing, and no doubt mistook the mailclad figure of Esmer for that of Gairner.

"I have it!" he cried hollowly. "A moment more and I rejoin—"

I yelled something at him—a wild cry of warning—but he paid no attention. I saw that it was useless. As for Esmer, he stared agape at the figure; for by now Sir Gaimar had started toward the second platform. Then he laughed softly, caught up his revolver and so stepped off the aisle.

Let me give the man credit for his bravery. I freely admit that I would not have trodden that path to save all our lives, and the life of Edith Gairner into the bargain. But Esmer was no fool, either; for he understood the peril, and had weighed it in that brief instant before he started out.

Sir Gaimar, I think, was out of his head, because, though I yelled at him again, he paid no attention whatever, but reached the second platform and started on for the first, the one nearest us. Esmer picked his way more slowly, but with infinite care. Not once did he stumble or slip, and when at length he came to the first platform he stood there and waited.

Sir Gaimar approached, looking ever down at the way he trod, and as he came near enough Esmer stretched out his left hand, and we could distinctly hear his laugh as Sir Gaimar gave him the golden casket.

With that the knight leaped to the platform. Esmer stepped back to the farther edge, raised his revolver, and deliberately fired twice. I saw Sir Gaimar settle back against the legs of the statue and slowly slump together. Esmer Bey paid him no more heed, but opened the casket. Then he took out the papers that had been inside and idly flung the casket away. It clattered from seat to seat; what became of it I do not know. Esmer lifted his head and looked at us.

"And so—I win!" he cried in Arbi. "And you, Suleiman, lose!"

"Suleiman cannot lose!"

A deep, heavy voice, sonorous as Esmer's own, broke upon us all. One startled cry burst from John as we turned. There, standing in the doorway behind and above, was no other than Akhbar Khan, the Afghan, and behind him were more men still, while faint shots drifted to us.

"Allah curse you!" screamed Esmer and whipped up his revolver.

Not yet realizing what had happened, thinking it all some wild dream, I could bear no more. I felt myself reeling as I stood.

But before my senses slipped away from me I saw what happened below and above. Above, Akhbar Khan lifted a rifle and shot once. Below, the slumped-up figure that had been Sir Gaimar straightened itself with an inarticulate cry and fell upon Esmer.

The Osmanli writhed and twisted, but Gaimar's steel-clad arms were about him. Then he fired, again and again, his revolver full against the side of Sir Gaimar. But at the final shot he went backward, screamed once, and the two men, with arms locked, plunged downward into the groove beneath.

As they went my senses fled—but I had caught a gleam of something white in the hands of Esmer and Sir Gaimar and I knew that Esmer had won, even in death.

CHAPTER XXI

OUT OF THEMOUD

I T   W A S   the same room as that in which I had first found
myself in the castle—the one with the outlook over the
desert. By my side sat a woman, young, but with lines of sadness
in her face. She was Edith Gairner; on her lap sat a curly-headed,
fair-headed boy—one of those who had been made motherless
and fatherless upon the night of massacre.

At my feet sat a man who looked out over the desert. He, too,
was young, very pale as if from illness, but with a strangely beautiful face, upon which was stamped a look of great resolve and
grief and strength. That was Bertrand—Count Bertrand now.

On the floor in a corner, with two children playing about him,
sat a swarthy man who laughed much, babbled much in Arbi,
but all very softly, as if he were afraid to speak aloud.

Sometimes he would touch one of the children and laugh,
whereupon they would laugh, too, and he would gaze down at
them with vacant, staring eyes. That was Omar ibn Kasim, the
Hazrami—mad, but harmless.

Sitting upon the bed, holding my hand, was a stranger figure
yet. He was a very old man, to judge by his deeply lined face, his
snow-white hair, and his broken-down frame, yet this was oddly
belied by his blue eyes, very wide and very blue and very pathetic
sometimes. That was John Solomon. He was talking as of old.

"No, miss; beggin' your pardon, but I don't agree with you. 'E
ain't so werry old, nor 'e ain't so werry young, but enough. If 'e

ups and goes with us, miss, 'e 'as a mortal lot to learn about the world, which same ain't good for a man of 'is time o' life.

"But if 'e stays 'ere, miss, why 'e ain't so bad off. No one is a going to come 'ere again, you can lay to that. 'E 'as a good bit o' land 'ere, miss, wi' them four esquires what we found alive. What's more, 'e 'as them there knightesses and children, miss, to be a looking out for. That's a werry good start indeed, I says."

"But, John," said Edith softly, "think how terrible it would be here for him, after all that has taken place, and how much better—"

"Excuse me, miss! Right you are as 'ow things 'd be main bad for a bit, but men wasn't made to 'ave easy times of it, I says; and the 'arder time 'e 'as getting straightened out, why, the more of a man 'e'll be when so be as 'e gets it all done, says I."

"John is right, Edith," I said, at which Bertrand turned and smiled at me, for he did not understand English, yet knew that we were settling his case. "John is quite right, I think. Bertrand would never be at home in the outer world, and these poor women and boys who are left would be absolutely helpless. Besides, these children, if you will notice, haven't that brooding look of hopeless doom which we noted in the faces of the older people. Bertrand hasn't it himself. Why shouldn't he rear up a new race here on the ruins of the old?"

Edith shook her head, not yet convinced. It was her idea that Bertrand should go out into the world with us. So we outlined our arguments to him, and left him the choice in the matter. He smiled somewhat sadly.

"Dear Lady Edith, I thank you. But it was in my mind also that our people are not wholly dead. By right of birth I have a duty to them, and duty to the outer world I have none. No; it is best for me to dwell here where my fathers dwelt—and, to tell the truth, there is that daughter of Sir Gaimar—"

And now he paused and looked somewhat red, at which Edith laughed suddenly and declared that he had better stay after all.

But I had best go back and explain, lest my tale run away with
me. That genius of intrigue and mystery named John Solomon
had foreseen that Count Hugo and his people would rather die
than leave their country—as, indeed, they had done. So he had
arranged with Akhbar Khan that the latter should go out into
the desert, for Akhbar thought he knew a place where he could
find his cousin, Yar Hussein, who had accompanied Mr. Gairner.
As I have said, Yar Hussein had been captured by Esmer, only
to escape.

So Akhbar Khan had finally made his way through the salt
desert and had come upon his cousin, also upon some assembled remnants of Solomon's dispersed band. These had easily
been persuaded to join the two Afghans, and the whole party
had struck for Themoud.

They had not reached the place without terrible suffering,
however, in which three men died and two more went mad; but
eventually they had reached it, coming to the castle in time to
wipe out the last of Esmer's men and learn what had happened.
Upon this the Afghans had pushed on through the passages,
surprising the guards, until they reached the place of the flaming Seal.

"And Esmer?" I asked John when he told me all this after
I had come out of the wasting fever that had seized upon me.

"Why, sir"—and something of his old look came into his
eyes—"why, Mr. Sargent, sir, 'e won't never trouble no more
honest girls, as the 'ousemaid said when she looked down at the
old gent when 'e was laid out in the vault."

And since that day I have never heard of John's "old gent"
further, which, to my mind, is not a good sign.

Well, in time I had my health back again, and we considered
our journey out. For one thing, we had Esmer's entire supply
of camels, and this ultimately proved our salvation. There were
nine men of us all told. As for poor Omar, we decided to leave
him there in Themoud. Poor fellow, he was past all hope and
was slowly wasting away, for that unspeakable few hours had

destroyed his mind altogether. Bertrand promised to care for him while he lived, which I suspect was not very long. Uriel Gairner was in both our minds, though none of us ever mentioned him after John told Edith how he had died.

Edith went with us, of course. Since we had nearly two hundred camels, and most of these could be laden with water, we decided to hit for Bosra, and from there to the railroad which would take us to Beirut. But even with our great caravan of beasts and our good water-supply that was not a journey pleasant to recall.

Our main reliance during the trip was placed in the two Afghans. So in the end we rode safely into Bosra.

We made no halt, however, until we reached Beirut. Here John visited the Crédit Lyonnais, where he had some trouble in proving his identity; I myself, who was well known, had changed so much that we aroused no little curiosity. This was increased when we passed our things through the customs, for we had brought with us certain coats of mail and other things the like of which had never been seen before—and that was how the first news leaked out to the press.

But all things have an end—happily; and in no long time we were homeward bound. I say "homeward" advisedly, because I had sworn to myself, as I looked down on the Seal of Solomon, that if ever I got home again I would put the past behind me.

And for John, too, our country was home. He had cut all ties behind him and dismissed all his men save the two Afghans, who were wild to accompany us to America. Their devotion to John is almost pitiful; but of late I have noticed that John has been having long talks with them, and has been regaining a good share of his old manner. I am afraid that the East is calling him, in spite of all.

We were cutting out into the Mediterranean the second day aboard ship, and I was standing watching a drizzle of rain and thinking many things, when Edith Gairner came up to me and slipped her arm in mine. Obediently I turned, and we walked aft.

"Well?" she said at length.

"Well," I echoed, smiling—"and then what?"

"Why, I was thinking! Do you remember once that you said to me you would like to settle down—"

"Of course I remember; and I've been trying to keep from telling you."

"Why should you do that?"

Now this was a very sensible question, and I did not see the twinkle in her eyes, so that for a little I was not sure what to say.

"Well," I said at last, "I want—I want to settle down with *you*, Edith!"

She was silent; but when I looked up I found her laughing at me—and all the rest belongs to me. So now we have our little house, not far from our trolley-line. As for the teaching—well, I have had offers enough, but somehow or other I have no time for teaching. I am busy learning—learning just to be happy.

ABOUT THE AUTHOR

H. BEDFORD-JONES is a Canadian by birth, but not by profession, having removed to the United States at the age of one year. For over twenty years he has been more or less profitably engaged in writing and traveling. As he has seldom resided in one place longer than a year or so and is a person of retiring habits, he is somewhat a man of mystery; more than once he has suffered from unscrupulous gentlemen who impersonated him—one of whom murdered a wife and was subsequently shot by the police, luckily after losing his alias.

The real Bedford-Jones is an elderly man, whose gray hair and precise attire give him rather the appearance of a retired foreign diplomat. His hobby is stamp collecting, and his collection of Japan is said to be one of the finest in existence. At present writing he is en route to Morocco, and when this appears in print he will probably be somewhere on the Mojave Desert in company with Erle Stanley Gardner.

Questioned as to the main facts in his life, he declared there was only one main fact, but it was not for publication; that his life had been uneventful except for numerous financial losses, and that his only adventures lay in evading adventurers. In his younger years he was something of an athlete, but the encroachments of age preclude any active pursuits except that of motoring. He is usually to be found poring over his stamps, working at his typewriter, or laboring in his California rose garden, which is one of the sights of Cathedral Cañon, near Palm Springs.